633 Squadron:
Operation Cobra

Frederick E. Smith

CORGI BOOKS
A DIVISION OF TRANSWORLD PUBLISHERS LTD

633 SQUADRON: OPERATION COBRA

A CORGI BOOK 0 552 11824 9

First publication in Great Britain

PRINTING HISTORY
Corgi edition published 1981

Copyright © Frederick E. Smith 1981

This book is set in 10/11 California

Corgi Books are published by
Transworld Publishers Ltd.,
Century House, 61–63 Uxbridge Road,
Ealing, London, W5 5SA

Made and printed in United States of America by
Offset Paperbacks, Dallas, Pennsylvania.

Frederick E. Smith was born in Hull and, after completing his education, served as a Local Government Officer for Hull Corporation until 1939 when he joined the RAF Volunteer Reserve. He served in Britain, Africa and the Far East until the end of the War. His wartime experiences and the people he met were later drawn upon and used in his novels, *Saffron's War*, *Saffron's Army* and the *633 Squadron* series.

Between 1947 and 1952 Mr Smith worked in South Africa and on returning to Britain he decided to become a professional writer. Today his novels are read in more than twenty-five countries. He has published twenty-seven novels, sold the film rights of five and had two major films made, one of which, *633 Squadron*, broke many box-office records. He has also published two plays, numerous articles and more than sixty short stories.

His main hobbies are travel, sport, conversation and yoga — something he learnt in the Far East when, almost dying from a tropical disease, an Indian Yogi helped him to full recovery. Today Frederick Smith lives in Bournemouth with his wife and two sons.

The author wishes to acknowledge his debt to the authors of the following works of reference:

Bekker, the Luftwaffe War Diaries (Macdonald);
Adolf Galland, The First and the Last (Methuen);
Alfred Price, Instruments of Darkness (Wm Kimber);
Richards and Saunders, Royal Air Force 1939–1945 (H.M.S.O.);
Sir. C. Webster and N. Frankland, the Strategic Air Offensive against Germany 1939–1945 (H.M.S.O.);
History of the Second World War, Purnell.

To
Barry and Rita
With love

1

The barometrically-fused flare exploded at its pre-set height of 2,500 feet. As its parachute broke free, the magnesium candle burst into blinding luminescence.

The effect was as dramatic as an arc-light illuminating a stage. Below was a sleeping airfield, the shadows of its hangars, Control Tower, and billets jet-black in the icy light. Like winged insects caught at rest, the shapes of aircraft carrying RAF rondels could be seen at their dispersal points. Neat arable fields surrounded the airfield and a row of poplars marked its southern boundary. Its northern boundary was a road containing a single, slate-roofed building. The navigator of the Messerschmitt 410 that had dropped the flare gave a shout. 'There's our marker, Major! The Black Swan.'

A second flare added its brilliance to the scene. With a word to his bomb-aimer the gruppe commander, Major Ernst Neumann, put his 410 into a dive and made for the north-west corner of the airfield. As the road and airfield perimeter met in his crosswires, the bomb-aimer released a target indicator. Falling less than fifty feet from a gunpost, the marker burst in a splash of green fire.

Levelling out, Neumann made for the north-east corner while on his left a second 410 laid markers on the two southernly corners. The lack of response from the gunposts suggested that the immunity given to RAF airfields during the last year had impaired their crews' efficiency. Releasing his second target indicator, Neumann climbed to 5,000 feet. By this time, although the parachute flares had burned out, green splashes of fire on each corner of the airfield defined its limits perfectly to the orbiting German aircraft. Protected by Junker 188 night fighters, they dived down one by one and released their bombs.

The result was devastating. Many of the 410s and 188s were carrying 1,500 kilos bombs and they tore through the soft-shelled buildings like bullets through butter. Great explosions ripped hangars apart; administration buildings and billets erupted into matchwood; and the Control Tower was hurled to the ground. More salvos of bombs blasted holes in the runways and ripped the dispersed aircraft into cardboard fragments. When the last bomber had swept over, the airfield resembled little more than a huge rubbish tip on which the remains of buildings and aircraft were burning pathetically.

With his mission completed Neumann led his exultant crews back into the darkness. With a last look at the burning airfield Neumann's navigator, Rudi Ulrich, gave a chuckle. 'What are the Tommis going to call it, Major? Being caught with their trousers down?'

Neumann smiled. 'Don't count your chickens, Rudi. Their night intruders could still take their revenge.'

Ulrich was clearly enjoying the mission. 'I don't think they're going to make it tonight, Major.'

Back at the gruppe's base in Holland the landing lights switched on and off briefly as the aircraft landed. A few minutes later the crews filed into their Intelligence Room. Behind a large table two high-ranking officers were talking to the Fliegerhorstkommandant of the Station, Martin Lemke. One was a Generalmajor in the Luftwaffe, a tall man with a good presence. The other officer, shorter in statue, was a Obergruppenführer in the Gestapo. On seeing Neumann enter the hut, Lemke waved the young Gruppe Commander towards him. Lemke was smiling. 'I understand the mission was successful, Ernst?'

Neumann, a dark, lean, good-looking man, smiled back. 'I don't think we left much standing, sir.'

'Good.' Lemke turned towards the stocky Gestapo officer. 'I don't believe you have met Obergruppenführer Welter. Herr Obergruppenführer, this is

Major Neumann, our gruppe commander.'

The Gestapo officer had close-cropped ginger hair and a harsh Saxon accent. His eyes, small and curiously unblinking, assessed Neumann as the younger man came to attention and saluted him. 'Your Station Commander tells me you have expressed curiosity over your mission, Major.'

Seeing Neumann's hesitation, the tall Luftwaffe Generalmajor answered for him. 'I think I understand Neumann's problem, Obergruppenführer. When I was asked to form this unit, I was under the impression myself that its purpose was to punish the English for their terror raids on our cities and to damage their industrial production. I had not expected one of my best gruppes to be diverted and used in this way.'

The stocky Gestapo officer, fully acquainted with the Generalmajor's brief, shrugged at the implied criticism. The formation of Fliegerkorps IX, on paper a force of some 550 aircraft, was the brainchild of Hitler himself. Infuriated by the incessant night and day pounding of his cities by the RAF and the United States 8th Air Force and yet adamantly refusing the advice of his senior Luftwaffe officers to give the utmost priority to his fighter defences, he had given Fliegerkorps IX the task of retaliation. The officer put in charge of this formidable task was Dietrich Magnus Peltz, an extremely experienced and capable officer.

"The Little Blitz" as it was popularly called had begun quite successfully. Using the "Pathfinder" technique developed by Bomber Command of marking their targets with flares and then dropping their bombs in the shortest possible time to keep losses to the minimum, the Junker 188s and Messerschmitt 410s of Fliegerkorps IX had bombed London, the Home Counties, and towns on the southern coast with some degree of success. The raids had started on the night of January 21st 1944 and on average had consisted of between 50 and 170 bombers. Yet in spite of never flying during the full moon periods, Peltz's losses had never been less than ten per cent and by this time, mid-April, Fliegerkorps IX was beginning to show the strain. With losses so high, it was hardly surprising Neumann had been puzzled when three days ago his squadron had been withdrawn from the fray and given specialised training. Now, as the stocky Gestapo officer motioned the officers out of earshot of the crews, he wondered if he were at last to hear the reason.

The man's unblinking eyes fixed on Neumann's face which was still bearing the imprint of his face mask. 'What I am going to tell you must not be told to your crews, Major. It is not necessary and it would be politically unwise. Do I make myself clear?'

Neumann almost said no, then changed his mind. 'I understand you are speaking in confidence, Herr Obergruppenführer.'

'Then I shall explain.' The Gestapo officer spoke for over two minutes during which time neither Peltz nor Neumann took their eyes off his face. 'You will both now see,' Welter finished, 'that in attacking this particular squadron, Number 633, you are not just attacking an RAF unit, formidable although this unit is. You are attacking a new concept of war which, if it were to succeed, might greatly hamper the political arm of the Third Reich.'

'You say there have already been such attacks made?' Neumann asked.

'Yes. There was one at Amiens and another in The Hague. Not by this squadron but even so both were relatively successful. Certainly successful enough for the enemy to call in this special unit of Mosquitoes. As yet, because these attacks require a high degree of skill and experience, we don't believe the enemy has many other squadrons to call on. But clearly if this squadron proves successful, it will be used as a seedbase for others. For all these reasons it must be destroyed on your first strike. The enemy is no fool and if you were unsuccessful he would make certain there was no repeat performance. How soon can you be ready?'

Peltz glanced at Neumann. The younger man shrugged. 'I suppose we are ready now, Herr Obergruppenführer. All my crews, including the reserves, had a good workout on that mock airfield tonight. But we shall have to wait for the next moon free period.'

Welter frowned. 'Why?'

Peltz answered the question himself. 'We cannot make an attack of that nature in moonlight of any kind. The enemy's night fighters and defences are far too efficient.'

'Surely darkness does not make all that difference?'

Peltz' voice was dry. 'It makes all the difference in the world and, as you've just pointed out yourself, we can't afford to fail.'

The Obergruppenführer's small eyes moved from Peltz to Neumann before he gave a nod of displeasure. 'Very well. If a moonless night is so important, then you had better resume normal operations with the Fliegerkorps until the first one arrives. But remember this. When it does arrive, you do not waste another moment. This enemy unit could be brought into action at any time and the damage it might do could be out of all proportion to its size.' True to his kind, Welter felt it judicious to end with a threat. 'If that were to happen, questions would almost certainly be asked why you and I were so dilatory in carrying out our orders.'

Although it was mid-April and the sun was bright, the wind that blew from the Massif de la Vanoise had the cutting edge of a razor. Snow still covered its peaks and lay in hollows down the mountainside. The small town that spread along the foot of the narrow valley looked subdued by the bitter cold. It was fed by two access roads, one winding in from the west, the other from the east.

A girl was taking cover behind a pile of icy rocks. In her mid-twenties, she was tall and supple, with grey eyes and an attractive, intelligent face. She was wearing a fur-lined coat and her dark hair was covered by a thick scarf. As the wind keened again, bringing up a flurry of snow, she turned to a young man at her side. She spoke French without an accent. 'When did the last convoy arrive?'

The man, Pierre Delacourt, was twenty-seven years old, slim and eager, with good Gallic features. 'Tuesday,' he told her.

'Tuesday. So that's two convoys in four days?'

As the Frenchman nodded, the girl lifted a pair of binoculars. She was watching three German transports escorted by motor cycles and sidecars moving along the western road towards the town. 'Have they all been this size?'

'Yes. Four transports is the most I've seen in a convoy.' The young man was showing both curiosity and admiration for the girl. 'What's your real name?'

Her voice turned curt. 'You call me Lorenz. The less you know about me the better for your safety. Tell me more about your friend Jean — the one who recognised Professor Werner.'

Delacourt shrugged. 'There isn't much to tell. He was a student of chemistry before the war and Werner came to give them a few lectures. When he recognised him in Gestapo uniform coming out of the Institute, he felt it was something we should know about.'

The girl had turned back to the town as she was talking. A large modern building, set in spacious grounds, stood somewhat incongruously in the centre of the old town. 'You did well to tell us. It might be very important. When was the Institute built?'

'In 1936. Three years before the war.'

'Was there much fuss when your town was chosen?'

The young man gave another shrug. 'There was some. No one likes an animal vivesectional centre right among them. But it soon died down. Most people here work on the land and they're not as sentimental about animals as townspeople. I suppose that's why they built it here.'

Nodding, the girl held out her hand. 'Let me see the photographs your friend took.'

Slipping off a glove, Delacourt fished inside his coat and drew out three prints. All were photographs of an open-topped German staff car with two officers sitting in the rear seats. Two prints were blurred but the third was in good focus, showing one officer to be young and the other elderly with a lined but distinguished face. Both men were wearing Gestapo uniform, the older man bearing the rank of Standartenführer.

14

The girl slipped the prints inside her coat. 'I'm keeping these, Pierre. They must go off to London at once.' Seeing the eager young Frenchman was about to question her again, she countered his curiosity by nodding at the bleak mountainsides around them. 'Didn't you say you had a relative who is a hill farmer?'

Delacourt nodded and pointed at a stone cottage lying inconspicuously in a corrie at the far side of the valley. 'That's his place. He's my wife's brother.'

'Who lives there with him?'

'No one. He's a batchelor.'

The girl eyed the cottage with renewed interest. 'He can survey the entire town from there. Is he to be trusted?'

'Etienne? He hates the Nazis.'

'Then can you arrange for a twenty-four hour watch to be kept on these convoys? I want to know everything, how many come in and if there is any pattern about their arrival. Anything in fact that might be useful to us.'

Delacourt hesitated. 'I'll have to get Jean to help. I've got my job to do and Etienne has to attend to his animals. Michelle can help too. She often comes up to visit Etienne, so no one will suspect her. Don't worry. We'll work something out.'

The girl had given a start. 'Have you told Michelle what you are doing?'

The young Frenchman gave a self-conscious laugh. 'I had to. We've only been married a few months and she was beginning to think I was seeing another woman. But it's all right. She's as eager to help France as I am. She won't give anything away.'

'You do realise what would happen to her if she did? The Gestapo would stop at nothing to make her talk.'

In the bitter wind Delacourt's face looked chilled. 'We know that. But we can't just sit back and do nothing, can we? Don't worry. I'll tell her to be careful.'

The sharpness left the girl's voice. 'Very well. But you bring in no one else. Remember that if our suspicions are correct, there'll be spies and informers everywhere to check there are no leaks. Don't try to contact me directly.

You'll be told how to pass messages on.'

The couple talked for another minute, then Delacourt started back down the mountain. The girl waited until he had disappeared round a rock shoulder, then raised her binoculars again. The transports, whose canvas covers were tightly laced down, had now reached the research centre and were passing through a huge steel gate. As it swung closed behind them, the wind came sweeping down the valley, agitating the trees and whipping up the pockets of snow. This time the bleakness of the scene brought a shiver from the girl as she turned away.

2

It was a fine spring morning when Air Commodore Davies' Miles Master appeared over the southern perimeter of Sutton Craddock. To be more definite it was 09.15 on April the 17th 1944. Already forewarned of the event, "Pop" Henderson, the Station O.C., and Adams, the Station Intelligence officer, were both seated in a jeep at the base of the Control Tower. As soon as the aircraft appeared, Henderson gave Adams a nod and sent the jeep bounding over the grass parallel to the north-south runway.

The point of the exercise could be seen half a minute later. The Master, as light as a ballerina, circled the airfield once and then floated over the hangars and settled down on the runway. Spray rose like smoke from its wheels as they touched down: there had been a shower of rain just after dawn. The sun had taken full command now, however, and dew was sparkling on the grass. The few clouds still present on the northern horizon had lost their winter gauntness and a couple of larks were trilling in the sky. To Adams, a southerner, spring had come to Sutton Craddock after a long hard winter, although there was no doubt that the locals, with their customary Yorkshire caution, would have dampened his optimism with the warning that only a fool casts his clout before May's out.

With its short landing run completed, the Master had already swung round on the runway and with blipping engine was taxiing back. Seeing the approaching jeep, Davies swung the aircraft towards a nearby dispersal point. As he switched off the engine a bleary-eyed

17

corporal appeared at the door of the hut. Giving a look of horror at recognising Davies, he turned and yelled at an ACII who was sprawled asleep on one of the duty crews' beds.

Scowling at the absence of a ground crew, Davies shrugged out of his parachute harness and threw it over the port wheel of the Master. Wearing only his service uniform, he was a small, spry figure with sharp features and eyes as alert as a sparrow's. As the jeep halted alongside the Master, Davies made towards it.

Henderson jumped down from the driving seat and saluted. The O.C. was a big, brawny Scot with a good-natured face and a voice that contained just a trace of Highland brogue. 'Good morning, sir. You're right on time.'

Giving a grunt, Davies jerked a thumb at the two red-faced mechanics who, to avoid his eyes, were making a great fuss over the parked Master. 'It's more than you can say for those two characters. What've they been doing? Drinking meths or something?'

Henderson hid a grin. 'Everyone's been up half the night, sir. The boys had to do that marshalling yard job this morning.'

Glancing round the airfield Davies noticed for the first time that only a few aircraft were standing at their dispersal points. 'Christ, yes; I'd forgotten. Any news yet?'

Henderson exchanged a furtive glance with Adams. To put it mildly it was unlike the small Air Commodore to forget the movements of the special service unit of Mosquitoes that he himself had created. Moreover, he had sounded uncharacteristically depressed when he had phoned through the previous evening. 'No, sir, it's too early yet,' Henderson pointed out. 'We don't expect them back before 10.45.'

'In that case you'll probably miss their return. Sorry, but it can't be helped.'

Along with his curiosity Henderson was feeling resentful. It was almost unheard of for a Station Commander to be absent when his squadron returned from a mission.

18

Before he could protest Davies turned towards Adams who had also climbed out of the jeep. There was an air of enforced cheerfulness about his greeting. 'Hello, Frank. How are you these days? Got over Norway yet?'

The bespectacled Adams, a somewhat portly officer, winced slightly at the reminder. It was barely six weeks since the squadron had carried out its spectacular feat of destroying the last of the German heavy water stocks in Norway, and Adams, who had conceived the daring operation, was still suffering sleepless nights at the memory. Forced to ambush and kill young German soldiers to prevent them reporting the squadron's hiding place, Adams found it more than ironical that the deed that still haunted him should have earned him Davies' supreme accolade, the use of his Christian name.

'I'm fine, thank you, sir,' he said. 'Will you be wanting breakfast before we go?'

Davies shook his head. 'No; there won't be time. But I wouldn't mind a cup of coffee.'

Adams stood aside for the Air Commodore to climb into the jeep, then took the rear seat. As Henderson accelerated out of earshot of the mechanics, he turned to Davies. 'Couldn't this meeting wait until the boys get back, sir?'

'Not a hope, Jock. They've even got Staines up here.' Davies' tone changed. 'Anyway, it's out of my hands. A joker from SOE has taken over. Lock, stock, and barrel.'

At first Davies' meaning did not register on Henderson. 'You mean Brigadier Simms?'

'No. This joker's senior to him. It's he who's called this conference.'

As the penny dropped, Henderson slowed down the jeep. 'You're not saying he's taken over the squadron?' When Davies nodded, even the Scot's phlegmatic temperament could not hide his dismay. 'But how can that happen? I thought we were a specialist unit under your direct command.'

Although the jeep was still in the middle of the airfield, Davies took a glance around before replying. 'It's this bloody invasion that's coming, Jock. New units are being formed, squadrons are being shifted about — it's all a shambles at the moment. I've fought it like hell but they've attached you to the 2nd Tactical Air Force under Coningham and he's loaned you to SOE. I stay as liason commander and advisor but I take my orders from this SOE character.'

Behind the two men Adams was sharing Henderson's concern. Special Operations Executive seldom concerned itself with straight-forward military objectives. With General Staines of the American 8th Air Force also participating, there seemed little doubt something big and complex was brewing. Adams leaned forward in his seat. 'How long is this arrangement to last, sir? Do you know?'

Davies scowled. 'Christ knows. Possibly until the invasion.'

'But that might not be until next year,' Henderson protested.

'Not a chance, Jock. It has to be soon or the Russians will go on strike.'

As Henderson halted the jeep outside the Officers' Mess, Davies made an effort to lift the general gloom. 'So you're back at full squadron strength again, are you?'

'Yes, sir. We've even got a couple of reserve crews standing by.'

Davies managed his gnome-like grin. 'Is that a fact? You've been having it too good, Jock. Your boys must be getting bored.'

Henderson did his best to respond to the banter. 'With all these randy Yorkshire lasses about? My problem's making sure the young sods get enough sleep.' His tone changed as he switched off the engine. 'It's a pity we can't take Moore along with us, sir. It's always useful to have his views.'

Davies gave a grunt of impatience. 'It's no use, Jock. The meeting's scheduled for 10.00 hours and that's the end of it. We can put Moore in the picture later.'

At that moment the zestful wind that was blowing the cottonwool clouds across the sky swept around the Officers' Mess with a rush. Davies, the only man not wearing an overcoat, gave a sudden grimace. 'It's not as warm as it looks. Let's get inside and have that cup of coffee.'

In spite of Davies' comment about the weather, High Elms was showing distinct signs of spring that morning. Birds were singing their hearts out in the tall trees that gave the old country house its name and the rhododendron bushes that lined the paths of the estate were thick with buds. In the library, which had been the scene of many a momentous conference, the sun, streaming through the French windows, was enriching the panelled walls and giving an extra sheen to the large polished table. Three men, basking in the sunshine, were chatting quietly when a young lieutenant tapped on the door and led Davies and company inside.

'Air Commodore Davies and his staff, sir.'

The soldier the lieutenant addressed was an elderly Brigadier of distinguished appearance with a small grey moustache and sensitive features. Dwarfing him was a massive two-star American general with spiky hair and a granite-like face. Staines had once played quarterback for his college and even now one could feel sorry for his opponents. Both men were well known to Davies. The Brigadier had been his executive officer during 633 Squadron's sacrificial assault on the German heavy-water plant in the Swartfjord the previous spring. General Staines had joined the Committee for the next three challenges that had faced the squadron: the Rhine Maiden rocket plant in Bavaria, the radiolocation station in France, and the remainder of the heavy water stocks in Norway.

The third man, however, was a stranger to all of Davies' party. He was a Brigadier in his middle forties, a good six foot two in height, with an out-thrust jaw, black hair, and beetling eyebrows. To Adams he looked like a heavyweight boxer or wrestler who had slightly run to seed.

Punctilious and courteous as always, the elderly Brigadier introduced all three airmen in turn. 'MacBride, let me introduce Air Commodore Davies.

Davies, this is Brigadier MacBride who asked me to convene this meeting.'

As the junior officer of the party, Adams was the last to step forward. Although the crushing handshake he received made him wince, MacBride was showing no cordiality. Instead his deep-set eyes were running over Adams as if questioning why a mere squadron leader should be present. Adams, incurably sensitive about his non-military appearance, liked neither the man's abrupt manner nor his rough-edged voice and was relieved when the introduction was over and Staines' gravelly greeting enabled him to turn away from the soldier's stare.

'Hiya, Adams. Is your frostbite better yet?'

Adams smiled at the big, grinning American. 'Yes, sir. It wasn't very serious anyway.'

'You did a great job over there, Frank. Congratulations.'

Embarrassed although Adams was, he knew it was a moment he would never forget. 'Thank you, sir.'

Staines turned to the beetle-browed MacBride. 'In case you never got the details, he spear-headed the Valkyrie operation six weeks ago. Then he ambushed half-a-dozen Heinies who'd discovered the squadron's hide-out. I guess you can say that if it hadn't been for him the whole unit would have been destroyed and those IMI stocks gotten through to Germany.'

It was all too much for Adams' modesty. 'I doubt that it made any difference at all, sir. They still found out we were there.'

Staines' eyes twinkled. 'Stop being so goddamed English, Frank. You did a great job.'

Adams was reduced to another mumbled 'Thank you, sir.' MacBride was giving him a second look. Although fully conversant with the Valkyrie operation, he was clearly wondering if the American was pulling his leg about the Intelligence Officer's role. With the tact for which he was famous, the elderly Brigadier intervened.

'We have asked you to join us today, gentlemen, because Air Marshall Sir Arthur Coningham has kindly loaned us your services until the invasion. Not that after the admirable feats you have performed for us we are strangers to one another, but as it is the first time you have been directly attached to us, Brigadier MacBride expressed the wish to welcome you personally and to explain your duties. As he also wants to give you details of your first mission, I will ask him to take the chair.'

The tall SOE officer moved to the head of the table. Something in his expression gave Adams the feeling he was enjoying his brief and he wondered how much the presence of an American general was adding to that enjoyment. Inviting his audience to sit, MacBride gazed at each man in turn. His forceful voice seemed ideally suited to his aggressive personality.

'All right, gentlemen, I will get to the point straight away. It will be no surprise to any of you — in fact it will be no surprise to the enemy either — that some time this year we are going to invade Europe. Because of the defences Jerry has put up, we know it's going to be a hell of a fight. It is therefore critically important that we pin down as many of his combat troops as we can in the areas well away from the invasion beaches. For this purpose we in SOE have been dropping arms to Resistance groups in all the occupied countries and urging on them the importance of giving us all the support they can when the invasion begins. As soon as they receive our orders we want sabotage on a massive scale. We want arms dumps blowing up, bridges destroyed, rolling stock sabotaged, everything possible done to prevent Jerry rushing up his reserves to the beaches we have chosen to invade. To put it briefly, we want Europe in flames.'

Prone to irrelevant thoughts in moments of high importance, Adams, who secretly prided himself on recognising accents, was trying to place MacBride's. The North-West was his guess, although he suspected a touch of Irish too. Pulling himself together he listened to the gruff, forceful voice.

'It is obvious we must provide leadership for such a campaign even for no other reason that it is properly co-ordinated but it is no easy task. We send over all the agents we can but they are limited in scope by the weapons they can carry and also by the tactics of the Gestapo. As you might know, they shoot ten or even a hundred hostages for every German soldier killed or every act of sabotage committed. This causes problems for our agents and for Resistance leaders because if too many civilians are executed, a backlash might develop that could have exactly the opposite effect intended.

'But even the Gestapo can hardly use this weapon of terror if our own armed forces are seen as the *agents provocateur*. That, gentlemen, is your first brief. To use your aircraft in every possible way that can aid and abet the Resistance Movements in Occupied Europe.' When Henderson opened his mouth to speak, MacBride anticipated his question. 'No, you won't be doing cloak-and-dagger stuff at night. In any case your aircraft aren't suited for spy-dropping. You are going to provide support, encouragement, and sometimes direct intervention according to the circumstances. With Winston's permission we have already tried an experiment or two. The results have convinced him and us that by using a unit of your skill and experience we can add a new dimension to the Underground War. That is why, with the consent of the Air Staff, we have been given your services until the invasion begins.'

As Henderson showed some relief, MacBride turned back to the attentive Davies. 'Now to your second brief. This could involve you in a mission as important as any you've carried out so far. I can't give you any details today because as yet our suspicions aren't confirmed. But I can say that if they are, you won't find your talents wasted.'

Davies was frowning. 'You can't give us a hint what it's about?'

'Not at the moment. But as it could still involve them, you can say that from today your squadron is declaring war on the Gestapo.'

3

MacBride paused to gauge the effect of his words. Staines was looking both puzzled and quizzical as if enjoying some secret joke. Davies, alerted by the possibility of another large-scale mission for his beloved squadron and resentful at his temporary loss of command, was doing his best to grin and bear it but was being markedly unsuccessful. Adams, who like the others was still uncertain what the squadron's new role entailed, was limited by a personal reaction. By nature disliking aggressive men, he also disliked name-dropping and with MacBride's relationship with Churchill almost certainly nothing more than a servant-master one, he found the use of the Prime Minister's forename ridiculous. Indeed he wondered if it accounted for Staines' quizzical expression. Henderson was clearly apprehensive. In the past, although he had often made protests against Davies' over-ambitious schemes for his ace squadron, he had at least known that behind those schemes there was a genuine affection for it. Now Henderson was gaining the impression it was in the hands of a man who saw it purely as a tool and would therefore use it ruthlessly. Seeing MacBride had paused to light a cigarette, the Scot seized on the opportunity for a question.

'Taking our first brief, sir, exactly how do we give support to the Resistance?'

From their expressions it was clear both Staines and Davies were equally curious as MacBride's gaze settled on Henderson. 'Do you know anything about the Danish war effort, Henderson?'

'No, sir. I'm afraid I don't.'

'Then I'll enlighten you. Until now, mostly for political reasons, the Danes haven't shown the same resistance to their occupation as other countries. Another reason is they've thought the Germans too powerful to be defeated. Yet with a determined Underground they could hold down half-a-dozen enemy divisions, maybe more. Knowing this, their Resistance leaders have suggested a way of overcoming their apathy. Every April in Copenhagen the Jerries put on a parade to celebrate Hitler's birthday. It's a big show with brass bands and full trappings and the Danes have come to see it as a spectacle. In addition there's a rumour their Quisling leader, Scavenius, might attend this year. Now supposing a flight or two of Allied aircraft were to join in the fun and games by flying low and dropping leaflets? The Jerries would drop their drums and trombones and dive for cover and the news would be all over Denmark in a few hours. Result — the Danes would take new heart and start flocking to join their Resistance.'

Henderson was looking aghast. 'You're saying they want us to put the squadron at risk just to disrupt a birthday parade, sir? Do they realise how far we are from Copenhagen?'

MacBride's voice was heavy with sarcasm. 'We can all read maps, Henderson.'

Equally shocked, Davies came to his surbordinate's assistance. 'You surely haven't agreed to this?'

He received the Brigadier's aggressive stare. 'I have. You've got to remember, Davies, that war isn't just a matter of shooting down enemy aircraft and hitting his production lines. It has a psychological side that is just as important. If we can put heart into the Danes and make them resist, we'll be doing more damage to the enemy than a month of air raids.'

Davies' face was a study as he received this lecture on matters military. Adams was feeling sympathy for the Danes. A fun-loving people over-run by the mighty German Army, it seemed to Adams they were showing good sense in keeping their heads down until the world found its sanity again. At the same time Adams allowed that he could be prejudiced. In the days of his puberty his parents had taken him on holiday to a small hotel in Bournemouth where a young Danish girl had been staying with an English family. A beautiful nubile creature, she had shown an interest in Adams and the shy, idealist boy had immediately imbued her with every virtue in the female calender. As she was the only Dane he had ever met, Adams had found himself thinking well of her country ever since.

Noticing Davies' expression, the elderly Brigadier made one of his tactful interventions. 'I don't think Air Commodore Davies is only concerned about the distance involved, MacBride. I believe I am right in thinking the parade takes place around midday. This means the flight would have to be made there and back in daylight.'

MacBride's curtness to a man almost old enough to be his father heightened Adams' dislike of him. 'We've taken all that into account, Simms.' He turned back to Davies. 'Wasn't it your squadron that carried out a daylight raid deep into Bavaria?'

'That's right,' Davies said. 'But we had over a hundred B17s giving us radar cover almost to the target. I doubt if we'd have got through without them.'

MacBride's glance at Staines said the obvious. The huge American gave a laugh of disbelief. 'A force of B17s to bust up a birthday party! You can't be serious, MacBride. You any idea what it costs to lay on a B17 mission?'

The army officer did not retreat an inch. 'I'm fully aware what it costs, General. But I'm also aware what it will cost in British and American lives if German reserve divisions are not diverted from the invasion beaches.'

Staines shrugged impatiently. 'No one's disputing that. I wouldn't have left my Air Force back in East Anglia for the day if I didn't think it important we help the Underground Movements. But Jesus, this is only speculation. The Danes might just split their arses with laughter and go back to making butter.'

'This squadron still has to carry out the mission,

General. And we haven't long. Hitler's birthday is on the 20th April.'

Two red spots, warning signs Adams knew well, were burning high up on Davies' cheeks. 'Where do these orders come from?'

'That depends on the circumstances. Sometimes from higher up, sometimes from my own Committee.'

'And where does this one come from?'

MacBride's tone made it clear he was answering Davies' questions as a favour rather than a right. 'As in part it is a political decision, it comes from higher up.'

Fully aware of the ambiguity of the expression 'higher up' Davies was showing suspicion as well as defiance. 'My boys are the best, as you well know. But they're not miracle workers and I certainly don't intend sending them to certain death now or any other time. I hope your Committee realises that.'

The look he received would have withered lesser men. 'Regrettably such decisions have been taken out of your hands for a while, Davies. In a way your squadron has only itself to blame. If it hadn't such a record for carrying out difficult missions it wouldn't have been chosen in the first place.'

There was a grunt of disbelief from Staines. Davies was showing bitterness. 'You're saying it has to pay a price for its success?'

'For God's sake, Davies, no one intends sending your boys out to certain death: we value their skills too highly. At the same time certain missions are necessary and must be carried out.' Here MacBride glanced at the frowning Staines. 'Knowing some will have to be carried out in daylight and aware the Americans have become expert in daylight operations, we thought it good sense to ask for their co-operation. However, if for reasons of their own they feel unable to give that co-operation, then we have no choice but to go it alone.'

With the ball put firmly in his court, Staines was breathing hard. 'Let's get this straight, MacBride. I'll co-operate when I think your schemes make sense because we're in the same war. But brass bands and birthday parties, no!' His expression changed as he turned to Davies. 'Sorry, Davies. But that's how it is.'

Davies was given no opportunity to reply. The jut of MacBride's jaw made Adams concede that whatever else the man might be, he was a fighter. 'You have the right to pick and choose, General. But if you give us a chance I think you'll find out our schemes aren't as bizarre as they first sound. Apart from having a great deal of experience, we take advice from Resistance leaders as well as our own agents, as in the case of this Danish mission. And it's hard to deny they know their own people better than we ever can.'

From the way Staines opened his mouth, then closed it again, Adams felt MacBride had won a point. Growling something under his breath, the Texan turned to Davies. 'Did you come up in that Miles Master of yours this morning?'

Davies looked surprised at the question. 'Yes. Why?'

'I'd like your offer of a lift back today. That'll give me the chance to have a beer and to meet Moore and your boys again.'

Realising it was the American's way of telling him he wanted a private talk, Davies nodded willingly. 'Yes, sir, of course. We'll be delighted to have you. The boys should be back by then.'

'You mean they're out on a mission?' When Davies nodded, Staines glanced across at the fidgeting Henderson. 'Then what's Jock doing here?'

Davies slanted a glance at the burly MacBride who was showing impatience at the cross talk. Without hesitation Staines turned back to the soldier. 'Are you going to need Henderson and Adams much longer, MacBride? Any C.O. worth his salt wants to be around when his boys get back.'

MacBride, as shrewd as he was aggressive, was wondering if Staines' request of Davies suggested a change of heart over the Danish mission. With no wish to prejudice the possibility he shrugged, 'Not if Davies is prepared to brief them on anything else we might discuss.'

Giving Staines a grateful look, Henderson rose to his feet. 'Thank you, sir. But I'd like to ask one question before we go. How will orders come down to me?'

MacBride nodded at the elderly soldier alongside him. 'We shall transmit them to the Brigadier and he will contact Air Commodore Davies. He will then brief you as before.' The man's gaze moved on to Staines. 'Naturally you will be informed of our every move, General, so that you can co-operate when you approve a mission.'

Unsure how much sarcasm was packed in the comment, the usually good-natured Staines gave a non-committal grunt. 'Leave out the birthday parties and we might get somewhere.'

Wasting no time, Henderson and Adams were already at the door. Seeing the elderly Brigadier motioning to them, they waited. Drawing them out of the room, he said something in a low voice that made them both start. 'That's good news, sir,' Henderson said. 'It'll cheer him up no end to hear it.'

The Brigadier smiled. 'I know it will. But tell him to keep it to himself.'

'Don't worry, sir. He will. Thank you for telling us.'

With another glance at his watch, Henderson started down the polished corridor. Hurrying after him, Adams found he could not match the Scot's long strides and fell behind. At the doorway that led to the courtyard, Henderson paused and stared back. 'What the hell are you doing, Frank? If we hurry we might still get back in time.'

Without waiting, he ran down a flight of steps towards his waiting car. Cursing the fate that had made him as he was, Adams scampered after him.

4

Henderson spotted the Mosquitoes as his staff car reached the top of the long, shallow hill that stood between the town of Highgate and Sutton Craddock. It was a point from which the southern reaches of the Yorkshire Moors could be seen. Sutton Craddock lay three miles to the east, a smallish airfield resting on a counterpane of neat fields, hedges, and clumps of trees. A whitewashed building, tiny in the distance, stood almost opposite its main entrance. Halting the car, Henderson pointed through the windshield. 'There they are! They're just coming in!'

Adams squinted through his spectacles. Before he could answer Henderson threw open his door and stood on the running board to gain a better view. Beyond the airfield tiny liverish specks were appearing in the hazy April sky. Seeing a smudge of black smoke, Henderson jumped back in the car and accelerated down the hill. Adams, who had been about to climb out himself, was thrown back into his seat. Recovering, he turned towards the Scot. 'Could you count them?'

'No. But one of them has taken a hiding. It's laying smoke all over Yorkshire.'

Ahead a Bedford 25cwt was trundling towards the airfield. As Henderson sounded his horn the driver put a hand from his cab and gave the V sign. Cursing, Henderson jabbed his hand on the horn again and swerved past with his wheels thumping on the grass verge opposite. The Bedford driver's yell choked in his throat when he recognised the staff car and the irate Wing Commander.

Down at The Black Swan the resident barmaid,

31

Maisie, was showing an equal interest in the Mosquitoes' return. She had first heard the distant hum of their Merlins when stacking empty beer crates in the back garden. With a shout 'Joe! The lads are back,' she had run up the private path to the wicker gate where she was now standing gazing anxiously skywards.

To anyone who flew at Sutton Craddock Maisie was an institution as permanent as Bishop's Wood or the line of graceful poplars that marked its southern perimeter. Dark-haired, black-eyed, with bold handsome features and breasts guaranteed to make any self-respecting airman's eyes glow like Very lights, Maisie seldom failed to welcome back her beloved lads. Even in the icy light of dawn, she was often seen in her dressing gown at the wicker gate. Eye-sore and dog-weary after a night of battle in German skies, crews would see her waving to them and know that indeed they were home again.

The hum of Merlins was growing louder. To the east three black shapes appeared. With one Mosquito pouring smoke from its starboard engine and the other two keeping station on either side, they were like two men supporting a wounded comrade. Noticing the smoke Maisie turned and dashed back along the path, passing on her way the innkeeper, Joe Kearns. A white-haired, portly man in his fifties, Kearns gazed after her with concern. 'What's the matter, lass? Are they in trouble?'

Ignoring him the girl dashed into the inn and ran upstairs into the unoccupied front bedroom. Over on the airfield sirens had begun wailing and an ambulance and two fire tenders were accelerating towards the north-south runway. Ground crews at the dispersal points were standing in anxious groups and pointing eastwards.

As they neared the airfield the two leading Mosquitoes released their wounded comrade and went into a wide orbit. The rest of the squadron joined them, great birds circling the field while the one in greater need landed first. Not all of these were unscathed. One was trailing a thin stream of glycol and others had battle scars on wings and bodies. The noise of their engines was deafening now, rattling loose window panes in the inn.

With the morning wind from the south, the approach path of the crippled Mosquito brought it almost directly over the inn. The cough of its damaged engine sounded like a man with blood in his lungs. As the pilot throttled back, the whine of airfoils became a thin scream of pain.

The girl threw the window open and leaned out. As the Mosquito passed unsteadily over she could see blackened flak scars on its starboard wing and a landing wheel dangling like a broken claw. Although the crew could not have seen the girl, the Mosquito dipped its wings before sinking gingerly over the airfield fence. Acknowledging Maisie's loyalty had become as much a part of the squadron's tradition as Moore's crate of whisky after a successful operation.

An anxious voice sounded at Maisie's elbow. In his undemonstrative Northcountry way, Joe Kearns was as attached to the squadron as the girl herself. 'You see that, lass? One of his wheels has gone.'

The girl felt for his arm and gripped it. The Mosquito had now levelled off above the runway. The fire tenders were racing alongside it, their asbestos-clad crews ready for the worst. The aircraft held off for nearly a hundred yards, then, as if its strength had given out at last, suddenly sank down. A cloud of spray rose, followed by a rending crash. The Mosquito's tail rose high into the air as if it were about to pitch over. Instead the tail fell back as the aircraft skidded on its belly towards the grass verge. There it almost somersalted again before completing a ground loop and coming to rest.

The fire tenders reached it within seconds. Leaping out, crews drove their extinguisher hoses into the heart of the smoking engines. As white foam began covering them, other men leapt on the wings and began levering back the cupola.

With the danger of fire eliminated, Maisie's grip on Kearns' arm eased. The pilot and navigator of the Mosquito were now being lowered to the ground. One, although unsteady, pushed away his helpers and bent over his comrade who a moment later was laid on a stretcher and slid into the ambulance. Waiting for the other crewman to jump in after him, the ambulance turned and sped away.

It was a signal for the rest of the Mosquitoes to land. Throttles back, dipping their wings in turn, they swept down in quick succession to the runway. When the last was down, Maisie turned to Kearns. 'At least they all got back. Tom Davidson and Bill Arnold were in the plane that crashed.'

'Don't tell me you could recognise 'em this far off,' Kearns said.

'I didn't need to. I know all their aircraft numbers.'

Kearns eyed her with respect. Then, noticing her slight pallor, he led her to the door. 'Let's crack that spare bottle of whisky, lass, and have a drink. I can do with one myself.'

Ian Moore dropped to the ground and pulled off his helmet with a sigh of relief. As he turned to look at the foam-covered Mosquito sprawled out on the grass, the April breeze ruffled his wavy fair hair and cooled his cheeks. His navigator, a small astute Cockney nicknamed Hoppy with a thin, pinched face, noticed his glance and said something to him. Neither Moore nor Hopkinson himself heard the words: both were suffering from the temporary deafness that afflicted all crews after a lengthy flight.

A corporal giving orders to the Mosquito's maintenance crew saw the helmet dangling from Moore's hands and took it from him. In return he received a smile. The young Squadron Commander seldom failed to show courtesy to his ground crews: one reason he received their loyalty.

There was din and movement everywhere as aircraft came in and taxied to their dispersal points and trucks drove crews towards the de-briefing room. Moore was unzipping his flying suit. The Mosquito was a warm aircraft and they had flown back at low level. As he threw the fur collar back the ribbons of the DSO and bar, the DFC and the American Congressional Medal of Honour could be seen.

Hoppy tried again, pointing at the crashed Mosquito. 'They were bleedin' lucky they didn't go arse over tip, skipper.' He glanced at the corporal. 'How did they come out of it? Do you know?'

'I think Mr. Arnold had shrapnel in his leg, sir. Mr. Davidson was just shaken up.'

The Cockney grimaced as he turned back to Moore. 'Considering the flak train, skipper, I reckon we got off lightly.'

Moore had a cultured voice with good enunciation. 'I'll go with that, Hoppy.' He started towards the crashed Mosquito. 'Let's go and see how bad the damage is.'

Hoppy fell into step alongside him. Although a veteran on his third tour of operations − and regarded by most crews as the best navigator on the Station − the Cockney was still a victim of the unwinding process that afflicted most crews after a mission. 'Did you see those trains, skipper? They were goin' up into the air like kids' toys.'

The smile Moore gave at the Cockney's euphoria puckered a small scar on his right cheek, the result of a 37mm shell bursting just outside his cockpit the previous year. 'They'll have the mess cleared in a week, Hoppy.'

Half a dozen pilots and navigators were already examining the wreck. One of them was a tall, raw-boned Squadron Leader with a face that was all planes and angles. Frank Harvey was B Flight Commander, a Yorkshireman who, in spite of his dourness, was highly protective towards his crews. His craggy face turned towards Moore as the Squadron Commander approached. 'These stupid bastards are lucky to be alive, Ian. They went against my orders and flew too low over that flak train. I've a damn good mind to charge 'em when they come out.'

His comment was overheard by a pilot standing on the opposite side of the fusilage. Dark-haired, full of humour, and the darling of the Waafs, the good-looking Tommy Millburn had joined the RAF before the U.S. had declared war and despite his constant disparagement of all things Limey, obstinately refused to change

35

uniforms even though the 8th Air Force periodically offered him promotion and pay that was astronomical beside British standards. As he spoke, he winked at Moore.

'Take it easy, Frank. They did lay a salvo right across the engine sheds. Which is more than the rest of us did.'

Harvey turned towards him with a scowl. 'When I want your opinion, Millburn, I'll ask for it.'

The American grinned. 'Don't bite me, Frank. I was a good boy today.'

Harvey's scowl deepened. 'Belt up, Millburn. Go and clown somewhere else.'

With tension unwinding after a mission, crews would occasionally pass comments that would make an eavesdropper flinch. Among the men themselves, with a camaraderie forged by battle and interdependence, they were seldom taken seriously. Nevertheless, knowing how Harvey felt about his crews taking unnecessary risks, Moore thought it best to intervene. 'You'd better get over to the de-briefing room, Tommy. Sue Spencer's filling in for Adams until he gets back.'

'O.K., skipper. We're on our way.' With a cheerful nod at Harvey, Millburn turned to the navigator alongside him. 'C'mon, boyo. Let's go and tell Sue how we're winning the war.'

Moore could not hide a smile as he watched the couple make their way towards a waiting transport. The navigator, Johnnie Gabriel, was a small, wiry man with gnome-like features that could look both young and old at will. Although older than the squadron average, Gabby, as he was known to all, had a thirst for excitement and was as famous for his mad pranks and tireless pursuit of women as was Millburn himself. At the same time the ill-assorted but inseparable pair were a highly capable crew who had once led Harvey's flight when the Yorkshireman had been hospitalised.

Gabby, a Welshman, had a somewhat lugubrious voice. 'What did you mean — you were a good boy today? You bloody nearly killed us when you tried to clobber that flak post.'

The tall Millburn grinned down at him. 'You binding again, boyo? I got you back in one piece, didn't I?'

'Only by luck. One of these days you're going to take one risk too many. And who's going to be the loser?'

Millburn slapped the indignant Welshman's shoulders. 'I'll tell you who, boyo. That big blonde I'm taking out tonight. She'd lose the best thing that's ever happened to her.'

Gabby sniffed. 'You think you're God's gift to women, don't you? You're heading for a fall one of these days, Millburn. Just wait and see.'

Millburn was not listening. He pointed across the airfield to the dispersal point where a Miles Master was parked. 'I didn't notice Davies' kite when we came in.'

Gabby, who was in one of his darker Celtic moods, followed his eyes. 'Since when do you notice anything? You know what it means, don't you?'

'Trouble?' Millburn suggested.

'What else when Davies comes? You'll see, Millburn. Any day now we'll be going out on another Valkyrie job.'

Millburn grinned. 'You're a real little ray of sunshine this morning, aren't you? Do you really want to know why he's here?' As the Welshman turned towards him, Millburn's grin spread. 'He's come to check how many Waafs you got pregnant last month. If it's as many as they say, you're in for a nasty operation, boyo.'

A camouflaged staff car speeding alongside the runway drew both men's attention. Gabby turned to watch it as it shot past. 'I thought Pop Henderson was at a conference this morning.'

'Maybe he's worried about the Waafs too,' Millburn quipped.

Henderson's target was the crashed Mosquito. Jumping from the car, he hurried towards Moore. 'How bad is it, Ian?'

'Not bad at all, sir. Arnold has a piece of shrapnel in his leg and Davidson had a shaking. They'll soon be back.'

'Any other casualties?'

'No. There's a spot of damage to the kites but the rest of the boys are O.K.'

Henderson relaxed. 'So it went well?'

'I think so. We left the engine and repair shops on fire.'

'What about the rolling stock?'

'Yes, we dropped a few sticks along the tracks. The damage was quite heavy.'

Henderson expressed the fear all Station commanders had at that period of the war. 'Do you think you killed any French civilians?'

'We tried to keep all our bombs on the target, sir.' Moore nodded across the airfield where a team of Waafs were removing the camera pack from the squadron's photo-reconnaissance Mosquito. 'But I'd rather see the photographs before sticking my neck out there.'

Knowing Moore's way was always understatement, the Scot was satisfied. He turned to Harvey. 'I've got some good news for you, Frank.'

He led the Yorkshireman and Moore out of earshot of the salvage team who were now assembling round the wrecked Mosquito. 'It's about Anna Reinhardt. I saw the old Brigadier this morning and he said she'd been in touch with them quite a few times recently. So it doesn't seem you've anything to worry about.'

In Harvey's harsh world a man showed neither his joys nor his sorrows in case his enemies took advantage of either. His only concession to the news was to light a cigarette. 'Did the Brigadier say what she was doing?'

'No,' Henderson lied. 'Just that she was safe and well.'

There was a few seconds of silence while Harvey sucked in smoke. Then: 'Did Adams come back with you?'

'Yes. He's helping Sue with the de-briefing.'

'Then I'd better get over there in case my lads are chatting up the Waafs instead of getting on with their job.' With a nod at both officers, the Yorkshireman started towards the tarmac apron, a tall figure with the gait of a farmer rather than a soldier. In the distance a large black mongrel rounded a hangar and made helter-skelter towards him. Sam, Harvey's dog, had been released from the Yorkshireman's billet and was expressing his joy at his master's return in no uncertain manner.

Cuffing the dog's head affectionately, Harvey ordered it to heel and continued on his way towards Adams' hut. As the two officers watched him, his shoulders straightened and he began whistling tunelessly. Moore smiled. 'He's really on Cloud Nine.'

The Scot nodded grimly. 'He wouldn't be if I'd told him everything.'

Moore gave a faint start. 'What does that mean?'

Remembering what Adams had told him the previous year, Henderson was already damning himself for making the comment. It was Adams' belief that Harvey was not the only man on the squadron who had fallen in love with the courageous German girl during the few days she had spent at Sutton Craddock. 'You want to hear it, Ian?'

Moore's voice turned sharp. 'Yes. Why not?'

It was a response that the Scot felt confirmed Adams' suspicions but it was too late to turn back now. 'It seems she was ill with jaundice for a while and her friends over there had problems getting her medical treatment. But she's recovered now and is working on some job in south-west France. The old boy wouldn't go into any details but I've reason to believe the Gestapo are involved.' For a moment Henderson's admiration outweighed his sensitivity. 'Imagine it. A German girl, working against those bastards for Allied Intelligence. Christ, I wish I had that kind of courage.'

For a moment a muscle twitched in Moore's cheek. Then he nodded after the retreating figure of Harvey. 'Tell him that and he'll go crazy. Let's find out how the de-briefing is going.'

5

As the huge automobile rolled from the courtyard and started down the tree-flanked drive of High Elms, Staines leaned forward and closed the glass partition between himself and the driver. Pausing to light one of his cigars, he turned to Davies. 'O.K., now we can talk. What do you think about this new ball game?'

Although he had known Staines for nearly a year now, Davies remained a regular serving officer and a General's invitation to talk frankly still caused him reservations. 'Do you mean how do I feel about losing 633 Squadron to the SOE, sir?'

'I don't need to ask you that, do I?' Staines grunted. 'I'm talking about the trend itself. All the reports I get suggest the Kraut's secret police are taking control over their Armed Forces. I think we're starting to move in that direction ourselves.'

Davies was looking startled. 'Do you really believe that?'

'Yeah, I do. Maybe it's the effect of total war. But one thing's for sure — with guys like MacBride pulling the strings there's going to be a lot more of the dirty stuff. The underground jobs, the half-military, half-political missions, and so on.'

'Like this Copenhagen raid?' Davies asked.

'That's right.' Staines eyed Davies through his cigar smoke. 'How're you feeling about that? Still sore?'

Davies' hesitation betrayed the second thoughts he had been having. 'I'm not certain. They do say the surest way to topple tyrants is to laugh at them. Perhaps if the Jerries can be made to look ridiculous it might just work.'

At that moment the car halted at the drive entrance. Recognising the two officers, the sentry saluted and waved them on. But with Staines' cigar now burning like a smoke bomb, Davies used the excuse to open his side window. 'General Staines and Air Commodore Davies,' he said.

The sentry saluted again. 'Yes, sir. I had recognised you.'

Aware the man had brought his ploy into the open, Davies nevertheless left the window down as the car swung out on the road. Eyes twinkling, Staines motioned at his cigar. 'You smoked one of these once, didn't you, Davies?'

'Twice, sir. And both times they nearly killed me.'

Staines' big laugh boomed out. 'You should persevere. I'm told they're good for virility.'

Davies almost retorted there was nothing wrong with his virility but refrained as the American's tone changed. 'So you think this Copenhagen raid could be worth the risk?'

'I wouldn't go that far,' Davies said. 'But I haven't any choice, have I?'

'Not by the sound of it. You'll have to watch that MacBride, Davies. He's a ruthless bastard.'

Feeling not to deny the charge was concurrence enough, Davies changed the subject. 'Is it true you've been given two wings of the 9th Air Force, sir?'

'Yeah. Right out of the blue. And Christ knows why. You aren't the only one who's been screwed up by this invasion, Davies. No one knows his arse from his elbow. That's if you leave out the Krauts.'

No one could have sounded more innocent than Davies. 'What are your squadrons, sir? Mustangs?'

'Yeah, one or two.' When Davies nodded, the Texan grinned. 'So what the hell am I doing not lending you a few for the Copenhagen job?' As Davies opened his mouth to protest, Staines' grin broadened. 'It's no use, Davies. I've been working with you British too long not to know how you frame your complaints. You think I'm letting you down, don't you?'

'Not if you have the right to pick and choose, sir. That's fair enough.'

Staines' grin turned into a frown. 'Having a free hand doesn't mean I throw my friends to the lions, Davies. It doesn't mean I throw away my boys' lives either. That's why I wanted this private talk. Like you I was dead against this Copenhagen junket until I'd time to think about it. Now I'm wondering too.' He turned in his seat. 'How many kites are you thinking of sending?'

'If I had protection I'd send only one flight. But now it looks as if I'll have to send the entire squadron.'

'A flight of eight ships?'

'Yes.'

'O.K. Then how would a dozen Mustangs grab you?'

Davies gave a start. 'A dozen Mustangs would make all the difference, sir.'

'O.K., you've got 'em. I can't spare any more because all our bombardment groups are supposed to be employed from dawn to dusk on these interdiction raids. We'll sort out the details when we see Moore.' Waving aside the relieved Davies' thanks, the Texan changed the subject. 'What about this other thing MacBride hinted at? You got any guesses what it is?'

'None at all.' Then Davies noticed Staines' expression. 'What have you heard, sir?'

'Just a rumour, nothing more. But it concerns the Krauts' ZWB.'

Davies' ears pricked. ZWB was the code-name for Germany's clearing house for reports on new weapons. It had been a ZWB leak, picked up by an Allied agent, that had resulted in the successful Rhine Maiden operation the previous year. 'What kind of rumour, sir?'

'Nothing specific, worse luck. But it was the reason I didn't bitch about attending MacBride's party today.'

'I noticed you had a private talk with him afterwards. Did you learn any more?'

The big American gave a grunt of disgust. 'No. He's one of those egotistical bastards who enjoys keeping things close to his chest. But he didn't deny it, so I reckon there must be a connection.'

Davies was looking puzzled. 'But if there is, where would the Gestapo fit in? I thought ZWB was a scientific-military establishment.'

'There's your secret police trend again. Maybe the Boche keep their boffins up to scratch by putting thumb-screws on 'em now and then.' Staines' grin was rueful. 'One thing for sure. If the ZWB are involved, it's going to be a lot harder for me to keep that free hand I was bragging about.'

6

Adams felt a twinge of heartburn as he hurried towards the Intelligence office. Having spent over an hour interrogating the crews, he had decided on a quick lunch. Although one could never be quite certain what the volatile Davies might do next, MacBride's conference that morning had seemed to leave the Air Commodore with little room for manoeuvre and Adams felt it wise to have all his preparations made.

The Intelligence Room, nicknamed "The Confessional" by the crews, was a Nissen hut packed with the mass of diverse information that poured out almost daily from Group and Central Intelligence. Collated from a hundred sources, there was everything from photographs of the enemy's latest flak posts to pamphlets dealing with German Mess habits. In theory the processing of all this "bumph", as it was known to one and all, should have made Intelligence officers the best informed airmen on the Station. In fact pressure of time forced them to burn eighty per cent of the pamphlets unread. Nevertheless the highly conscientious Adams made a point of reading anything that could remotely affect the safety of his men, one reason he had little free time in the evenings.

A young Flight Lieutenent was just closing the door of the hut as he came hurrying round the corner. Before the man turned away Adams recognised Tony St. Claire. Of all the pilots on the Station, he was the one Adams envied most. Tall, slim, with a face that was Byronic in its good looks, St. Claire had been making a name for himself on the concert platform as a pianist before he had volunteered for the RAF. Moreover he had the love of a girl that in Adams' eyes made even these considerable assets pale into insignificance.

'Hello, Tony. Is Sue still in there?'

The pilot turned, recognised him, and nodded. 'Yes.' Hesitating a moment, he went on: 'I haven't been wasting her time, if that's what you're getting at.'

Adams pulled up short. 'I wasn't getting at anything, Tony. What on earth made you think that?'

The young man looked both shamefaced and sullen. 'The way you asked me, I suppose.'

'All I did was ask if she was there.'

'You knew all along she was there. She's been waiting for you to get back from lunch.'

'But I didn't ask her to wait.'

With a shrug, St. Claire walked away. Feeling ridiculous for making explanations he had no need to make, Adams gazed after him for a moment before entering the Nissen hut. 'Sue!'

The girl was bending over the open drawer of a filing cabinet. With her back to him and with his eyes needing a moment to adjust to the light, Adams had the impression it was a posture of distress. Yet her voice was under control when she straightened. 'Hello, Frank. Have you had a good lunch?'

He watched her carefully as he threaded his way through the chairs that were scattered over the floor. Reaching his large desk at the far end of the hut he paused, noticing the girl had still not turned to face him. 'We'll have to spend this afternoon seeing what we've got on Denmark and Copenhagen. I can't see any way Davies can get us off that operation.'

Her hand lifted briefly to her eyes, then she turned to face him. A tall, willowy girl, she had been his assistant for nearly a year and during that time an affection had entered into their relationship. It was not the kind of affection for which the lonely Adams craved but it was still one he needed and valued. With her gentle ways and her understanding, Sue Spencer was the antithesis of the waspish woman his wife had become.

45

'Has he come back to the station yet?' she asked.

'I don't know. He wasn't in the Mess but he could be in Henderson's office.' He moved nearer to her. 'You've been crying.'

'Don't be silly. Of course I haven't.'

He reached out and touched her wet cheek. Seeing his expression she tried to laugh but only succeeded in making her tears flow again. Biting her lip, she turned away. 'I'm sorry, Frank. I'll be all right in a moment.'

His concern was the greater because he had seldom seen her courage and self-discipline fail her. Even after St. Claire had been shot down the previous autumn, she had insisted on doing her full stint of duty the following day. Nor had she faltered during the agonising weeks that followed when the Red Cross had been unable to affirm or deny her fiancé's death. It had been Adams' task to inform her that the young pilot and his navigator had survived the crash and were safe in the hands of the Belgium Resistance and her joy that day was something he would never forget.

Because of the broken leg St. Claire had suffered, the Resistance had not been able to smuggle him back to England until late January. Sue's euphoria, however, had been short-lived. With St. Claire convalescing after his ordeal at his parents' home, Adams had arranged for the girl to spend a long weekend with him. Expecting her to be starry-eyed on her return, he had found her quiet and dejected instead.

At first Adams had believed he knew the reason. Before his crash, St. Claire had been struck by a flak shell at the moment he was releasing a rocket, an accident that had resulted in the deaths of a dozen American prisoners of war. It was the kind of tragedy that could well prey on a sensitive man's mind, particularly after months of inactivity, but to Adams' surprise the girl had denied it was the reason for her concern. When she had refused to say any more, Adams had been baffled. The obvious reason — that his affections had strayed elsewhere — was certainly not true of anyone on the Station. With St. Claire's good looks and talent, Waafs tended to swoon if he as much as glanced in their direction, but instead the young pilot was spending more and more time in the Mess where his heavy drinking was causing concern to his Flight Commander.

Sighing, Adams sat down. 'I'd like to help, Sue. You do know that?'

'Of course I know, Frank. But there's nothing anyone can do.'

Adams drew out his pipe and frowned down at it. 'Are you sure of that?'

'Yes. Quite sure.'

There was a note of reproach in Adams' voice. 'It doesn't make any sense. A few months ago we all believed he was dead. Instead he survived by a near miracle and on top of that he escaped. You ought to be overjoyed. And yet look at you both.'

'I know,' she said quietly. 'It seems wicked, doesn't it? Only it's not that simple, Frank.'

To give himself courage Adams pulled out his tobacco pouch and began opening it. 'Is there someone else, Sue? Someone he's met since he's got back?'

The Nissen hut went very quiet for a moment. Then she moved towards her desk. 'No. In a way I wish there was.'

He stared at her. 'You wish there was? What does that mean?'

'I could fight that, Frank. Or at least live with it.'

'You're making it more mysterious by the minute.' Without intending to, Adams was looking hurt. 'We've shared confidences before, Sue. Why can't we share this one? Sometimes it helps to talk and it won't go any further than me.'

She was gazing at the walls of the Nissen hut as if it were a prison. 'I can't, Frank. I can't talk here.'

'Then what about somewhere else?'

She toyed with a pile of interrogation forms on her desk. For a moment she sounded almost sullen. 'Why should you bother about my problems? You've quite enough of your own.'

Sensitive as always, Adams began wondering if his

concern was beginning to look like curiosity. 'I don't want you to think I'm prying, Sue. If you'd rather not tell me, I'll understand.'

Her tone changed immediately. 'Of course I don't think you're prying. Where would you like to go?'

The suddenness of her assent surprised him.

'We could go to the Swan. There aren't any guests there at this time of the year and I know Kearns would let us use his private lounge. Or we could go into Highgate. I know the people who run the Kettledrum so they might push the boat out a bit for us.'

She shrugged. 'I don't mind either.'

True to himself, Adams was having an afterthought. 'No, come to think of it, perhaps we'd better make it Highgate.'

Something in his tone drew her attention. 'Why?'

His eyes moved down to his pipe into which he was pressing tobacco. 'Nothing,' he said lamely. 'I just thought it would make a change. But that's stupid. Make it the Swan. It's easier to get to.'

In some ways she knew Adams better than he knew himself. 'You were thinking it might make Tony jealous to see me out with another man, weren't you? What's wrong with that? It might do him good.'

It had been Adams' original thought but he had immediately dismissed it as ridiculous. That even at this moment the girl could bolster his self confidence by pretending such a thing were possible perhaps explained why Adams had become devoted to her. 'I can't think of anything less likely. But let's stick to the Kettledrum. When shall we go?'

She moved back to one of the filing cabinets. 'I haven't much call on my free time these days. Let's go the first night we're both off duty.'

London was not at its best that late April morning. Well-muffled pedestrians were hurrying unsmilingly along the wet pavements, the traffic sounded surly, and the Cockney sparrows, usually so chirpy, were huddled in tiny groups on window ledges as if discussing whether a policy of migration should be included in next year's agenda.

A small group of them had settled on the Whitehall window behind which the elderly Brigadier was standing and their earnest discussion drew his eyes as MacBride crossed his office and rummaged in a steel cabinet. His attention was quickly restored as MacBride threw an enlarged photograph on a polished table.

'It's Werner all right. We've had it double checked by the faculty at Oxford.'

The Brigadier gazed down at the photograph. 'I suppose there's no possibility he is a genuine member of the Gestapo?'

'At his age? And a world famous scientist to boot? You think the Germans would waste the talents of a man like that by making him a political policeman?'

The Brigadier nodded. 'You're quite right, of course. So what's our next move?'

MacBride picked up the photograph and stared at it. 'We could assassinate him.'

The elderly soldier gave a start. 'But we aren't certain yet our suspicions are correct. He could be carrying out experiments that are harmless to us.'

'Then why would he be wearing a disguise? And why would the Waffen SS and the Gestapo be guarding the town?'

'I agree it all looks suspicious. But as yet we've no real evidence to justify assassination.'

'We haven't?' MacBride sounded truculent as he tossed a sheet of paper on the table. 'Lorenz has made friends with one of the civilian staff working there. Her radio report came in last night. Read it.'

The Brigadier looked shocked as he picked up the transcript. 'That girl takes too many risks. We shouldn't allow it.'

MacBride gave a shrug of indifference. 'She's a German. That makes it easier for her. Read her report.'

As the Brigadier obeyed, MacBride moved to his elbow. 'Note what the man said. "When the experiments are finished England will pay for her crimes against the

49

Fatherland". Does that sound as if Werner is working on a vaccine for foot-and-mouth disease?'

'But Werner is a scientist of world renown. He was on the short list for a Nobel prize in 1937.'

'So what? You think that means he won't work for the Nazis? There's a whole bunch of eminent scientists carrying out experiments in the concentration camps.'

The Brigadier was only too aware it was true. 'But isn't there a possibility this man might just have been showing off to a pretty girl?'

'Yes, that's possible. But you know Lorenz as well or better than I do. Do you think she's the type of agent who wouldn't see through a man's boasting?'

The Brigadier shook his head. 'No. She's highly intelligent.'

'Then there you are. Something big is going on in that research centre. As I see it we've plenty of reasons to assassinate Werner.'

Aware of the nature of the man, the Brigadier was careful to keep all sentiment out of his objection. 'I think it's too dangerous. If Werner is killed the Germans are certain to take heavy revenge on the town and that could cause a backlash. French Resistance groups might decide we're acting too arbitrarily and not giving enough thought to French lives. Apart from that, Werner must have assistants fully acquainted with his experiments. If we kill him, they'll be alerted and simply move their faculties elsewhere.'

MacBride's scowl told he had been working along the same lines. 'It's a hell of a pity because assassination wouldn't have been difficult. All right, let's consider the alternatives. We can't bomb the place because it's slap in the centre of the town and anyway, at this point in time, we'd never get De Gaulle's permission. I'm wondering if I shouldn't have this German assistant Lorenz is seeing kidnapped by one of my Maquis groups. If I picked the right group, they'd soon get the truth out of him.'

The Brigadier looked aghast. 'You can't do that. It would put Lorenz under immediate suspicion.'

'For Christ's sake, we might be playing for high stakes

50

here. We can't pussy foot with our agents. She could always pack her bags and get out once she'd laid on the kidnapping.'

Shrewd in spite of his gentle manner, the elderly Brigadier knew there was only one way of controlling the man's ruthlessness. 'If we did that, Lorenz would be no further use to us. And I've found her invaluable. A better idea would be to have one of the convoys ambushed and its contents examined. Lorenz has already sent us their route and times of arrival. Once we have a sample of the contents we'll be in a far better position to know if our suspicions are correct.'

It was a plan so simple that MacBride was clearly puzzled why he had not thought of it himself. He gave a grudging nod. 'All right; let's do it that way. You never know – civilian assistants might travel with the convoys. Or the military escort might know what's going on. I think I'll use Ferot. If anyone can squeeze information out of men, he can.'

The older man could not hide his distaste. Ferot was noted as being one of the most ruthless of the Maquis leaders and a man he himself seldom used. 'How will you arrange the ambush? Through Lorenz?'

MacBride consulted the transcript. 'If the Jerries keep to their timetable – and thank Christ they usually do – there's one due tomorrow. So there's no time to waste.' He moved towards the door. 'I'll see a message goes straight off to Ferot, with orders that Lorenz stays in overall charge and all information obtained is to be channelled through her. That'll keep everything neat and tidy.'

He returned ten minutes later, radiating confidence and efficiency. 'All taken care of. I've also arranged for a boffin to be flown out tonight if the weather holds. Then he'll be on the job to examine the stuff the moment Ferot brings it in.'

The Brigadier nodded his approval. 'That's an excellent idea. So, with luck, we might get a report from him the day after tomorrow?'

'If Ferot can move the stuff quickly, we might even get

51

one tomorrow night. I'd like you to stay down here if you will. Once his report comes we might have to convene our Committee.'

'Yes, of course. I'll arrange it.' The Brigadier paused. 'What action are you planning to take if the threat is as grave as you fear?'

The man's sudden irritation betrayed his indecision. 'Then I suppose we'll have to go to De Gaulle and get his permission to bomb.'

'Do you think he'll give it?'

'How the hell do I know? If the threat's that serious, he's going to find it hard to object.'

'I wouldn't be certain of that. He's already vetoed quite a number of targets Coningham and Spaatz want to attack.'

MacBride scowled. 'Don't tell me how pig-headed he can be. We've had problems with him ever since I took over the department.'

Although the Brigadier had sympathy with the French leader in his concern for his countrymen's lives, he saw no purpose in making a case for him at this moment. Before he could think of a reply MacBride's change of tone illustrated the man's resilience. 'We'll meet the problem of De Gaulle when it arrives. At the moment I want you to take a drive with me down into Hampshire.'

'Hampshire?'

MacBride steered the elderly soldier towards the door. 'It's the second reason I asked you down here today. There's one of our research establishments there and two boffins I want you to meet. One knew Werner when he was at university and the other worked with him for a time when he was doing research in Cologne. They've also got one of my French agents with them: someone who had to get out of Europe in a hurry last week. He's brought a rumour with him that the boffins think might add the last piece to the jigsaw puzzle.' When the Brigadier showed curiosity, MacBride grinned maliciously. 'You'd better brace yourself. If they're right you're going to find out Werner's hardly working for the benefit of mankind.'

7

The road ran eastwards for half a mile, then disappeared round a sharp bend. Trees and felled logs flanked it on either side: the Bois de St. Jouin was dense right along the hilltop. Lifting his head Ferot gazed down the foresters' path opposite. Although the tailgate of the old truck he had brought could just be seen behind a clump of bushes he felt it unlikely to be noticed by a passing vehicle. Satisfied, he dropped back behind a pile of logs where six other men were crouching. Wiry, with gaunt black hair and a broken nose, he looked like a bird of prey. He spoke to the man alongside him, his words slipping characteristically from the corner of his thin mouth.

'You know what to do, Delacourt?'

The younger man, armed with a Sten, was looking worried. 'I don't like this place. I still think it's too near St. Julien.'

Ferot's grin showed a mouthful of bad teeth. 'What's your problem? Are you afraid for that pretty wife of yours?'

'Yes, I am. Wouldn't you be?'

Ferot grinned again. Born in the slums of Paris he had moved south before the war to find work. A natural hater of authority, he fitted into the Maquis like a bullet into a gun barrel. Although some of his methods revolted his colleagues, his toughness and courage could not be dispensed with in the ruthless war the Gestapo were waging. His laugh sounded like a butcher's saw cutting through bone. 'Maybe I would at that. I'd exchange beds with you any time. But you worry too much. If we attack any further west we'll be too near the Boche garrison at

Moutiers. Anyway, how can they suspect we're from St. Julien when they've got the SS guarding both exits?'

'I get out without any trouble,' Delacourt said. 'They must know it's possible.'

'It's not possible to get back in again with a truck and captured Boche stores, is it?' The man laughed again at Delacourt's expression. 'You didn't think of that, did you? When they find out we've emptied the transports, St. Julien's the last place they'll suspect.'

At the far bend a man had run out on the road and was waving an arm urgently. Waving back, Ferot gave Delacourt a push. 'Go back to your section now. They'll be in sight in five minutes.'

The partisans had spotted the small German convoy ten minutes earlier, crawling up the mountain road from Albertville. Led by two motor cycles and sidecars, it consisted of three large transports followed by another couple of motor cyclists. Every Frenchman in Ferot's contingent knew the occupants of the sidecars would be armed with machine guns. From their initial invasion of Poland and France, the Germans had proved the motor cycle and sidecar to be a mobile and effective weapon and today its highly-trained crews were feared and respected.

Ferot watched Delacourt drop behind a pile of logs behind which another section of six men were crouching. Satisfied, he turned to the five partisans at his side. 'Keep your heads down until I open fire. Then shoot the pigs. For Christ's sake don't miss. If one of their motor cyclists get away he'll bring half the Boche army down on our backs.'

In the silence that followed the cawing of rooks could be heard and the scurrying of an animal through the bracken. Then a low hum sounded, rising and falling as gears were changed. Ten seconds later the leading motor cycle and sidecar rounded the bend. It was followed by the second escort, then by the tall ungainly transports. With his chest pressed against a frozen log, Delacourt could feel the pounding of his heart. Each pulsation seemed to jolt his body and he wondered how such a small muscle could withstand such a strain.

The leading motor cycle and sidecar was picking up speed now as the hill flattened out. Squatting low on the road, with its driver and gunner goggled against the icy wind, the vehicle looked like a creature from another planet. Ferot was watching it with some concern, knowing that if it stretched the gap too far between itself and the following vehicles, the ambush might fail. To his relief the gunner leaned towards the driver and shouted a warning. Responding the driver slowed down and allowed the convoy to close up.

Cocking his Sten gun, Ferot waited until the vehicle was almost abreast of him. Then, taking careful aim at the driver, he pulled the trigger.

It was a signal for all the ambushers to open fire. The first motor cycle swerved crazily as it shot past Ferot and careered into a ditch. The driver, already dead, slumped on the road. The gunner picked himself up, ran a couple of yards, then fell under a hail of bullets.

The second motor cyclist recognising his danger, gave a shout and accelerated wildly while his gunner swung round his machine carbine and fired a long burst at the pile of logs. Bullets ricochetted off them and one Frenchman was flung back with his skull cracked like an egg shell. With a hail of bullets following it, however, the vehicle's escape was short-lived. Swerving violently, it overturned, one wheel of the sidecar spinning crazily. The driver lay motionless, his neck broken. The gunner lay kicking his feet on the frozen road.

With the three transports blocking their way of escape, the rearguard motor cyclists suffered the same fate from the bullets of Delacourt's men. But the near escape of the second escort had given the driver of the leading transport a chance and he took it. Putting his foot down, he sent the huge vehicle careering past the pile of logs before the partisans could fire through the windshield.

It was a move that put the entire vehicle between the crew and their ambushers. Conscious of the danger to his men if it escaped, Ferot jumped up and fired a long burst at the rear tyres. The transport swerved violently, then skidded into a pile of logs and fell over on its side. Fearful for their lives, the half-stunned crew stayed inside their cab.

With all four motor cycles and sidecars out of action, the remaining transports had halted. While their crews were dragged from their cabs and bundled to the roadside, Ferot and a large bearded partisan were hurriedly unlacing the canvas of the second vehicle. As Ferot jumped inside, Delacourt heard his exultant yell. 'Look what we've got in here!'

Jumping in after him Delacourt saw two terrified civilians trying to hide behind a pile of wooden crates. A number of large metal drums completed the consignment. Ferot prodded one of the men in the ribs with his Sten. 'Deutschlander?'

The frightened man swallowed. 'Ya.'

Ferot glanced at Delacourt and gave his feral grin. 'Those soft-handed gentlemen in London are going to be happy about this, mon ami.'

Before Delacourt could reply, shouts of discovery from the rear transport made the two Frenchmen jump down to the road. Waved forward by excited partisans, they found half a dozen manacled men inside the vehicle along with more wooden crates. Wearing filthy clothes, clearly suffering from ill-treatment, they were delirious with joy as they answered the questions of their rescuers. As Ferot's harsh voice stilled the din, a partisan turned to him. 'They're Frenchmen, padrone! Members of the Maquis.'

'The Maquis?'

'Yes. They've been in the Gestapo prison in Lyons.'

Ferot addressed the nearest of the prisoners, an unshaven, emaciated man in his middle forties. 'Why are you in this convoy?'

The man shook his head. 'We don't know. But they've taken batches like this before. Usually six at a time.'

Ferot turned to Delacourt. 'Get back to the overturned truck and see what's in there.' His voice rose. 'The rest of you get these transports off the road and over to our truck. Move fast! A Boche patrol could come at any time.'

Reminded of their danger, the partisans scattered. As Delacourt returned he saw Ferot herding the six German soldiers into the wood. All were looking terrified and one was pleading in German. 'Where are you going?' he asked.

Ferot grinned. 'The Boches' legs are stiff after their long drive. I'm taking them for a little exercise. What was in the truck?'

'Only more crates and drums. You can't shoot these men. Not in cold blood.'

Ferot pointed at the runes on the nearest German's collar. 'These bastards are SS.'

'I know who they are. But I don't want to be as filthy as them, do you?'

'Wrong, mon ami. I want to be so filthy they will run back to their Fatherland to escape the smell. Get over to our truck and wait for me there.'

As Delacourt hesitated, Ferot swung the Sten in line with his stomach. 'Men who hunt with my pack get only one order, Delacourt. If they disobey it, I shoot them. Get over to the truck.'

Delacourt heard the rattle of automatic fire as he was turning down the narrow foresters' path. A flock of rooks, only newly settled after their first disturbance, clattered again into the cold sky. As a single scream came, there was a second and last burst of firing. Wincing, Delacourt hurried towards the waiting partisans.

There was a loud murmur of disbelief in the Operations Room when Davies finished speaking. With the Air Commodore's presence usually signifying a mission of high importance, the crews were finding an Alice-in-Wonderland quality in the briefing he was giving them. A past master at knowing when to pause and consolidate, Davies turned away from the large map of Denmark fixed to the screen behind him. 'Any questions before I go on?'

Half a dozen hands shot up immediately. Davies chose someone likely to provide humour. 'Yes, Millburn.'

'If it's a birthday party, sir, can't we drop something a bit livelier than leaflets?'

'Such as?' Davies asked.

Millburn grinned. 'What about a few stink bombs? And can't we give them a squirt or two? We're not likely to hurt any Danes if we fire at the big drums and the trombones.'

Davies gave a disparaging grunt. 'You think you're Deadeye Dick, Millburn? Of course you can't fire at the parade. The streets will be lined with Danes. If we kill any of 'em, we're hardly likely to have 'em queuing up to help us, are we?' He glanced at Moore who, along with other specialist officers, was sharing the platform with him. 'I think they'd all better have their guns buttons on safe when you go down in case someone has a rush of blood to the head.'

When Moore nodded, Davies turned back to his audience. Only eight crews were present – without consulting MacBride the Air Commodore had decided against risking his entire squadron. Originally his intention had been to leave out Moore and to call for volunteers until Henderson had reminded him that it was a squadron tradition on such occasions for all men to step forward. Left with no other option, Davies had been forced to ask Moore to choose eight crews. Although Moore had agreed he had made it clear without a word being said that his terms were participation. As was his way, Davies had not capitulated gracefully. 'You're being an obstinate fool, Moore. Apart from having two of the best flight commanders in the business, you've got a bunch of men so highly trained they could probably do the job without any leadership at all. I want you around to carry out operations whose results can be measured, not imagined.'

Moore had been his usual urbane but cogent self. 'With respect, sir, if this operation isn't going to achieve anything, then none of my men should be risking their lives taking part in it. If it has a purpose, then I have a responsibility to share the risks with them.'

Knowing he hadn't a leg to stand on, Davies had been reduced to a growl of frustration. 'And I once thought *I* ran this squadron. Who was I fooling?'

Henderson, who had been present during this scene, had given Moore an amused glance. Since his meetings with Staines, which had been frequent during the last few months, it had been noticeable that Davies was picking up Americanisms. Davies, who had spotted the Scot's glance, had realised what he had said and bridled. 'All right, go and get yourself killed, Moore. Only don't put the blame on me.'

Reminded of this conversation now, Davies changed his tone. 'You'd better watch it, all of you. I don't want another American train job, with everyone screaming for our blood afterwards. You don't make a move that could kill a single Dane. Just make the Jerries look stupid and you've done your job.'

St. Claire was one of the pilots chosen for the mission and Adams, who was seated next to Moore, noticed him stiffen. Inwardly censuring Davies for his lack of tact, Adams saw one of the two Flight Commanders put up a hand. "Teddy" Young, who led A Flight, was the only pilot who had flown his shell-tattered Mosquito back from the Swartfjord. A tough, ginger-haired Australian, he was a man with a gritty sense of humour and a passionate love of horse racing. He was sharing a couple of chairs at the front of the assembly with Harvey, a privilege the Flight Commanders enjoyed on these occasions.

'Are the Yank Mustangs going to follow us down into the streets or not, sir?'

'No,' Davies told him. 'Their job is to give you cover.'

'But are only eight kites going to impress the Danes that much?'

'Of course they are. Don't forget all those Mustangs will be buzzing around as well. To civilians the sky will seem full of planes.'

Harvey's gruff Northcountry voice was in marked contrast to the Australian's twangy drawl. 'But I thought

59

you said the Yanks were only giving us twelve.'

Knowing Harvey had three of his crews going on the mission, Davies eyed him warily. The Yorkshireman's concern for his men had brought the two of them into friction before and this time the Air Commodore knew how wide open the mission was to criticism. 'That's right, twelve. That's nearly two escorts a kite.'

Harvey was frowning. 'It might seem plenty of kites to the Danes, sir, but it's not going to seem many to us if a minelayer or a flak ship spots us going out. Are you laying on any spoof raids?'

At times like this Davies wished the North of England were at the other side of the Atlantic. It was seldom if ever that Harvey failed to put his finger on the weakness of an operation, making the Air Commodore regret he had not carried out his usual practice of briefing the Flight Commanders before he spoke to the crews. 'There won't be any need for spoof raids this time. Jerry's fully occupied with the interdiction raids we and the Yanks are carrying out on his transportation system.'

Harvey's grunt was that of a veteran who had been given such yarns about the German defences before. 'Jerry's always got a few squadrons in reserve, sir, and that Baltic coast is lined with airfields. If a ship spots us, we could be in trouble.'

'Then you'll have to see to it a ship doesn't spot you,' Davies snapped. 'If your navigators keep their eyes open for smoke stacks, that shouldn't be difficult.'

Seeing Harvey was still not satisfied, Moore half-rose from his chair. He was forestalled by Young who kicked the Yorkshireman's leg. As Harvey fell back scowling, another hand rose. Deciding enough was enough, Davies ignored it, and turned to the table behind him. 'If you've any more questions you can bring them up later. I'm going to call on your Navigation Officer now to give you your point of rendezvous with the Yanks.'

8

The North sea was having one of its tantrums that morning and a fresh wind was blowing spindrift from its waves. Flying at ultra low level, the eight Mosquitoes were catching the brunt of its ill-humour. Spray kept hissing into their spinning propellers and splattering on their windshields. Acutely conscious that a half-second lack of concentration could mean collision and disaster, pilots were hardly daring to blink as the aircraft skimmed like stones over the tossing sea.

In such conditions surveillance for enemy activity was one of the many tasks of the navigators. In this they were lucky that a layer of cloud covered North-Western Europe that morning. Met. reports suggested it stretched as far as the island of Fano but then gave way to broken sky over Copenhagen. It gave excellent cover from any patrolling German aircraft but had one grave disadvantage. If the Mosquitoes were spotted, it would allow fighters to mass unseen and then pounce without warning.

The pros and cons of the sea conditions were less easy to evaluate. Some crews held that poorish light favoured aircraft because they were so much smaller to sight than ships. Others argued that camouflaged ships were difficult to pick up against a grey sea while aircraft, no matter how low they flew, were always silhouetted above the skyline.

At such times it was a comfort to any pilot to have Hopkinson along on an operation: the astute Cockney was acknowledged to have the finest eyesight on the Station. Flying with Moore in A-Apple at the head of the phalanx of Mosquitoes, he was glancing back at the twelve Mustangs that were keeping tight station behind.

His voice sounded in Moore's earphones. 'You know something skipper? For Americans those Yanks aren't bad.'

Moore smiled. 'You approve, do you, Hoppy?'

Hoppy was careful not to overpay his compliments. 'Mind you, it's still early days. We ain't seen 'em in action yet.'

Moore himself was impressed by the Mustangs' discipline. Knowing that the enemy's Freya radar scanners could now pick up Allied aircraft rising from their airfields, he had led his flight south as if heading for France. After making rendezvous with the Mustangs over Lincoln, he had then led both units south for another ten miles before dropping to ultra low level and swinging east. Now, hopefully below the enemy monitors, they were two-thirds of the way towards Jutland. In all the manoeuvres the Mustangs had kept station well: a relief to the Mosquito crews who knew that if just one aircraft rose into the beam of the enemy scanners all their precautions would be in vain. Moore adjusted his throttles. 'They look pretty good to me, Hoppy. It's a pity we have to keep radio silence. I'd like to find out who their leader is.'

Other crews were commenting on the Americans' discipline. Harvey, flying D-Danny, was never one to give gratuitous compliments but even he had given a grunt of approval when the Mustangs had swung into station barely a hundred feet above the fields of Lincolnshire. In T-Tommy, Millburn was making the most of the occasion. 'Take a look at those guys, boyo, and don't ever tell me again that Yanks don't know how to fly.'

Gabby, secretly impressed, gave a sniff. 'Wait until the shit starts flying. That's what sorts out the men from the boys.'

Millburn gave him a scornful glance. 'It's been a long time sorting you out, boyo. You're more like Rupert Bear now than when I first met you and that's saying something.'

With fuel an urgent consideration all the Mosquitoes were carrying drop tanks. In A-Apple Moore turned to Hoppy. 'What's our ETA for the Jutland coast?'

Hoppy glanced down at the notes strapped to his knee. 'Seventeen minutes, skipper. The wind's delaying us a bit.'

A hail squall swept out of the murk: April was being its usual fickle self. Ice rattled like bullets on the Mosquitoes' wooden wings and perspex windshields. The eyes of both pilots and navigators ached as they tried to pierce the white tracer that flashed past.

To everyone's relief the squall lasted no more than a minute before visibility opened out again. A seagull, trying to avoid the aircraft, smashed into Harvey's starboard propeller and disintegrated into a blur of blood and feathers. Half a mile to starboard a small fishing boat swept past. Navigators watched it nervously, praying it had no wireless.

Jutland came into sight sixteen and a quarter minutes later and Moore nodded his appreciation: Hopkinson was a superb navigator. With the beach backed by low grassy dunes, waves could be seen breaking on the sand. Enemy coast ahead! Every man present, however experienced, felt his stomach tighten at the sight. Waggling his wings, Moore turned on his fire-and-safe button and tested his guns. Behind him the Mosquitoes opened their ranks and spat jets of fire as each pilot followed suit.

Moving into a line-astern formation, the Mosquitoes swept over the coast. Two forks of tracer rose from behind the dunes but both fell short: the entry point had been carefully chosen to avoid heavy flak defences. It was the sky now that posed the main threat. Like all their defence units, the German Observer Corps was highly efficient and it would not be long before urgent alerts would be signalled to nearby fighter bases. The trick was to make it difficult for the Corps to vector fighters on to an interception course. Hoppy, now relying on dead

63

reckoning, was studying the ground intently. Half a minute passed, then he lifted his face mask. 'Ten degrees to starboard, skipper. Now!'

A-Apple banked gracefully, then straightened. The rest of Moore's pilots followed as if running on an invisible rail. The Mustangs, not certain when the manoeuvre would commence, lost station for a moment but closed up almost at once. With a grimace of approval, Hoppy turned to Moore again. 'You keep this course until we hit the Holstebro-Veile railway, skipper. Then we turn out to sea again.'

The route, apart from being designed to confuse the Observer Corps, was to enable the force to enter the Storebelt at Horsens and then jink through the islands until Kalunborg was reached. After that they were to make a straight dash to Copenhagen.

The flat but attractive Danish countryside was streaming below. With concentration at a premium for the pilots, only the navigators could follow landmarks with their eyes. A school playground, full of pupils enjoying their morning break, appeared from behind a clump of trees. Catching sight of the rondels on the Mosquitoes, the children turned hysterical, waving their arms and screaming with excitement. A church steeple rose and was flung past. Then came a wood, its leafless trees burnished with the sap of spring. Hoppy peered out at a hamlet sweeping past his starboard wingtip. Vind, he decided. A sharp question in his earphones made him turn. Moore had spotted rail tracks ahead. 'No, skipper, that runs back to the coast. We want the next one. Ten more kilometres.'

The Mosquitoes flew on. Behind them the Mustangs were also flying in line astern. Their leader was watching the Mosquitoes' progress critically. Although by this time 633 Squadron's exploits were legendary on both sides of the Atlantic, no one knew better than the serving soldier how the media as well as the public needed its heroes and how one outfit could be glamorised out of all proportion to its deeds. In this somewhat sceptical frame of mind Major Alan Dent had welcomed the escort mission, believing he would now be able to sort out the truth from the fiction.

So far he had been one hundred per cent impressed. It did not take a pilot as experienced as Dent to appreciate the precision of the Mosquitoes' manoeuvres. The crews were undoubtedly highly-trained and, from the confidence of their navigation, most ably led. However, the test of a soldier was on the battlefield, and like the Mosquito crews, the American was reserving his judgement on his Allies until their objective was reached.

Alan Dent was a New Yorker, a stocky man of medium height with thoughtful brown eyes and a good sense of humour. A couple of years older than the average pilot of his squadron, he had worked for Kodak before the war and had found it a grave impediment to his ambition to fly. Blinkered like the rest of their kind, his Selection Board had automatically ear-marked him as a recruit for the Army Photographic service. It said much for Dent's powers of persuasion as well as his determination that he had at last convinced them that as an administrator in the huge company he had needed to know no more about photography than how to load a box camera. After winning his case he had been transferred to the Army Air Force where he had proved himself an exceptional pupil.

After his posting on operations he had first flown in Thunderbolts. Then, three months ago, with the U.S. 8th Air Force at last receiving the long-range fighter it sorely needed, he had been given command of a squadron of Mustangs. They had given sterling service to the huge Fortresses on their daylight missions and some of his crews had shown resentment when told they were to escort a single flight of RAF light bombers whose only object was to upset a German birthday celebration. Dent, who had seen the reasoning behind the mission, had shamelessly used 633 Squadron's participation as evidence the mission must have value. (Dent's sense of humour made him the first to admit that when the occasion demanded it, he could be pragmatic.)

Ahead in A-Apple Hopkinson had spotted the second rail track and was pointing it out to Moore. Swinging to starboard, the Mosquitoes raced down it. Freed for the moment from the tyranny of dead reckoning, Hoppy lifted his head and squinted at the sky. The cloud base appeared to have lifted a good thousand feet and the Cockney decided the Met reports were correct and they were nearing the fringe of the low pressure area.

Below, the rail track and its telegraph poles were blurred by the speed of the aircraft. Moore eased back on the wheel, leap-frogged a bridge, and squatted A-Apple down on the rails again. The following Mosquitoes rose and fell in turn. Hoppy glanced back. The mental and physical strain of flying low for long distances were immense and although 633 Squadron existed for such precise operations, its crews still needed constant practice to keep them efficient. With the Mustang pilots used chiefly for high-level combat they could not be expected to sustain such a degree of concentration, but although some were beginning to show signs of strain, they were still flying low enough to avoid radar detection.

A skyline of buildings appeared ahead and Hoppy nodded at Moore's question. 'Herning, skipper. We keep going south-west.'

Warned by Adams there were flak defences within the town, Moore led the aircraft round its southern suburbs. With the surprised AA crews having no time to warm up their radar-controlled guns, the only flak came from automatic weapons. A 20mm shell punctured the wing of St. Claire's Mosquito and two Mustangs received bullet holes. Then the town fell back and the rail track could be seen continuing south-west.

All navigators were now intent on the lightening sky. If the German Observer Corps had not picked up the aircraft before, the guns crews certainly knew of their presence now and frantic alerts would already be reaching fighter bases. The problem of continuing along the rail track meant that it aided fighters to be vectored ahead.

Like a long line of cavalry, the aircraft raced on. Starlings, grubbing for seed and worms in the fields, scattered and fled in terror at the scream of the engines. Hoppy was intent on the rail track again, knowing there

66

were two branch lines ahead. The first swept past, then the second, and the Cockney relaxed. 'Only fifteen miles to Veile, skipper.'

Knowing Veile was a port which might contain enemy shipping as well as heavy flak defences, Moore by-passed it, entering the Vehle fjord three miles to the north. The water was calmer here and the Mosquitoes were able to flatten down until their slipstreams ruffled it.

At this point the Storebelt, the stretch of sea between Jutland and Zealand, was fifty miles wide. Knowing Hoppy would again be able to watch the sky, Moore relaxed slightly. Glancing in his mirror he had a glimpse of Harvey's D-Danny in perfect position above and behind him. The sight was oddly comforting. There had been a time when he and the Yorkshireman, with respective backgrounds of privilege and poverty, had hardly been able to exchange a word without dissent. Since the arrival at Sutton Craddock of Anna Reinhardt, however, and the subsequent mission in which Moore had saved Harvey's life, their relationship had been transformed. Although it was certain the dour Yorkshireman would die rather than admit it, the two men were now the closest of friends.

The island of Endelave appeared at 10 o'clock. A German patrol boat, low and wolfish with a saliverous bow wave, was sniffing along its southern coast. Another five minutes and the twin arms of the Kalundborg fjord could be seen reaching out into the Storebelt. Guiding Moore south of the town, Hoppy picked up the main road that ran eastwards. 'Copenhagen dead ahead, skipper. ETA in around 15 minutes.'

Moore could see patches of sunlight on the chequered fields ahead. As prophecied, the sky cover was breaking up. A village swept past. Girls on bicycles stopped, women ran out into gardens and waved handerkerchiefs. Gabby grimaced at Millburn. 'Why did I join the RAF? It's a hell of a waste up here.'

Millburn grinned. 'I'll tell you why you joined the RAF. Because you were too small a runt to foot slog. Why don't you get wise to it?'

An enemy staff car, coming into sight as the aircraft flew over a shallow hill, reminded the crews they were in enemy-occupied territory. Catching sight of the Mosquitoes, the driver braked and two officers leapt out. As they ran for cover one Mosquito dipped its nose and fired a burst of cannon. Without the pilot breaking formation, there was little chance of scoring a hit but the exploding shells made the officers dive into a water-filled ditch. In D-Danny, Harvey's voice was harsh. 'That was St. Claire, wasn't it?'

His navigator looked uncomfortable. 'I'm not sure, skipper.'

Harvey scowled. At the briefing Moore had been explicit that no ammunition should be wasted on irrelevant targets and the dour Yorkshireman was not one to brook disobedience. 'When we get back tell him to report to my office. On the double.'

In S-Sammy, the culprit Mosquito, the navigator was also showing discomfort. One of the squadron's recent recruits, Johnnie Webb had been crewed with St. Claire after the pilot's return from France and so found it well-nigh impossible to believe that once St. Claire had been a calm, composed, and engaging personality. Aware of the pilot's likely reaction, Webb took a deep breath. 'Better watch it, skippper. Our orders were to save all our ammunition.'

With his mask in position, there was little to see of St. Claire's handsome face but his voice said it all. 'I know what our orders are, Webb. You look after your business and I'll take care of mine.'

The pilots's disobedience had not escaped Moore, who spoke his thoughts aloud. 'You've no idea what's brought about this change in him, have you, Hoppy?'

The Cockney shook his head. 'No, skipper. He clams up as soon as anyone mentions it.'

While making a note to talk to the pilot, Moore was missing nothing of the scene ahead. Three miles to port a town dominated by a huge cathedral was rising into view. Memories of a trip to Denmark he had made with his parents when a schoolboy came crowding back.

Roskilde. With its magnificent cathedral the burial place of over three dozen Danish monarchs and queens.

As if it were on a great conveyor belt the town swept past. On the road below a convoy of camouflaged German transports appeared. Moore waited for another burst of cannon fire but this time St. Claire's guns remained silent. The sunlight was bright now and navigators were squinting anxiously upwards. By this time it was certain hunting packs of Focke-Wulfs and 109s would be casting about urgently for their scent.

Four more minutes passed and then Hoppy gave an exclamation and pointed ahead. 'How's that, skipper? Only a couple of minutes from our ETA.'

Moore's eyes crinkled. 'You're a marvel, Hoppy. You really are.'

The thunder of A-Apple's Merlins rose a note as Moore thumbed his throttles forward. Behind him crews braced themselves and three young Americans pushed fresh wads of gum into their dry mouths. A long, crenellated line of buildings was rising from the skyline. Copenhagen lay dead ahead.

9

The assembly point the Germans had chosen for their birthday parade was the area directly north of the Hans Anderson Boulevard. Friends of the Third Reich defended the choice on the grounds it was an ideal starting point and also had the space necessary for the exercise. Enemies of the Reich noted the area contained the Danish House of Parliament as well as the Royal Palace and drew their own conclusions.

Certainly the display promised to contain enough units of German military might to intimidate any city and its people. Since dawn they had been driving or marching in and by 11 a.m. the entire area was packed with impeccably-uniformed men and their war machines.

Precisely at 11.15 hours the parade got under way. From the tower of Radhuset a green Very flare soared into the air. An order was bawled out, a band struck up, and jackboots began their measured tread. Under huge photographs of the Führer, phalanx after phalanx of men marched round the Borsen, down Christiangade, and swung right into the wide Hans Anderson Boulevard.

The size of the parade was impressive. Every unit of the German military machine that had crushed Europe appeared to be represented: line regiments, Panzer Grenadiers, Stormtroopers, Paratroopers, The Luftwaffe, The Navy. Even units of the Allgemeine S.S., and the Waffen S.S could be seen. Their presence had caused some controversy. A few of the more sensitive German administrators had argued their appearance would prove an unnecessary exacerbation. Others, more

70

notably Scavenius and more hawkish Nazi officers, had argued no one had more right to be there. For one thing they were Hitler's pretorian guard and for another, as the real purpose of the exercise was intimidation, the parade would not fully achieve its effect without them. The hawks had won and the sinister Nazi elements marched in step with the rest.

It was impossible for the Danes to boycott the celebrations. All public employees had been ordered to attend and knew they would be punished if they did not. School children had been given the day off, marched to pre-arranged sites along the route, and then given Nazi flags to wave. Private employers had been ordered to close their businesses while the parade passed by. Morever, it was an impressive spectacle in its own right. Every now and then the marching men would halt while the massed bands played popular music. With the Danes as starved for colour and entertainment as the rest of Europe, it was at least something to alleviate their boredom and many watched it for no other reason.

The column was led by an armoured car followed by a bullet-proof automobile containing three high ranking German officers. One was the Military Governor of the city. Scavenius was not present for fear of assassination. Next in the parade came a large military brass band. The armoured car and the automobile were just crossing the Gyldenlovsgade bridge when the sirens began to wail. The blare of trumpets, cornets and trombones faltered and ceased as the musicians stared at their bandleader. Their halt brought about a chain reaction the full length of the parade. The bandleader, a plump, ruddy-faced Bavarian called Schultz, stared up at the sky in dismay. Surely the Allies were not going to bomb the parade, not with thousands of Danish women and children in the streets! Yet the raid could not be a coincidence. The sound of aircraft engines could now be heard and the graceful shape of a Mosquito swept from behind the Radiohuset. The musicians began showing distinct signs of panic. In the distance Schultz could hear alarmed orders being shouted. Yet what could he do? There were no shelters nearby and the streets behind were blocked with men and vehicles.

The sound of revving gears, followed by the scream of brakes made him turn. A haughty but angry face was leaning out of the bullet-proof automobile. 'Why are you standing there like that? Don't you realise you are holding up the entire parade?'

'But, Herr Generalmajor, the sirens have gone.'

'What if they have? The raiders cannot attack us, not without killing hundreds of Danes. In any case, there is no time to retreat. Get your band moving, you fool! At once!'

'Yes, Herr Generalmajor.' Gripping his baton tightly, Schultz shouted his orders. For a moment the musicians stared at him as if he were mad. Then, with more than one trumpet and cornet giving a squawk of misgiving, they obeyed. Behind them, like a serpent with a will of its own, the huge parade began moving again.

With concealment no longer possible or even desirable, Moore led his Mosquitoes up to 1,500 feet. In spite of the sirens wailing below, Copenhagen looked deceptively peaceful and serene. As he led the aircraft into a wide orbit, Moore studied the sky above. It was now a typical April day with patches of sunlight and large castles of cumulus. He switched on his R/T. 'Spoilsport to Kittihawk leader. Will you give me cover now?'

Dent responded immediately. 'You've got it, Spoilsport leader. Grab a trombone for me, will you? I've always wanted to play one.'

Moore smiled. 'I'll do my best. See you in a few minutes.'

The parade, packing the streets all the way from the Borsen to the Radhuspladsen, was clearly visible now. Studying it, Moore realised that if the Mosquitoes were to traverse its full length, they would have to pass over the docks either at the beginning or the end of their pass. He could see at least two German minesweepers among the ships anchored there, as well as a number of E boats, and knew their crews would be frantically stripping the tarpaulins off their AA guns in preparation to engage. Making a typical snap decision, Moore made for the docks.

Below, Copenhagen revolved like a huge wheel. The Mosquitoes, still flying in line astern, looked like a drawn bow as they followed A-Apple. Behind them the twelve Mustangs detached themselves and climbed up to the base of the drifting cumulus which Hoppy now estimated was around 4,000 feet.

Enemy activity was beginning to make itself felt. Although the heavier AA guns had not yet warmed up, LMGs situated on rooftops and in parks were pumping up bullets and shells and with the Mosquitoes flying at only 1,500 feet they were well within range. As a row of jagged holes appeared in Millburn's starboard wing, the American grimaced at Gabby. 'For guys who're not supposed to get much practice, they're not doing a bad job, boyo.'

'Why aren't you weaving?' Gabby grumbled.

Millburn grinned. 'I thought it might make a sprog like you air sick.'

Gabby's scowl deepened. 'It's all right for you, Millburn. You've got armour plating under your arse. But what about poor bastards like me?'

It was a familiar complaint of Mosquito navigators that their seats were unprotected. Although Millburn was secretly sympathetic, he was not one to miss the chance of a quip. 'What's that you're always telling me – that I'm only a bus driver and navigators really run the show? It doesn't look as if the designers think that way, boyo. They must rate you guys as ten a penny.'

'You know something, Millburn? Without me to get you home, you'd end up in Germany or Switzerland.'

'You kidding? Switzerland, with all those girls and ski parties? The sooner you get those bullets up your arse the better, kiddo.'

After a quick circuit out to sea, Moore was now leading the Mosquitoes back towards the Hans Anderson Avenue. He had completed the manoeuvre as quickly as

73

possible in order to cross the docks before its AA defences were fully operational. In addition, to give the ship gunners the most difficult targets possible, he had ordered his pilots down to zero height again. Tracer from automatic guns was arcing towards them but by jinking round the ships below mast height the Mosquitoes made it difficult for the gunners to avoid firing on one another. A-Apple leapt over the Amager Boulevard and Hans Christian Anderson Boulevard lay ahead.

Moore opened his bomb doors and felt them quivering in the airflow. Along the broad avenue, the procession was marching again although hundreds of helmeted heads were staring apprehensively back. They streamed below like a river full of flotsam as A-Apple squatted down at roof top height. Moore's task was to cover the head of the procession, the following Mosquitoes to fill in the gaps behind.

Hoppy, holding the bomb release, was waiting for Moore's signal. Below images were leaping in and out of their vision: a girl leaning perilously from a third floor window to blow kisses at the Allied planes, a soldier flinging back a Dane who had run out excitedly on the road, an officer yelling orders for his men to keep in step. Ahead sunshine shone on a stretch of water. Seeing the wide bridge that spanned it and realising the armoured car and automobile on its far side was the van of the parade, Moore gave Hoppy a nod. 'Now!'

Hoppy pressed the bomb release and the Small Bomb Container tucked inside the belly of the Mosquito opened its doors. Above, one of the Mustang pilots let out a yell of delight that rattled the eardrums of his colleagues. 'Will you look at that, you guys? They're dropping toilet rolls!'

Grinning pilots peered down. As Mosquito after Mosquito dropped its first load, multi-coloured streamers went plunging down the entire length of the parade. Before packing the toilet rolls into the SBCs the armourers had made certain their ends were loosened. Some unwound quickly and fluttered in the sky for all to see. Others plunged down and wrapped themselves around the heads and shoulders of struggling German soldiers.

The Mosquitoes had not finished yet. Going into a climbing turn, Moore waited until his last aircraft had finished its run. Then, with a word of command to his pilots, he put A-Apple's nose down again.

His approach this time was towards the van of the parade. Ignoring the armoured car whose gunners were doing their best to punish the audacious Mosquitoes, he swept along the Aboulevarden, crossed Gyldenlovesgade bridge, and dropped to roof top height again over the Hans Anderson Boulevard. Making certain A-Apple was directly over the parade, Moore gave Hoppy another nod.

This time, mixed with thousands of fluttering leaflets, it was tin chamber pots that rained down. Landing with a great clatter, they leapt and bounded along the avenue. Believing from their shape they were a new type of bomb, the troops lost all semblance of discipline and scattered in all directions.

On the pavements the Danes were falling over one another. Fun-loving people at the best of times, they were hysterical at the sight of the once arrogant German soldiers covered in coils of toilet paper and now running for their lives from chamber pots. Nor was the hysteria confined to the Danes. Millburn almost crashed T-Tommy when he saw a pot fell a yelling, red-faced German officer. 'Oh, brother, just look at that! Why don't we do this all the time? They'd sue for an armistice in a week.'

Gabby was grinning like an exultant gnome. 'There's only one thing missing, mush. Those pots ought to be full.'

The radio channel was a bedlam as both Mosquito and Mustang crews added their ribald comments. It took sharp words from Moore and Dent to quieten them. The reason became obvious when Moore, who had attacked the rearguard of the procession, swept over the docks. Every AA gun there was now ready and the sky around A-Apple became peppered with shell bursts. Banking away as steeply as he dared, Moore gave cryptic orders to the Mosquitoes following him. 'Break as soon as you've dropped your load. I repeat — break smartly when your load has gone!'

One by one the Mosquitoes obeyed, climbing steeply to reform out of LMG range. Shells from 37mm and 88mm guns followed them, exploding and lashing them with white-hot steel. Dent was about to order his Mustangs lower in an attempt to draw off some of the fire when a sudden shout made him squint upwards. 'Bandits, Kittihawk Leader! Bandits in the sun!'

The bandits were a Staffel of 190s. For the past hour, like others of their kind, they had been searching for the mysterious raiders who had entered their air space. Their sudden appearance was due to a bright flight controller at Third Fighter Division's headquarters at Arnhem-Deelen who had remembered the birthday parade in Copenhagen. Ignoring the scorn of his colleagues that the RAF would risk aircraft on a target that could not be bombed, he had made contact with a Danish-based Control Centre. Seeing from their Observer Corps reports that he could be right, the Centre had vectored the Staffel towards the city. There its Fighter Leader had massed his three *schwarms* behind a bank of cumulus. Now they were all diving together to avenge the indignity inflicted on their comrades below.

With the Mosquitoes still short on altitude, it was a moment of danger for them that Dent was quick to see. Calling to his pilots, he led them straight at the attackers.

The air battle that followed was fierce. Fighters banked and dived, cannon hammered, and the radio channel filled with excited voices. 'Bandit at ten o'clock, Red.' 'I got one, skipper!' 'Look out, Blakey, for Chrissake! Watch your tail.'

Blakey had no time to take warning as a burst of cannon fire hit his main fuel tank. A huge oily fireball followed, only for a 190 without a tail unit to tumble down through it a moment later. Although the 190 Staffel was a seasoned unit, the Mustang pilots were attacking with great élan and making it difficult for

76

the 190s to break through to the climbing Mosquitoes.

Two did succeed, however, and plunged down like gannets. Two thousand feet below, Moore had ordered his Mosquitoes into a corkscrew formation and was making for a large bank of cumulus to the west. From there he felt confident he could play hide and seek until he reached the solid cloud cover that stretched back to England.

The first 190 tried to latch on to Moore's tail. As Moore swung A-Apple round on its corkscrew orbit it led the 190 in front of Harvey's guns. The Yorkshireman squinted into his reflector sight, fired a short burst, and the 190 turned over like a gaffed fish and began its dive to earth. The second pilot tried to line up on Millburn but fire from Van Breedenkamp, the South African flying in F-Freddy, forced the German to break off and climb away.

The flak had ceased when the 190s attacked but with the fight between the Mustangs and 190s drifting away, the guns opened up again. As bursting shells made A-Apple reel and plunge, Moore spoke into his microphone. 'Are you all right, Kittihawk Leader?'

Dent's voice came over the static a couple of seconds later, breathless but confident. 'We're O.K., Spoilsport. Go home and get the champagne out.'

Moore smiled. 'We might just do that. Thanks and good luck.'

Clouds closed around the Mosquitoes half a minute later. They left behind them a sky heavily disfigured by shell bursts but a city bursting with gossip and excitement.

10

The pretty WAAF with the freckles opened the inner door of the ante-room. 'Flight Lieutenant St. Claire is here, sir. Shall I send him in?'

Moore, seated at his desk signing requisition forms, glanced up. 'No, Tess. Give me a few minutes. I'll buzz you when I'm ready.'

'Very well, sir.' About to close the door, the girl paused. 'You shouldn't be working in this light, sir. You could damage your eyes.'

With surprise Moore noticed how dark the office had become. Since his return from Copenhagen de-briefing, aircraft inspection, and post-battle inquests had kept him busy until the late afternoon. Since then he had been trying to catch up with his office work load and had not noticed the advent of the evening. 'It is getting a bit dim, isn't it? Sorry, Tess; I'm keeping you from your dinner. Why don't you run along now? I can manage here.'

The girl gave him a bright smile as she switched on the lights. The young Wing Commander with his immaculate appearance and invariable courtesy was her idol and if the truth were known she would have worked herself to skin and bone for him. 'I'm not in a hurry, sir. So take your time.'

As she withdrew Moore picked up his telephone. He spoke into it for a couple of minutes before replacing it and pressing a buzzer on his desk. A few seconds later the door opened and the elegant figure of St. Claire appeared. The pilot's handsome face was sullen as he walked forward and stood to attention. 'You want to see me, sir?'

'That's right, Tony. Pull up a chair.'

After what he had done that day, it was the last invitation St. Claire expected. 'No, thank you sir. I'd rather stand.'

Moore's voice remained even and affable. 'And I'd rather you sat, Tony. So please pull up a chair.'

Sullenly the pilot obeyed and sat down. Moore pushed a gold cigarette case towards him. When St. Claire shook his head, Moore lit a cigarette himself and regarded the young musician through the smoke. 'I understand you've already seen your Flight Commander?'

'Yes, sir.'

'And he has reprimanded you?'

'Yes, sir.' The affirmation was made with extreme bitterness.

'He hardly had any choice, had he? Not after you deliberately disobeyed orders. You could be grounded or court martialled, you know.'

St. Claire opened his mouth, then closed it again. Moore lifted an eyebrow. 'You were going to say something?'

'No, sir.'

Moore eyed him a moment, then leaned back in his chair. 'I haven't called you in to admonish you any further, Tony. Harvey has done that, and if I know Frank, he'll have done a thorough job. My purpose is to find out why you're acting this way. Before you were shot down in Belgium, you were one of my most promising pilots. In fact I had you ear-marked as a future Flight commander. Now you've suddenly gone right off the rails. Why?'

In the silence that followed the muffled roar of a Merlin under test could be heard. Moore tried again.

'Everyone here understands what you must have been through these last few months but some things aren't making sense. For one thing you don't seem to appreciate how lucky you are to be back with the squadron. Normally escapees are either grounded or sent out to the Far East because if they were shot down over Europe a second time, it wouldn't take the Gestapo long to make

79

them give the names of their rescuers. The reason given me was that you hadn't seen anything that could be of value to the enemy. Yet you were in the hands of the Resistance for months. So how is that possible?'

The young pilot did not meet his eyes. 'You've asked me this before, sir. The group I was with were very careful not to let me know their real names or any details of their organisation.'

'But you were with them for months, Tony. You must at least have known what part of Belgium or France you were in.'

When St. Claire did not answer, Moore went on: 'All right, let's try it a different way. Why did you fire at those two Germans in that car today?'

This time the pilot glanced at him. 'I think they were Waffen SS officers.'

'What if they were? I want to know why you felt it worth-while to disobey orders by firing on them.'

The expression on the pianist's face made Moore feel he had suddenly joined two high-voltage wires together. Believing it was an emotion too powerful to be contained, he waited. Instead St. Claire took a deep breath and returned his gaze to the wall. Moore tried again.

'The St. Claire I used to know was never bloodthirsty, Tony. Like the rest of us, you shot down aircraft and bombed enemy installations because you knew that if we didn't defeat the enemy we'd become a slave nation like Poland or France. You didn't kill for the sake of killing.'

St. Claire's lips curled. 'Isn't that hypocritical?'

Moore sat back. 'Tell me why?'

'If we kill men, isn't it far healthier to have a genuine hatred of them? It seems to me that if we don't have that hatred, we oughtn't to be killing them at all.'

Moore was silent for a moment, then gave a shrug. 'Idealistically I have to agree with you. But isn't that the moral problem all wars present? Some power-mad tyrant tells his lies and goads his people to fight and his victims have to kill the innocent with the guilty or go under.'

'How do you distinguish the innocent from the guilty?
Aren't the people who make the guns and the tanks as big
a threat as the men who use them?'

'That's the philosophy of the Nazis, Tony. They call it
total war.'

'Then perhaps they are right. No one is innocent. And
certainly not the SS and the Gestapo.'

Moore studied the pilot's handsome, defiant face, then
ground out his cigarette. 'One of these evenings we'll call
in Frank Adams and one or two more of our intellectuals
and have a thorough discourse on the philosophy of war.
But this is neither the time nor the place. You still haven't
told me why you have become so bloodthirsty. What
happened over there?'

'Nothing,' the pilot muttered.

When Moore wanted to show disapproval, the effect
could be chilling. Nodding, he rose to his feet. 'Very well,
you wish to keep the reason to yourself. Now I want you
to remember this. From this moment on, whatever your
personal feelings, you will obey orders to the letter. One
slip — just one more — and you will be grounded and
punished. Is that clearly understood?'

Erect to attention, St. Claire gave a sullen nod. 'Yes,
sir.'

'All right. Now you can go.'

Highgate was in one of its least hospitable moods when
Adams parked the bull-nosed Morris in the market place.
The blackout was complete and rain was drenching
down from the night sky. Shrugging up his greatcoat
collar, Adams jumped out. When the car door failed to
close he remembered and lifted it upwards as he
slammed it. This time it latched and held.

His association with the car dated back to Harvey's
promotion to Flight Commander. To celebrate the
occasion the Yorkshireman had bought it from a Highgate dealer for thirty pounds. Although few men dared to
beg its loan from the redoubtable Harvey, it was always
available to his friends and Adams was high on that list.

He peered across the market place. Although the moon

81

was well hidden behind the sodden sky, there was enough light to see water running in rivulets between the cobblestones. A moment later rain on his spectacles distorted the view like a reflection in a funfair mirror.

Sighing, Adams wiped them and made for the street opposite. Until today, although fully aware his date could offer no more than it promised, he had been looking forward to it with the eagerness of a man half his age: a tête a tête with Sue outside the rigid formalities of the Station had seemed a thing to savour in its own right. Moreover he was genuinely concerned about St. Claire and anxious to hear what had caused such a change in him. Yet as he crossed the market place all his sense of expectation seemed to have died.

Although he knew the true reason lay within himself — Adams had always had a sense of inadequacy with women which his marriage to the dissatisfied and carping Valerie had done nothing to dispel — he felt the weather was also a contributor. Adams was one of those people weather affects, and though he felt autumn and winter were better fitted to the vileness of war, he was basically a Spring man. And tonight Spring seemed to be withdrawing its first tentative steps as if it had finally decided the violent world it served was unworthy of its coming.

He paused halfway across the square as three Army transports swung round a corner, their tyres hissing and their slitted headlights shining like oriental eyes. A lone car followed them. Reaching the opposite pavement Adams heard singing and laughter: the Red Lion in High Street was doing good business tonight. As he neared the darkened entrance, light flooded out as two men emerged. A yell came from the far side of the road as an air raid warden, tin-hatted and wearing a rain-soaked cape, spotted the infringement. Hearing the indignant warden shout again, the men laughed and ran away into the shadows. Both were in uniform and Adams wondered if they were airmen from Sutton Craddock.

Half a minute later he reached the doorway of the Kettledrum. Pushing through the blackout curtain he felt the warmth inside wash his chilled face. He caught sight of Sue immediately, sitting in one of the partitioned alcoves that made the restaurant so popular with courting couples. Shrugging off his greatcoat and quickly wiping his spectacles, he made towards her. 'Hello, Sue. I thought the rain might keep you away.'

She looked surprised at the comment. 'Why should it do that?'

He decided it was a question best left unanswered. 'I hope you didn't get too wet. How did you get here?'

'I had some shopping to do first so I begged a lift on the airmen's transport.'

She was wearing a green dress and a cream cardigan. With 633 Squadron something of a law in itself, Waaf officers were allowed to wear civilian clothes when off duty. Neat as ever, with the slim-fitting frock matching her blond hair and emphasising her natural grace, Adams thought how attractive she looked. He felt his mood slip away as he dropped into the chair opposite. 'I hope you've had a drink?'

'No. I thought I'd wait until you arrived.'

Adams motioned to the middle-aged waitress beside the cash desk. 'What can we have to drink, Mrs Jeffries?'

The woman had been weighing up Sue for the last few minutes and her response suggested approval as well as curiosity. Glancing round the half-empty restaurant, she lowered her huge bosom conspiratorially over the table. 'I think I might be able to find a bottle of wine for you tonight, Mr. Adams. If you don't spread the news around, like.'

His gratitude heartfelt, Adams put a finger to his lips. 'That's marvellous, Mrs. Jeffries. Not a word. What's on your menu?'

'We've got mutton and spam. Oh, aye, and a bit of gammon.' She turned to Sue. 'That's what I'd have, Miss, if I were you, the gammon. We don't get it often and this is a bit of good stuff.'

With restaurant meals in Britain now down to a cash limit of five shillings, the offer of gammon was one neither guest could refuse. Scribbling on her pad the woman turned back to Adams. 'What about your wine, sir? Do you want it now or with your meal?'

Adams made no attempt to determine its colour or quality: to be offered both wine and gammon in a Highgate restaurant at this time of the war was riches enough. 'We'll have it now, please, Mrs. Jefferies.'

'Righto, sir.' With another curious glance at Sue, the woman bustled away. The girl smiled.

'Wine and gammon? She must fancy you, Frank.'

Adams grinned wryly. 'She's not that hard up. She's married to a bricklayer about six feet six tall and four feet broad. She knows me because I think I'm the only customer who tips her. They don't go in for it much in these parts.' His eyes moved from her face. 'I like your dress. It suits you.'

'Thank you. But haven't you seen it before?'

'I don't think so. In fact I don't think I've ever seen you in civvies.'

She laughed. 'I've never seen you in anything but uniform either. Isn't it ridiculous?'

Aware what the tension was between them he was tempted not to keep her to her promise: on a personal level it would make the evening more enjoyable. Almost immediately Adams pushed the temptation away. If the subject were not raised she might believe he had gained the date under false pretences. Moreover it was always possible she might find relief in discussing her problem with a fellow professional. Whatever had affected St. Claire, Adams had no doubt that it stemmed from his experiences in Europe.

He was hoping she would bring up the subject herself but she made no mention of it during the meal, although the increased brittleness of her conversation told it was in the front of her mind. By the time their plates were cleared and their wine glasses re-filled Adams knew time was running out. He decided on an oblique approach. 'You studied medicine before the war, didn't you, Sue?'

The question clearly took her by surprise. 'Yes. For two and a half years.'

'Why did you give it up?'

Her voice was full of self-disparagement. 'I found I wasn't suited to it. I knew that if I ever began to practice I'd become too depressed and involved with my patients.' Her eyes lifted. 'Can you understand that?'

'Yes. I'd be just the same. Is that why you didn't become a nurse?'

She hesitated. 'I suppose it was. Not that there was much chance to think about it. The war started the same week I came back from medical school.'

'All the same, you must have gained quite a bit of medical knowledge. Doesn't it help you to understand what's happened to Tony?'

The look he received told him how clumsy his approach had been. 'One doesn't need any medical knowledge to understand what's wrong with Tony, Frank.'

Adams took a deep breath. 'And yet none of us can understand him. The Tony I used to know fought only because he believed this was one war that had to be won. We often discussed it together. But he hated killing. He couldn't help himself. Tony's an artist — someone who values life.'

'He still values life, Frank. That's what has changed him.'

'But not German life. His navigator says there's something personal in the way he fights now.'

'It is personal. Very personal.' Seeing his expression she made an apologetic gesture. 'I'm sorry, Frank. I'm making too much of a mystery about it, aren't I? But it's such a private thing to him and I did promise not to tell anyone.'

Adams sat back. 'Would you rather leave it? If so, I'll understand.'

She hesitated, then shook her head. 'No. Although he's promised to obey orders in the future, he might go off the rails again and if you know the cause I feel you might help him. I'm being quite selfish, you see.'

Adams smiled. 'Go on.'

'Promise me one thing before I do. You won't tell a soul

unless he breaks orders again.'

Adams laid a hand on his heart. 'Scouts' honour.'

Smiling back at him, she lit the cigarette he gave her before continuing. 'I believe his troubles began the moment the Belgian partisans pulled them out of their wrecked aircraft and spirited them away. As you know, Simpson, his navigator, wasn't badly hurt, so the partisans were able to feed him into their escape line right away. But with Tony having to be nursed back to health first, it meant he had no other airmen to confide in. I'm sure that in the long run this told against him.'

Adams nodded. 'Who looked after him?'

'A Belgian family in the Ardennes. They couldn't take him far from the crash because of his leg. This meant he was still in the catchment area when the Germans discovered there was no crew in the Mosquito. So for over a fortnight the family were in great danger. Tony says their house was searched three times.'

'How did they manage to hide him if the Germans kept coming back?'

'After a doctor had set his leg, he was taken to an underground shelter a couple of hundred yards from the house. Tony says it was lined with logs and entered by a trapdoor covered with turf. Of course it hadn't been specially built for him. The family had been working in an escape line for nearly two years and dozens of airmen had used it.'

'How long was he there?'

'Over two months.' The girl gave a faint smile. 'Towards the end, when his leg had healed and his headaches gone, I think he almost enjoyed himself. It was autumn by this time and the falling leaves made his hideout doubly secure. And the family were very kind to him. When the heat had died down, they allowed him into the house in the evenings. As he was able to speak French, they made a big fuss of him. They also had a piano so he was able to entertain them and their friends.'

The imaginative Adams could understand this. Like the rest of his colleagues, St. Claire had been flying at maximum effort for some time and the enforced rest without any personal responsibility cannot have been entirely unwelcome. Moreover, for a young man the ever-present element of danger would have added spice to the situation. 'Who were these people?'

'They were called Arnoux. The man was a forestry inspector, his wife looked after a small holding, and their only child, a daughter called Francoise, was a teacher in a local school.'

Adams was growing more fascinated by the minute. 'So what happened?'

'By the time Tony was able to walk without a stick, both the husband and wife were called away. The man had to supervise another part of the forest for a sick colleague and his wife had to go and nurse her mother who'd had an accident. This left only Francoise with Tony and as she was at the school all day she could only keep an eye on him in the evenings.'

As the girl paused, Adams tried to read her expression, but she was toying with the stem of her wineglass. A clatter of plates in the kitchen drew her eyes before she continued. 'The weather was getting cold now and against Francoise's advice Tony had started taking walks in the woods. One afternoon he ran into a woodcutter he hadn't seen before. Although Tony was in civilian clothes and spoke to him in French, the man was obviously curious and said he'd walk with Tony for a while. It put Tony in a spot because he didn't want to walk much further in case he ran into any Germans or collaborators, yet at the same time he daren't put Francoise at risk by walking back towards the house. When the man wouldn't take hints, Tony had no choice but to be rude to him. The man went off grumbling and although Tony took great care going back, he had the feeling he was being followed. Eventually he decided to hide in a clump of bushes until it was dark.

'When he thought it was safe he started back again. On his way he saw a torch flashing and heard his name being called. Francoise, half-frantic, thought he had been caught. Still afraid he was being watched, Tony told her to go back to the house. She did not want to leave him but he made her go and later in the night he crept back to his hideout.'

'Francoise was still alone in the house?' Adams interrupted.

'Yes. She had left food in the hideout and after eating it Tony fell asleep. He awoke in the morning to find the woods full of German soldiers. Lowering the trapdoor he wondered what he should do. Francoise would already have left for school and if he tried to warn her and was caught, which seemed certain, she would be implicated. All he could do was wait and hope the Germans did not suspect her.

'The Germans remained in the woods and around the house for the rest of the day. Around midnight the trapdoor opened and a man's voice whispered to him in French, telling him Francoise had been arrested and taken away. He was to go with the newcomer to another hiding place.'

The girl paused and took a sip of wine. Adams knew she was bracing herself for what happened next.

'He was taken away in a farmer's cart, blindfolded and covered in straw so he had no idea where he went. When the blindfold was removed he found himself in a farm storeroom. For the next two days he saw only the face of the Belgian who brought him food but he could hear other men in the house. The man was very unfriendly and he knew they were all blaming him for Francoise's capture. When he asked what would happened to her the Belgian only shrugged his shoulders.

'Tony learned the truth the second night. He had discovered that if he lay with his ear to the floorboards at one end of the storeroom he could hear people talking in the room below. Around six o'clock someone burst into the room and there were shouts of relief. Then he heard Francoise's name mentioned. When the Belgian brought his food later, Tony again begged for news of her. This time the Belgian was so bitter he told Tony everything.

'It seemed that one of his friends, who spoke German, had also been under suspicion and had been taken to the same Gestapo Interrogation Centre as Francoise. Although he was kept there for two days, unlike her he had been able to prove his innocence. But during his second night in the cells he had heard Francoise being interrogated.'

The girl paused, drawing deeply on her cigarette. Seeing her expression, Adams lowered his eyes and fumbled in his tunic pocket for his pipe and pouch. He was thumbing tobacco into the pipe bowl before she spoke again.

'They were torturing her. Her screams went on right throughout the night. God knows what they did but the following morning, when the Belgian was taken into the Commandant's office, a young Gestapo officer entered and said the girl was dead. When the Commandant asked if she had given away the hiding place of the RAF officer, the man admitted she had not.'

A flake of tobacco dropped on Adams' lap but he made no effort to move it. The warmth of the restaurant seemed to have drained away, leaving him numb and chilled. He listened to the girl recounting the last details of a nightmare.

'After that Tony was kept under close guard and never allowed to see his rescuers' faces. He has never said why but I know. If he could have escaped he would have gone berserk and killed the first German he saw.'

Adams' throat was dry. 'Why in God's name did they tell him?'

'Isn't it obvious? They blamed him for Francoise's death and later for her parents' arrest and in one way he was to blame. But it was a terrible punishment.' The girl paused, then went on quietly: 'Particularly as he had fallen in love with her.'

Adams picked the flake of tobacco from his trousers before lifting his head. 'Did he tell you that too?'

'Not in as many words, Frank. But he didn't need to. Now do you understand why he has changed so much?'

There was a long silence while Adams sought for the right words. 'He was a refugee in enemy-occupied Europe. A young girl risked her life to nurse him back to health and to keep him from the enemy. Sue, any one of us would love a person who did that for us. It's the way we're built. But none of this means he loves you any the less.'

'I'm not blaming him, Frank. And I'm immensely grateful to Francoise for all she did for him. If she had lived I would have given him to her with all my blessings.'

Adams shook his head. 'If she'd lived he wouldn't have gone to her.'

He realised what he had said the moment the words left his lips. 'So now you understand,' she said quietly. 'If she had lived I could either have fought her or accepted my loss. Now she is dead I can do neither one thing nor the other.'

It was all tragically clear to Adams now. 'That's crazy. Francoise's dead and Tony's alive. You have to make him understand this and make him relate to life again.'

'How do I do that, Frank? She gave her life for him. That means she can never disappoint him or spoil a single moment of the time they spent together. Remember Tony is an artist. His nature is more sensitive and vulnerable than ours. His feelings of guilt and responsibility are destroying him.'

It was one of those moments when Adams felt totally inadequate to offer advice or sympathy. 'You have to fight, Sue. You have to win him back for his sake as well as yours.'

Because the sob she gave was her only loss of control the entire evening, it seemed to Adams the more moving for it. 'How, Frank? How do I prove that I would die for him too?'

11

Staines gave a grunt of impatience as he gazed at the red light shining over the closed door. 'What the hell's going on now?'

None of the other four men seated at the long library table felt qualified to answer him. Although Moore looked his usual disciplined self, Davies, Henderson and Adams were all displaying a mixture of curiosity and concern. The hastily-called conference at High Elms, plus the attendance of Staines, suggested something more than a straightforward attack on a Gestapo base was under consideration.

It was five days after the Copenhagen raid. During that time 633 Squadron had carried out a further operation. This time it had been against one of the Gestapo's extraordinary filing systems. Invented by a man named Mehlhorn, the records of the Third Reich's possible enemies were housed in huge circular drums driven by electric motors, the systems being sited all over Occupied Europe. At the touch of a button, a card containing the personal details of any suspect could be obtained within seconds. The Dutch system was housed in a building in the surburbs of The Hague. Hearing the Nazis were about to carry out a purge to forestall Dutch help during the invasion, MacBride had sent in the Mosquitoes at low level. When they had finished with the blazing building, it was clear that however else Dutch patriots might be caught, it would not be with the aid of the pernicious filing system.

If Staines' presence at High Elms had not been a guarantee that MacBride had important news to impart, the security there would have been evidence in itself. Guard dogs were loose in the grounds and the visitors had been stopped twice before reaching the house. There, after a final check on their identity, a smart young Provost lieutenant had marched the five men briskly along the terrace into the library.

At first Staines had appeared unconvinced that the request for him to attend had valid reasons and his first pugnacious words to MacBride were to this effect. The reassurance MacBride had given him seemed borne out by the man's manner. Although still full of aggressive vigour, it had a slightly subdued quality that hinted he was sharing the obvious concern of the elderly Brigadier who had greeted the visitors with his usual courtesy.

'Thank you for coming so promptly, gentlemen. With your permission we will begin proceedings immediately and have coffee later. The news we have recently received from France calls for a certain urgency.'

With their expectations high by now, the five officers had wasted no time in finding themselves seats at the long table. Yet MacBride had no sooner risen to address them when a red light over the far door had begun flashing. Exchanging glances, the two SOE officers had disappeared into the room beyond it. Frustrated like his four colleagues and denied a reply to his earlier question, Staines turned to Davies. 'It'd better be something we can get our teeth into this time! None of that birthday party hokum.' Then the American's sense of humour returned as he glanced at Moore. 'Mind you, it must have been a hell of a sight to see those piss pots and toilet rolls going down. Dent says his guys wet themselves laughing.'

Moore smiled back. 'I think it amused the Danes too sir.'

'Let's hope it did more than amuse 'em,' Staines grunted. He turned back to Davies. 'Have you heard any reports yet?'

Davies looked surprised. 'Haven't you been told, sir?'

'Not a damn thing. But who does hear anything out in the sticks in East Anglia?'

'The Brigadier told me yesterday the first reports are good. It looks as if the story was all over Denmark in twenty-four hours. And their Resistance groups report a big increase in volunteers.'

Staines gave a grimace. 'Maybe MacBride knew what he was doing after all. Were you happy with your escorts?' he asked Moore.

'Very happy, sir. They did a fine job.'

'Yeah, Dent's a good man. You ought to meet him sometime.'

'Yes, I would like to . . .' Moore broke off as the end door opened and the two SOE officers re-appeared. Conferring with one another for a moment, they made their way back to the table. The low buzz of conversation among the seated men died as, after a final word with his older colleague, MacBride turned to face them.

'Sorry for the interruption, gentlemen, although later on you'll realise it couldn't have come at a better time. I've asked you all to attend today because I'm now in a position to give you details about your second brief that we discussed a week ago.'

The grunt from Staines suggested it was not before time. As MacBride turned his deep-set eyes on the American, Adams felt his pulse quicken. A glint in them suggested that an important piece of information had just been added to a jig-saw already nearing completion. The man's forceful voice, with its hint of self-satisfaction, added to the impression.

'What I am about to tell you is top secret. If news of it reached the general public it might cause alarm or even panic. So I must ask you not to repeat a word you hear this afternoon to anyone who has not been cleared by our respective security units. Is that understood?'

Nodding, men leaned forward to listen. Unable to suppress a nervous cough Adams received a frown from the burly SOE officer.

'To put you right in the picture, I'll begin at the beginning. Some time ago — never mind how — we got word the enemy was developing a new weapon.' As Staines met Davies' eye, MacBride went on: 'In itself that

93

wasn't particularly startling – we know Jerry has a number of projects in the experimental stage – but in this case we took notice because our French agents had reported high security measures being taken around a small town in south-west France. The Gestapo had taken over as their headquarters a large institute of animal vivisection right in the centre of the town and units of the Das Reich SS had put up road blocks at both ends of the valley. Of course the Gestapo Headquarters could have been established to police a wider area than the valley itself but the presence of the Waffen SS seemed without point. Accordingly we sent an agent to investigate and she came up with a startling piece of information. A certain Doctor Werner had been seen entering and leaving the Institute. With Werner a chemist of international repute, that was curious enough but when we heard he was wearing Gestapo uniform we were forced to investigate further.'

All five men were looking puzzled. 'A scientist in the Gestapo?' Staines asked.

'So it appeared. Our agent had also discovered that small convoys arrived at the Institute at regular intervals. Deciding they could be the key to the mystery, I ordered a Maquis group to ambush one and steal its contents. At the same time I sent a boffin to France to see if the contents were what we suspected.'

As MacBride paused, the only sound that could be heard in the library was the ticking of a clock and the chirruping of birds outside. Clearly enjoying his moment of drama, MacBride moved his eyes from face to puzzled face.

'Yesterday an agent brought us this boffin's report. Some of the drums contained the constituents of a gas called Sonam.'

Both Staines and Davies gave a violent start. The other three men gazed at MacBride with varying degrees of puzzlement and concern. 'Sonam?' Henderson said.

The SOE officer nodded. 'Yes. As it is classified, some of you won't have heard of it. It is a nerve gas – that means it acts by destroying the enzyme cholinesterase

94

which enable the nerves to transmit messages. Even a small dose turns a man into a twitching wreck and death usually comes because of inability to breathe. It is particularly dangerous because gas masks are useless against it – it works through contact with the skin. We've known about it for some time because it is the end product of a series of such gases which began with one called Tabun. Needless to say, we haven't lagged behind and today have a whole range of sophisticated nerve gases ourselves. This is one reason we haven't believed the enemy would use them. He knows we possess more offensive aircraft than he does and that means we could kill far more people. But this discovery has made us put two and two together and we've realised we've been too smug in our assumptions.'

Davies' voice was at least half a tone sharper than usual. 'Are you telling us Jerry's going to start using poison gas against the U.K.?'

MacBride turned to him. 'Yes. After this discovery, that's what we fear.'

Adams felt frozen with dismay. Like the other men in the library he knew that the bakelite-lined cylindrical cylinders officially called Smoke Curtain Installations that every bomber airfield kept in its armoury had another and far more sinister purpose than the laying of smoke screens and in his worst nightmares he had seen armadas of aircraft from both sides laying a deadly mist of mustard gas over cities. Hideous although the vision was, there had been some comfort in the thought that if gas masks and protective clothing were issued in sufficient quantities they could minimise the horror. But if MacBride were right about the nerve gases, that last comfort was ripped cruelly away.

Davies' question told he was sharing Adams' dismay. 'But how can Jerry use gas? If he tries it, we can saturate him.'

MacBride nodded. 'As things are at the moment, you are quite right. But supposing he delivers gas in a different way? Supposing it comes over in vehicles plentiful enough and fast enough to saturate our defences?'

About to ask what vehicles could do that, Davies gave a sudden start. 'Do you mean those rockets he's developing? The ones we're bombing on the Belgian and French coasts?'

MacBride could not prevent a smile of triumph. 'Yes. We know he's producing them in vast quanties. We now believe he intends using some of them to carry this gas.'

'Jesus Christ,' Staines muttered. In the silence that followed, the slam of a door somewhere in the large house sounded like an explosion. Then Davies found his voice again. 'But how does this institute come into it?'

'There were other chemicals apart from nerve gas constituents in the transport and samples of them were brought back by our boffin. They've now been analysed and their nature confirms our suspicions. They are diffusing elements — chemicals that would help the nerve gas to disperse quickly once a rocket had come down. They are necessary because rockets can't spray gas like an aircraft can and, unless a strong wind were blowing, without dispersal elements the gas would tend to lie in pockets where it would do minimal harm. The problem is to introduce these elements into the gas without weakening its killing power and we believe these are the experiments Werner is carrying out in St. Julien.'

Staines sounded hoarse. 'But why in a French town, for Chrissake?'

The burly MacBride shrugged. 'Doesn't it make sense? To begin with, a large animal research centre will be ideal for the experiments with its modern equipment and vacuum-sealed laboratories. On top of that our aircraft are reaching right across Germany and Austria these days. No place is completely safe, as Davies' men proved during the Rhine Maiden affair. So now the Germans are relying on our queasiness to protect their experiments.'

Henderson exchanged a glance with Adams. 'Queasiness? If you're right about all this, sir, a raid on that centre could spread poison gas right across the town.'

The look he received made it clear MacBride did not take kindly to interruptions from junior officers.

'However, that is not the only reason they have chosen a site in France. When our Maquis agents ambushed the convoy they found six French Resistance prisoners tied up inside one of the transports. Also, most fortunately for us, two of Werner's assistants were in charge of the chemicals. The Frenchmen had no idea what was to happen to them but the two German civilians knew and after a little persuasion they talked. As you must know, experiments on human beings have been going on for years in German concentration camps. First it was mental defectives, criminals, and their own dissidents who were the guinea pigs. Then it was Jews, Poles and Russian prisoners. Now apparently it is the turn of the French Resistance and the Communists.'

Staines' rugged face was a study as he leaned forward, his chair creaking beneath his great weight. 'You're telling us that Werner is experimenting on Frenchmen? With this gas?'

'There seems no doubt about it. According to the German prisoners, Werner has not yet solved the problem and this means constant experimentation on the prisoners brought in. Some apparently die; others become physical and nervous wrecks.'

Adams felt an urgent need to breathe clean air and to wash his face and hands, but the forceful voice offered no respite.

'When you think about it, it is all quite logical. With our invasion imminent, the Maquis and similar Resistance Movements represent a grave threat to the Nazis and what could be a greater deterrent than to use their members for these experiments.'

At that moment Staines appeared to be the only listener sufficiently recovered to ask questions. 'But you say this place and its experiments are a secret.'

'Naturally it has been the Germans' intention to keep it that way. But by using French political prisoners they were hedging their bets. If the truth leaked out, as it now has, the effect is twofold. The presence of French prisoners in the Institute is a deterrent against bombing it and the thought they might end up as guinea pigs in such

97

experiments must deter some Frenchmen from joining the Resistance.'

Staines was shaking his spiky head. 'I don't believe it. I thought this was the Twentieth Century. Does De Gaulle know what's going on?'

'Of course. We've had to keep him informed from the beginning.'

'What's his reaction?'

MacBride's scowl gave an answer before his words. 'He won't allow us to attack. Not on any count.'

'You can hardly blame him at that,' Staines said. He threw a wry glance at Davies. 'At least you know now why the SOE grabbed your squadron.'

MacBride nodded. 'With Jerry using these new tactics, we needed crews who could take out one building among hundreds. We had plenty of targets but since then this has become the big one.' The man's facial muscles tightened. 'If I had my way your Mosquitoes would be out at first light tomorrow. And if they didn't do the job I'd ask the General to send in his B17s.'

'Even though the town would be wiped out or its people gassed?' The shocked Henderson could not hold back his comment.

The scowl the Scot received was black with aggression. 'Yes, by God. Until now I thought the French were realists. But on this they're acting like timid women. So far we've only talked about the threat to civilians but there's a far worse one. If Werner overcomes his problems with the gas and it goes into the rockets, they could smother our troops at their assembly points before they even cross the Channel. In other words the invasion could become a disaster.'

Staines gave a groan. 'And before I came here today I thought we were winning the war. If we aren't allowed to bomb Werner's laboratories, what can we do?'

MacBride turned away from Henderson. 'That's another reason I wanted to see you all today. It's imperative we delay this project while our politicians have a fresh go at the French because if Werner completes his experiments and moves out there'll be no stopping the threat. Our boffins have told us the chemicals we captured are both difficult and dangerous to manufacture and so likely to be produced in only a few plants. They've given us some names but because we can't afford to waste time bombing the wrong targets I told my Maquis group to question the German prisoners again. The result was radioed to London and given to us a few minutes ago.'

There was not a man in the room unaware of the reality behind the man's matter-of-fact statement and all were showing varying degrees of distaste. Ironically, because of his experience in Norway, it was Adams who could best understand the ruthless MacBride's order. Forced to choose between the cold-blooded killing of half a dozen German soldiers and the capture or death of all his colleagues, the sensitive Intelligence Officer had learned the hard way that wars could not be fought with clean hands and unsullied integrity.

Staines' response sounded more like a bark than a question. 'Well! What did they find out?'

'The chemicals come from two factories, a large chemical works in the Rhur and a small, specialised factory on the river Weser. I want those factories destroyed, gentlemen. As soon as possible.'

'But if Werner and his assistants are still active, won't they just switch production over to another factory? The Krauts are the best in the chemical business. Everyone knows that.'

'Yes, of course they will. But we shall gain a week or two. And even a week could be vital.'

Davies decided it was time he made his presence felt. 'So far you've made it sound as if the Jerries don't know we're on to them. If we attack these two factories, won't that tip them off? And in that case won't they pack in more French prisoners to make it even more difficult for us to bomb Werner and his laboratories.'

'Yes. That's more than possible. But until the French relent, we've no other choice. We must try to slow down the experiments.'

Adams felt the need to make one humanitarian

suggestion. 'Wouldn't it be possible for the French to evacuate the town, sir?'

The glance he received made his cheeks burn. 'Don't you listen to what you are told? The institute is a Gestapo headquarters and the SS are guarding both ends of the valley. So how the hell can the people evacuate the town?'

Staines gazed round at the silent men. When no one offered a suggestion he shrugged his massive shoulders. 'If that's the best we can do, then let's get those factories bombed.' Glancing at the darkening French windows, he turned back to MacBride. 'Mind you, there's no way we can fit 'em in today. What about you, Davies?'

The small Air Commodore was doing swift calculations. 'It depends which job we get. The Ruhr's out of the question because of the smoke. But we might just manage the Weser job.'

Across the table Moore was shaking his head. 'There won't be time, sir. To begin with Lindsay hasn't enough Target Indicators in store.'

Aware his offer was too ambitious, Davies gave in testily. 'All right then. Tomorrow.' He glanced at Staines. 'Perhaps we can get our heads together on this, sir?'

'That's for sure,' the American grunted. He turned back to MacBride, his dislike for the man showing in his sarcasm. 'Just one last thing. When you bribed those two German prisoners with candy and cigarettes, did they give you any idea how soon Werner hopes to finish his experiments?'

There was something brutal in the man's terse reply. 'Yes, they did. He's been given a deadline of two weeks but he's hopeful of finishing sooner.'

12

It was 20.15 hours when Henderson braked the car outside the Control Tower and dropped back in his seat. 'You know something? I feel like a drink.'

He was sharing the car with Moore and Adams. Leaving Staines and Davies still discussing details of the forthcoming raids with the SOE officers, the three airmen had driven back to Sutton Craddock to make certain the station was ready when the teletype machine began clacking. Moore, who was in the front seat, turned to the Scot. 'Why don't we go to my billet? Or would you prefer the Mess?'

In the darkness of the rear seat Adams was showing surprise. In all the time he had known the young Squadron Commander he had never seen him drink when action was imminent. Henderson's voice hinted the Scot was equally surprised. 'You pushing the boat out, Ian? What have you got there?'

'Whisky. Or brandy if you feel like it.'

'Brandy? You haven't been holding out on us and landing in France, have you?'

Moore smiled. 'Nothing so spectacular. My family sent me a couple of bottles the other week.'

With a grunt Henderson heaved his big frame out of the car. 'Never let it be said a Scot refused a free dram. Anyway, I couldn't face those cheerful young bastards in the Mess tonight. But I'll need a word with the Duty Officer first. He'd better alert the SWO and get all crews and airmen rounded up. You two go ahead and I'll meet you in your billet.'

Moore shook his head. 'We'll wait here for you.'

Henderson was back in less than five minutes and the three men made their way on foot to Moore's quarters. Although the sky was dark the afterglow on the horizon was blood red. A heavy drone made all three men glance up. Henderson's grunt was aimed at no one in particular. 'They're early tonight.'

As Moore nodded, Adams knew what was in their minds. With the moon now in its third quarter and only rising after midnight, Bomber Command had brought its nightly raids forward in the hope its heavies would be homeward bound before they were exposed to the rapacious enemy night fighters.

A minute later Moore pushed open the door of his billet. Sparsely, even austerely furnished, it contained little to betray the young Squadron Commander's wealthy background. Nodding at Moore's question, Henderson dropped into a chair with a suggestion of weariness. 'Yes, thanks, Ian. I'll try the brandy.'

'You have the same, Frank?' Moore asked.

Adams, who had noticed there was only one spare chair, was sinking down on the bed. 'Please, Ian. I think I need a brandy tonight.'

His comment was an instant catalyst. The stare Henderson gave him was almost hostile. 'You think you're alone? Christ, I never thought I'd live to hear the things MacBride told us today.' He turned to Moore who was standing over a small bedside cabinet filling three glasses. 'Do you think he's right about those French prisoners?'

Moore nodded quietly. 'Yes, he probably is.'

'Then who the hell are we fighting? Fiends?'

Moore handed him a glass before answering. 'No. Just men like ourselves.'

Henderson stared up at him resentfully. 'What the hell does that mean?'

Moore took a second glass over to Adams. 'What it says. I don't believe that basically we're any different to the people we're fighting.'

'You're saying we could torture men or experiment on them with germs or gas?'

'Yes. In the wrong circumstances I think we could.'

'Then why don't we? We're at war with the bastards.'

Moore dropped into the other chair. Adams, who had never seen the big, good-natured Scot in this mood, watched in fascination as Moore shrugged. 'We were doing things just as brutal two hundred years ago.'

'Two hundred years is a long time. We've changed a bit since then.'

Moore took a sip of brandy before shaking his head. 'The emotional side of our natures hasn't changed since we were cave men, Jock. We're still the savagest animal on earth. What we have done is develop institutions to curb that savagery. It was the only way we could live in communities. But get rid of those institutions, as the Nazis have done, and we'd be back in the Dark Ages with the best of them.'

Although Henderson was looking less hostile now, Adams thought it wise to intervene. 'You're saying it's our institutions, not our consciences, that civilise us, Ian?'

Moore turned to him. 'In the sense that our institutions shape our consciences, yes. The Nazis threw theirs out of the window and replaced them with the cult of the Superman. Yet if history has taught us anything, it is that the man who believes himself superior to others is already depraved.'

With brandy warming his stomach and softening the outlines Adams was revelling in a philosophy that was so like his own. 'I couldn't agree more. That's always been my problem with religion. Every religious creed believes itself the true faith and so, by implication, its followers must be the chosen ones. Once men believe that, it's only one step from believing they've a God-given right to burn people at the stake in order to convert them.'

Henderson, who had finished his brandy, was frowning heavily. 'Religion! Burning at the stake? What are you babbling about, Frank?'

Adams realised his enthusiasm had carried him too far. 'I was trying to compare religious bigots with the

Nazis,' he said lamely. 'I think there is some similarity.'

The Scot's snort dismissed the unfortunate Adams' theory without ceremony. 'All I can say is that the two of you must have a hell of an opinion of human nature if you believe we're all tarred with the same brush as those murderous bastards over there.'

Moore's quiet voice came to Adams' rescue. 'Jock, it's only twenty-five years since the most brutal war in history. How many died — thirty, forty, fifty million? Nobody knows but it was a holocaust. Yet here we are at it again. It must say something about man's nature.'

'We didn't start this war,' Henderson grunted. 'Or have you forgotten that?'

'No. But we've started a few in the past.'

'Past, past, why do you keep harping on the past? The only thing I ask myself is if we're right in fighting this one. And if I wasn't sure before, by the Lord Harry I am after all I heard today.'

Moore nodded as he reached for the Scot's glass. 'I'll go with that. This is one war that has to be fought.'

Henderson's grimace showed his good humour had returned. 'Thank God for that. I thought for a moment you two were turning into conscientious objectors.' Shaking his head, he rose to his feet. 'No, I won't have another or I'll be as pissed as you are. I'm going to my office to give Davies a ring. They must know what they want by this time.' As both men rose, he waved them back. 'No, you stay and get it out of your systems. I'll let you know when I want you.'

As his footsteps died away outside, Moore took Adams' glass. 'Beneath all that Highland phlegm, Jock's a sensitive man. That news today shocked him.'

'It shocked us all,' Adams said with feeling. 'In fact I'm still finding it hard to accept.' He paused. 'Do you really believe we're all a mixture of Jekyll and Hyde, Ian?'

'I'm certain of it. When I see a fighter shoot down a friend of mine I want to tear it apart with my bare hands.'

Adams thought what he had so often thought before — that no one really knows anyone else. 'Yet we all think of you as the coolest and most clinical pilot on the squadron.'

The young Squadron Commander hid his expression from Adams by turning towards his cabinet. 'I suppose I hide it better than most. But although, God knows, I loathe it, I carry the mark of Cain like the rest of us.'

As he poured brandy into Adams' glass the drone of more heavy bombers could be heard. Moore's eyes lifted. 'There they go. Thousands of youngsters, every day and every night, going out to kill or be killed. Does anyone stop to think what it's doing to us, Frank?'

Adams was quick to offer comfort. 'It won't change them that much, Ian. It didn't after the last war.'

Moore's low laugh told Adams he had misunderstood the question. 'I wasn't suggesting we'd turn into killers or enemies of society. I was wondering how we'll face civilian life again.'

Adams was floundering a little at this sudden switch of mood. 'Will it be that difficult?'

'I think for aircrews it's going to be traumatic. Think of it, Frank. Day after day we fly into the bright blue sky or among the stars with thunderbolts in our hands. We press switches and our enemies fall from the skies or die in their hundreds on the ground. Even when we die ourselves there's no humility in our passing. We go down in flaming coffins with the wind screaming our loss to the world. The gods of Olympus couldn't do better than that.'

Hearing for the first time the innermost thoughts of the cultured young pilot, Adams could do nothing but swallow and listen.

'But one day soon it's going to end. If I survive I'll have to take over a chain of shops. Instead of that limitless sky I'll have to drive to an office every day where I'll shuffle papers from one drawer to another. But I'll be lucky. What about men like Harvey? How will he feel when he turns into a builder's clerk again after years of playing God? Every day he'll shrivel and die a little. But who'll understand? Who'll sympathise with him when he kicks the cat or gets fighting drunk?'

Although Adams longed for the day when the atrocious waste of life ended, his own vivid imagination had sometimes asked the same question. 'But surely there'll be compensations, Ian?'

Moore's laugh made him wince. 'It's quite a world when you have to ask a question like that, isn't it, Frank? The truth is, I don't know. They took us from our schools and universities, they honed and sharpened us into fighting machines, and then they gave us winged chariots and thunderbolts to play with. Are there compensations for young men who've been forced-fed with drugs for six years and then had those drugs snatched away? Will the world show them patience and understanding?'

When Adams made no reply, Moore took another sip of brandy. His voice mocked his forebodings when he spoke again. 'Perhaps we'll all be so glad we've a chance of dying in our beds that we'll settle down without any problems. But one thing I'm sure about — ex-bomber crews won't stay popular very long. As nations form new power blocks and old enemies become allies, we'll become an embarrassment. Before long they'll make us so ashamed at what we did that we'll keep it from our best friends, never mind our children.'

After two large glasses of brandy, the sentimentalist in Adams found this too much to bear. 'I hope I never live to see the day, Ian.'

Moore's reply betrayed the complexity of the young pilot. 'Why? It might be a good thing if the world forgets its soldiers. They've had a long run.'

'Forget all this courage and sacrifice? In a war to free half the world from tyranny and genocide? You can't be serious.'

Moore's smile showed his earlier mood had lifted. 'You're a romantic, Frank. But you'll see it'll happen, just as it happened after the last war. Soldiers, even heroes, have a short life in more ways than one.'

13

Sutton Craddock broke into life at 20.55 hours, the time the teletype bell in the Operations Room rang. The Duty Sergeant, lying on his camp bed reading a paperback, jumped up with a start and ran across to the machine. The Duty Officer, who had been listening to the radio, grabbed the telephone and ordered all outside communications to be cut. With the Station sealed off from the outside world, the DO began alerting the specialist officers. The C.O., the Squadron Commander, the Intelligence Officer, the Engineering Officer – as each phone call was made the list was meticulously ticked.

Outside the Tannoy began rasping orders. All available Mosquitoes had to be ready for dawn air-tests. Cursing mechanics emerged from their warm Messes or dispersal huts and began swarming over their wards. As NCOs yelled orders, men caught their shins on picketing hooks and bruised their chilled hands on spanners and screwdrivers. To the uninitiated it would have seemed chaos. In fact all the men were craftsmen and the stand-by procedure was well rehearsed.

To Maisie in The Black Swan, whose young customers, aircrews and mechanics alike, had been hustled out half-an-hour earlier by Special Police, it was a fascinating sight. Muted headlights, moving hither and thither across the black airfield, gave tantatising glimpses of yelling NCOs and running airmen. Storm lanterns formed pools of light around dispersed aircraft. As an accompaniment to the general din there was the occasional cough and roar of a Merlin under test that scattered sleeping birds from the hedges and trees of Bishops Wood.

Just before 21.45 hours a staff car swung into the camp entrance. As an SP walked in front of it, a corporal shone a torch through the side window. Although the man stiffened to attention on recognising Davies, he did not move aside. 'Good evenin', sir. Who is that with you?'

'It's General Staines of the United States Air Force.'

'Might I see his pass, sir?'

'He hasn't got a pass,' Davies snapped. 'I'm vouching for his identity. Tell that chap of yours to get out of the way. We're in a hurry.'

'Sorry, sir, but I'll have to get the W/O's permission. It won't take a moment.'

Breathing hard, Davies watched the corporal walk somewhat leisurely towards the Guardroom. Staines grinned. 'Your guys take security seriously.'

Davies gave a snort. 'Not as seriously as this. The bastards are up to something.'

The two officers had just made a speedy dash from High Elms. Details of their targets had come through shortly after Henderson and company had left and for the next thirty minutes Staines had been in argument with his Bombardment Group Headquarters. It had been an argument of some acrimony because when the Texan had emerged from the sound proof communications room he had looked as angry as if one of his erstwhile blockers had ducked a tackle and given away a touchdown. 'This goddam invasion's screwing up their heads back there. They're so set on smashing up the Krauts' transportation system, they can't see we could lose the war through the back door.'

As the journey back to East Anglia was a long one and with time at a premium, Staines had decided to base himself at Sutton Craddock for the next twelve hours. One factor was the red telephone in the Operations Room. Set up the previous year to link the American with his USAAF Headquarters for the Rhine Maiden Operation, it was still available for his use. A second factor was the way the two forthcoming raids were linked both in

108

application and purpose. From Sutton Craddock Staines felt he would be better able to monitor both of them. Knowing Staines' presence would ensure him the same facility, Davies was delighted with his decision.

Accordingly, after agreeing on a combined strategy with the American, Davies had put a call through to Henderson ordering all specialist officers and Flight Commanders to be present in the Operations Room. The rest of the aircrews were to retire to their quarters after being told they would be awakened at 05.00 hours sharp. Unsure what time the Air Commodore would arrive, and with all his officers having a dozen jobs to do, Henderson had told them to carry on as before but to be ready to run to the Ops Room the moment Davies' car arrived. He had then had a quiet word with the Station Warrant Officer, Bertram.

It took fifteen seconds for the massive figure of Bertram to stalk from the Guardroom. Known to one and all as Bert the Bastard because of the severity of his discipline, rumour had it that even the local blackbirds lined up before him for morning inspection. Coming to attention alongside the station wagon with a stamp of polished boots that made the ground shake, he lowered his peaked cap to Davies' window. 'Good evening, sir. What can I do for you?'

Davies glowered at him. 'What the hell's going on tonight, Bertram? Why are you holding up my car like this?'

'Just obeyin' orders, sir. All outside communications are cut, so we've got to be careful.'

'Damn it, man, you've seen General Staines before.'

The W/O motioned his corporal to shine his torch again on Staines whose rugged face was shadowed by a night's growth of beard. His disapproval of American standards was conveyed to both men without a muscle of his face moving. 'If you're vouching for him, sir, I suppose it's all right to let him through.'

Even Davies was bereft of words in the presence of such massive military imperturbability. With a last disapproving look at Staines, Bertram rose to his full height and nodded at the SP ahead. As Davies threw in the gears, the ground heaved again as Bertram snapped to attention. Grinning broadly, Staines glanced back. 'That's a fearsome sonofabitch. Who is he? Your Provost Officer?'

Davies was in the kind of mood when he wished Americans would use correct military titles and not weird colonial patois. Breaking hard on the road outside, he led Staines down the steps of the Operations Room. By this time most of the specialist officers were present. Noticing that some were breathing hard as they came to attention, Davies gave Henderson a hard look as they walked toward the platform at the far end. In no mood for a preamble, he got down to business right away.

'We've got an important job on tomorrow morning, gentlemen. As we're doing this one in conjunction with our Allies, I'm going to ask General Staines of the 8th Air Force to run over the broad outlines with you. We'll go into the details later. General Staines.'

With the majority of the officers present knowing nothing about the operation, the presence of an American general at a preliminary briefing was causing intense speculation. Aware of it, Staines gave a grin as he mounted the platform with Davies and faced his small audience. 'At ease, gentlemen, and stop looking so worried. No one's going to transfer you to the 8th Air Force.'

Among those present were the two Flight Commanders, Young and Harvey. Young had won a double at the races that day and had been celebrating in Highgate when the SPs had made their round-up. Although plied liberally with coffee on his return, the Australian was still in love with the world and his whisper to Harvey carried right across the room. 'Thank Christ for that sport.'

Davies looked aghast. Seeing the heavens were about to fall on the beaming Australian, Staines acted quickly. 'Yeah, you've sure got a lot to thank the big fella for. When I think of all that spam and soya links you guys get, I don't know how we manage on our mixed grills and ice-cream.'

As the Texan grinned maliciously, there were groans,

110

followed by appreciative laughter. With Davies under-
mined, Staines walked towards the illuminated map of
Europe that rose behind the platform and picked up a
pointer.

'Our targets, gentlemen. Two factories — one near
Hagen in the Ruhr and the other on the banks of the
Weser, here. As you'll all appreciate, the Ruhr target has
to be hit in daylight because of the smoke factor. The
Weser job, more easily identified, could be clobbered at
night and primarily was ear-marked for you. However,
now we've been given the exact locations, we've realised
we can do a combined job. Let me show you.'

As puzzled officers crowded nearer, Staines laid his
pointer flat on the map with one end resting on the East
Anglian coast of Britain and the other on the Belgian
coast. 'This will be our way in. With luck the Krauts will
think we're heading for transport centres in France.
Everyone's hitting 'em these days, so why shouldn't we?
Instead we've other ideas.' Holding the Belgium end of
the pointer firm, Staines revolved the other end until it
was pointing at the Ruhr. 'We turn sixty degrees at Ronse
and make straight for Happy Valley. Obviously some
fighters are going to track us, so it's not going to be a
picnic. But this time we'll have an escort of Mustangs. On
top of that the Krauts have got their britches stretched
tight with all the interdiction raids that are going on. So
with luck it won't be as tough as the last time.'

Seeing the expressions of his audience, Staines paused.
'Any questions so far?'

Moore's cultured voice made everyone turn. 'You say
us, General. Does that mean you're planning a similar
raid to the one we carried out last year in Austria?'

The Texan nodded. 'That's right; we're doing another
"Rhine Maiden". You'll fly at your maximum ceiling
above my B17s so that we mask you from the Kraut monitors. With their fighters occupied by our Mustangs, you
should reach Hagen undetected. Then, while we clobber
the complex there, you make straight for the Weser.
With any luck at all, the Krauts won't know anything
about you until the factory's gone up in smoke. Then you

111

move out fast. Whether you link up again with our Mustangs or head straight for home is something we can decide later.'

At this point a Northcountry voice broke in. As usual Harvey was blunt and unequivocal. 'I don't follow this, sir. If this is a daylight job and you're using your B17s, why are we coming along? You could just keep going after Hagen, prang both factories, and save us the trouble.'

From the way the other officers were nodding it was clear the Yorkshireman had spoken for them all. The Texan's grunt and change of mood gave evidence of what the nature of his altercation with his Group Headquarters had been. 'Yeah; that's a fair question. Originally we'd decided you could sit this one out. But right now every ship in your outfit and mine is knocking hell out of the Krauts' transportation system. As both Whitehall and Washington are behind this strategy, all they'd allocate me are fifty B17s.'

Somebody gave a whistle. Staines answered it with a grim nod. 'That's right. With all the smoke that's going to camouflage Hagen, they'll barely be enough. However, if we can't do both jobs ourselves, at least we can help you guys to reach Mindenberg by using our Rhine Maiden tactics. This way we ought to get an optimum result from the limited number of ships we've got. Any other questions before we get down to specifics?'

Harvey raised a hand again. 'What about photographs of the factories, sir?'

Staines glanced at Davies who stepped forward. 'Benson will have a Spitfire over at first light. To save time the pilot will fly back here and we'll process the film ourselves.'

Harvey had not finished yet. 'When do we brief our men?'

'As soon as they've done their air tests and had breakfast,' Davies snapped. 'At 07.30 prompt.'

At this Teddy Young winced, then gave a half-suppressed belch. Davies could contain himself no longer. He had already noticed the somewhat suffused eyes of Adams who was sharing the platform and although he had a shrewd idea why the Intelligence Officer had been drinking, he nevertheless felt his favourite squadron was presenting a poor image to the American General. The hapless Australian received the full brunt of his feelings. 'For Christ's sake go and get yourself a dose of bicarb, Young. Otherwise at 35,000 feet you're going to blow your poor bloody navigator right out of his flare chute.'

14

The clouds were in three tiers that late April afternoon. First a mixed layer of nimbus and cumulus. Then towering thunderheads. And finally flimsy ice clouds that reached almost into the stratosphere. From 36,000 feet, the height the sixteen Mosquitoes were flying, it was like looking down on some Antarctic landscape with mountains of black rock brooding over a fissured plain of snow and green water.

The Mosquitoes, painted PR blue for the occasion, were flying in battle order. Although far above the variations of weather, they were having to keep a looser formation than usual. The rarefied air was giving reduced support to their airfoils and the pilots were having to make constant adjustments as the aircraft dipped and yawed. An additional discomfort was the bitter cold which was affecting the crews' nervous systems and giving them a sense of detachment from the dazzling sky around them.

The fifty B17s who were giving the Mosquitoes radar protection were flying over two miles below. Grouped together in a tight combat box, they were driving forward through the towering thunderheads. The great crescents their condensation trails were forming betrayed the high wind that was sweeping across the upper limits of the troposphere. Other smaller contrails were criss-crossing above and through them as if some god of the sky were operating a giant loom. They came from the B17s escort of fighters, sweeping from side to side as they kept watch for enemy interception. Dent's Mustangs made up half their number: the rest were

114

Thunderbolts with drop tanks. Dent had made his rendezvous over Great Yarmouth: the Thunderbolts had made contact on the Belgian coast. Both escort commanders were surprised that an enemy counter-attack had not been made sooner. Now, as Hopkinson tapped Moore's arm and pointed, it was clear, at least to the Mosquitoes from their privileged viewpoint, that battle was only minutes away. Eight thousand feet below at 10 o'clock, a cloud of liverish black spots were darting forward through a layer of ice clouds. Hoppy lifted a pair of binoculars. '109s,' he announced.

As usual it had been the German Fighter Control at Deelen that had picked up the American bombers assembling over Great Yarmouth. With the Allied interdiction raids now in full swing, the Chief of 3 Fighter Division, Major General Walter Grabmann, had felt it more than likely that one of the marshalling yards in Northern France was their target and accordingly had ordered fighter units to take up positions near radio beacon Beate, north of Malmedy in Belgium. At the same time, being highly experienced in the feints and abrupt changes in course that the British and Americans had perfected, Grabmann had kept in reserve two gruppen of Jagdgeschwader I, one of his most experienced wings. These pilots had been standing by for the last half hour while Grabmann watched the formation track across his frosted screen. When he saw the formation suddenly turn eastward, his order had run in a swift chain of command to JGI's airfield where two loud speakers, previously blaring out dance music, rapped out an urgent order. 'Attention, attention! Heavy babies heading towards Essen. Take off and intercept!'

It was the first of these gruppen that Hoppy had spotted. Guided by ground control from one map reference to another, the Germans had now sighted the B17s and were preparing to attack. Because of their vantage point and the lack of cloud in the stratosphere most of the Mosquito crews had seen them but with strict orders not to reveal their presence they were helpless to do anything but watch the battle unfold.

115

It was a situation none of them relished. All the survivors from the Rhine Maiden affair remembered their feelings when they had been forced to sit aloft and watch the Americans suffer heavy losses. Now that helplessness was to be experienced by their younger crews.

Before the operation it had been hoped that the distraction of the interdiction raids would leave the Germans short on reserves to engage the B17s. The sight of the large gruppe sweeping in to intercept them made that optimism academic.

Under normal conditions Dent and his escort would have sighted the 109s and cut them off. Today, however, the condition favoured the Germans. The gruppe commander, a man with fifty such battles behind him, knew exactly what to do. Leading his 109s from cloud to cloud like a pack of Indians stalking a wagon train, he suddenly broke from cover above and behind the B17s.

At first the Mosquito crews believed he intended to attack from the rear, a tactic seldom employed these days because of the massive firepower carried in the Fortresses' waist and rear gun positions. As pilots and navigators exchanged puzzled glances, small dark objects suddenly began raining down on the tightly-packed formation. Hoppy gave a start. 'You see that, skipper? They're bombing the Yanks!'

The Cockney was right. JG1 had been the first German Fighter Wing to experiment with the tactic and to some extent had perfected it. With 109Gs capable of carrying loads up to 500lbs, fragmentation bombs could be highly effective even if they did not secure direct hits. Equipped with time fuses they had the same effect as if heavy flak were bursting in the heart of the combat box.

A huge oily fireball on the flank of the Fortresses told one had received a direct hit. A second reeled sideways and collided with the wing of a companion. As both ships went cartwheeling down, Millburn in T-Tommy gave a groan of anguish. A bulky, almost grotesque figure in his air-tight mask, pressure suit, and smoked goggles, the American was peering over the side of his cockpit. 'C'mon, you guys! Bale out, for Chrissake!

Only three parachutes opened. A fourth snagged on the tail of one of the giant ships and dragged its struggling crewman down. A few seconds later the tangled wreckage burst into flames and sank into a thunderhead.

By this time the startled Allied escort had sighted the gruppe and was climbing vengefully towards them. With the bombers heading towards their Fatherland, the 109s were equally prepared to take them on. Releasing the last of their bombs, they put their noses down. Within seconds the sky below turned into a giddy kaleidoscope of darting shapes and whiplashing tracer.

Forced to open their ranks during the attack, the Fortresses resumed their tight formation and flew doggedly on. But their troubles were not over yet. The second JGI gruppe, flying the latest 109s with the powerful Daimler-Benz 605 engine that gave them an edge over the Mustangs, had spotted the bombers' escort and also opted for cloud cover. Now, as the combat box swept over a sunlit pool, the 109s broke out from a black mountain ahead. Line abreast like a detachment of cavalry, they headed straight for the formation, firing their 21cm rockets at 1,000 yards range and their cannon at 800.

Once again the Americans suffered losses. Two of the giant aircraft reeled away, to become instant prey for the hungry fighters. Half the 109s broke left and right, to sweep round and attack from the beam. Other enemy pilots, full of desperate courage, went head on into the formation, spraying cannon fire as they went. Waist gunners, half-frozen in their open posts, raked them with .5 Brownings as they flashed past. Tuned into the B17s' radio channel, the Mosquito crews could hear shouts of warning and cries of success as 109s swooped in or fell like winged birds. They could also hear cries of pain as crewmen were cut down. As yet another B17 staggered and then wheeled away, Gabby turned to Millburn. 'If this goes on there won't be enough left to do the job.'

The American scowled. 'They'll have enough.'

Gabby was watching a wounded B17. As it reeled away from the combat box, two 109s were on it like wolves. One released a rocket which, by a stroke of fate, struck the giant aircraft full on its exposed bomb bay. Immediately a massive explosion rent the sky, its shock waves causing even the high-flying Mosquitoes to pitch and yaw. When the great fireball contracted, pieces of wreckage could be seen fluttering down. Millburn's voice was full of grim satisfaction. 'At least they took two of the bastards with them!'

The pressure on the B17s was beginning to ease. Recovering quickly from the surprise attack, the Mustangs and Thunderbolts were now at grips with the enemy. From high above, set dramatically against the backdrop of thunderheads and cumulus, the antagonists looked like tiny but voracious fish as they darted about and tore at one another in a frenzy of destruction.

In the way of air combat the duelling fighters quickly dispersed and the Fortresses, with only flak to contend with, were given time to attend to their wounded. As they swept over one of the great cloud canyons, the green fields below could be seen giving way to the haze of industrial towns. Moore glanced at Hoppy. 'How much longer?'

'No more than five minutes, skipper,' the Cockney told him. 'If that.'

Already the Fortresses were losing height. Ever since the Met forecast the previous night, it had been known conditions would not be good for high level bombing but the seriousness of the threat had given Staines no option but to order his men out. Now, to counter both the conditions and the industrial haze below, the B17 commander was forced to take his aircraft below the cloud base where they would be more vulnerable not only to the heavy flak that guarded the Ruhr but also to any more fighters the Germans might vector towards them.

Knowing that the enemy monitors were likely to pick up the Mosquitoes' presence now the gap between them and the Fortresses was widening, Moore decided it was time to part company. But before he could announce his intention to the B17's commander, Hoppy jabbed a finger downwards, where the tiny shapes of Mustangs could be seen overtaking the Fortresses. Once contact with the German fighters had been fully made, the escort's superiority in numbers had forced the Germans to break off their action. As if Moore's thoughts had been picked up below, an American voice sounded in his earphones.

'Betty Grable to Kestrel Leader. I guess this is where we part company. Have a good July 4th party.'

Moore smiled. 'Don't you mean November 5th?'

'Oh, hell, yes. I'd forgotten you guys are Redcoats. Good luck anyway.'

Sinking lower, the combat box of Fortresses disappeared into the bottom tier of cloud. Hoppy grimaced. 'I don't envy 'em, skipper. It's going to be hell down there.'

Nodding his agreement, Moore addressed his R/T again. 'Kestrel Leader to squadron. We're starting our descent now. Keep a close watch for bandits.'

The noses of the sixteen Mosquitoes dipped. With their radar cover removed, their ploy now was to find cover in the middle tier of clouds. Ironically the very conditions that posed problems for the B17s were acting in their favour. Navigators watched altimeters as the Mosquitoes sank down. 30,000 feet, 29,000 feet, 28,000 . . . . . . Pilots found their controls tightening as the stratosphere was left behind. Every man knew they were now visible on enemy monitors. The only question left was whether the fighters, already leaping off their airfields, would be able to find them in time. Experts at the deadly game of Blind Man's Buff, the Mosquitoes slid into a thundercloud and vanished.

Below the B17s were tracking towards their target. With the need to gain all the cover possible and yet allow his navigators a view of the ground, the Commander was flying through the underbelly of the cloud. It was a manoeuvre that meant the Fortresses flying in a looser formation to avoid collision but with cloud above him and the Mustangs at his back, the Commander knew his main enemy now was not fighters but flak.

Nor was he wrong. Nicknamed "Happy Valley" by the

RAF who had been bombing this heartland of Germany's industrial might almost since the beginning of the war, the Ruhr contained the heaviest concentration of flak guns of any German industrial complex. Over a thousand heavy guns were sited among its throbbing factories and the hundreds of wrecked aircraft that had littered its wastelands and slag heaps before they had been hauled away for scrap were testament to their deadly efficiency.

The problem of bombing the Ruhr had always been its permanent industrial haze. An added factor were the dummy factories and townships the Germans had built. While it was true that daylight bombing tended to ease these problems, on the other hand it meant the Ruhr's terrifying flak guns no longer needed to rely on their searchlights and radar "eyes". For this reason, when the Americans raided Happy Valley, they sent in massive numbers of aircraft in an attempt to overwhelm its defences. To send in a comparatively small force of fifty aircraft was playing right into the Germans' hands, the cause of Staines' frustration the previous evening.

To the German flak gunners the B17s looked like ghosts as they flittered in and out of the cloud base. The sight in no way impaired their expertise. Many of the guns were the terrifying 88s with a maximum rate of fire of 20 rounds per minute. With Ruhr crews having had more practise than any other flak gunners in the Reich, many were achieving that rate and the density of the bursting shells was awesome.

With the target one factory among many, the Fortresses were forced to waste costly seconds identifying it and ship after ship went down as white-hot steel ignited fuel tanks or sliced the arteries of feed lines. Yet when the target was sighted the ordeal for the crews had only begun. Precision bombing meant the ships had to close formation to increase the density of the bomb pattern and also to fly on a steady course. It also meant that if skill had played any part in survival so far, it played none now. Life or death depended entirely on the moving vectors of aircraft and shells. When they coincided, and the laws of chance made it certain some would, death by fire or mutilation was the outcome. A waist gunner screamed as his companion opposite was decapitated by a hissing steel splinter. A co-pilot grabbed the controls as his captain slumped forward, his flak jacket and stomach sliced open like the skin of a plum. Blood and oil ran in rivulets along metal floors, to mingle with empty shell cases. The air inside the giant ships stank of cordite, blood, and fear.

While all this hell was raging the Bombardier Leader was crouched over his bombsight, giving directions to his pilot. The factory, an ugly complex of buildings, sheds, pipes and storage tanks, was beginning to slide into his drift wires. Behind him the rest of the B17s had their bomb doors open. Squinting down, the Bombardier Leader waited, waited – then gave a sharp cry. Seconds later bombs tumbled out of the ships in their hundreds. Wobbling at first in the slipstream, they straightened out and plunged down like sinister dolphins.

With flak still lashing the ships, minutes seemed to pass before the bombs struck. Then a great pool of shuddering flashes appeared in the haze below. The flashes radiated out like an expanding fan as more bombs rained down. Exhausted voices tried to express triumph but men had little emotion left. The Commander silenced them. 'Betty Grable Leader to escort. We're going home. Stay with us.'

The surviving B17s, some with smoking engines, lifted themselves painfully into the clouds and banked away towards England. They left behind a great pall of smoke and a landscape littered with the funeral pyres of their comrades.

15

Hopkinson nodded at the sheen of water ahead. 'There's the Weser, skipper.' He studied the map strapped to his knee for a moment, then pointed to starboard. 'We need to follow it south for about four miles.'

Moore dipped his starboard wing twice, then banked parallel to the river. The troop of Mosquitoes behind him followed as if tied together by elastic. Then Moore lifted the nose of A-Apple again until grey mist swirled back and turned his canopy opaque.

Like the B17s, the Mosquitoes had been flying through the lower layer of cloud for the last fourteen minutes, descending into clear air only to establish landmarks. Although Moore had little doubt enemy monitors had picked them up, they would not be easy to find if they could keep out of sight of the German Observation Corps.

They emerged again from the clouds a minute later. The Weser, now off their port wingtips, could be seen swinging east a couple of miles ahead. In this sector it ran through a range of steep and wooded hills. Hoppy pointed at a smoke haze that hung over the valley. 'Mindenberg, skipper.'

Moore switched on the R/T. 'Kestrel Leader to squadron. Mindenberg's at 10 o'clock. Prepare to attack.'

Like well-rehearsed soldiers the Mosquitoes swung into a line astern formation. Putting A-Apple's nose down, Moore led them towards the river. A railway track and a road ran along its far bank. Crossing the river Moore banked until they were running directly below him.

Mindenberg was now dead ahead. Houses, some half timbered, appeared alongside the road and spread like a rash up the southern hillside. A complex of smoking factories, fed by the railway, lay on the river bend where the channel was deep. Half a dozen barges were moored at jetties and a stationary train was puffing at a siding. Needing to identify the chemical plant, Moore made a tight circuit of the town while Hoppy took his eyes off the photograph on his knee and examined the clustered factories.

Given a few seconds respite, Mindenberg was using them to advantage. Sirens were howling, factory workers turning off power and running into shelters, and gun crews stripping the covers off their weapons and switching on their predictors.

Like many of his pilots Moore was using the frustrating seconds to locate the flak posts. One gave its position away immediately as a chain of coloured shells rose from a blockhouse at the edge of a marshalling yard. Moore suspected others would be sited up the hillside but because of the dense trees they were invisible as yet.

A shout in his earphones brought back his attention. 'The factory's just past the river bend, skipper! The one with the tall chimneys and the pipelines.'

The discovery was made by Wall in S-Sammy: for once the hawk-eyed Hopkinson had been forestalled. Moore smiled at the disgruntled Cockney. 'You can't win them all, Hoppy.' Then his voice rose. 'Kestrel Leader to Squadron. We attack at twelve second intervals. Good luck.'

Leaving his Mosquitoes orbiting the town, Moore put A-Apple's nose down. The plan was to attack the factory at low-level with time delays. Although the remarkable Mosquito could actually carry the same bomb load as the much larger B17, sixteen aircraft were clearly not enough to saturate their target as the Fortresses had done. However, by attacking at low level – a tactic at which they were specialists – the squadron could achieve a degree of precision that would compensate for their lack of numbers. Moore's initial solo attack was to sound out the defences, a role that, despite Davies' disapproval, he always insisted on taking. Afterwards the Mosquitoes would attack in threes, with twelve seconds between each assault.

Through A-Apple's windshield the factory was growing larger by the second. It looked to be recently built or at least enlarged, with a weird structure of pipe lines, valves, and nodular containers towering over massive buildings, storage tanks, and transport bays. It reminded Moore of a petro-chemical plant he had seen up in Teesdale and he wondered if one of its functions was to refine spirit for the Reich's war machine. If so, it would be heavily defended.

The flak began in earnest when A-Apple was less than half a mile from the factory. As well as the coloured shells coming up from the marshalling yard, two more chains were rising from the jetties where the barges were moored. Then a vicious explosion lifted A-Apple's port wing. As more black bursts exploded nearby, a North-country voice came over the R/T. 'Watch it, Ian: They've got flak wagons down there.'

The two wagons Harvey had spotted were lined up on either side of the marshalling yard. If they were the standard type, Moore knew each would carry an 88 as well as a 37mm flak gun. Seeing that so far the crews had only one gun operational, he made a snap decision. The name of the game was surprise and if he went on and dropped his bombs, precious seconds would be lost while his men waited for the time delays to explode. Banking steeply away, he gave a terse order. 'Blue Section 1,2, and 3. Make your attack now.'

It was a decision instantly understood by his highly-trained crews and the words had barely left his lips before Young, Matthews and West swung into line abreast and came diving down. Without wasting a second Moore banked steeply over the northern hillside, at the same time calling in Millburn. Banking southwards, the American's Mosquito climbed like a rocket up the far hillside, then, dropping a wing, came sweeping back on a reciprocal course. With A-Apple having carried out the same manoeuvre, both Mosquitoes were now heading towards one another on a collision course with the marshalling yard their point of contact. Designed to confuse and distract gun crews, it was a manoeuvre that had served the squadron well in many a tight situation.

Meanwhile the first section of Mosquitoes had swept over the huge plant and dropped a mixed load of 250lb GP and 500lb SAP bombs. From a height of only seven hundred feet it was difficult to miss and navigators saw their bombs smash through roofs and disappear into the buildings beneath. As the aircraft climbed away and their navigators began counting the seconds, a second trio swept into line, opened their bomb doors, and prepared to attack.

Below, now approaching one another at over 600 mph, Moore and Millburn had their eyes fixed on the southern flak wagon which the Squadron Commander had decided to attack first. Heavily armoured from end to end and bristling with guns, it was a formidable sight as it swept towards them. Its 37mm and LMG gunners, busy tracking the first trio of Mosquitoes, failed to notice Millburn until the last moment as he came at roof top height over the town. As frantic orders were yelled one gunner did manage to depress his LMG but in the few seconds left to him his burst of fire was badly aimed.

Millburn's role, however, was that of decoy; to have opened fire might have meant the death of his Squadron Commander. The threat came from A-Apple whose bomb doors almost touched the water as she leapt across the river. Bomb release in his hand, Hoppy was watching Moore as the marshalling yard appeared and the flak wagon grew huge in the windshield. Seeing him nod, Hoppy pressed the button and a tail-fused 250 lb bomb dropped from the bomb bay. Skipping like a huge stone over the tracks, it smashed into one of the wagon's wheels, spun away a few yards, then came to a halt. Tracer from the wagon's LMGs beat a tattoo on A-Apple's fusilage as the Mosquito banked steeply to port. As Hoppy let out his breath, he discovered a calm

125

cell in his mind was counting: . . . 'three . . . . four . . . . five . . . .'

The bombs planted in the factory exploded first, a rolling salvo that sounded like the slamming of giant doors. A chimney toppled over as great columns of smoke, severed pipelines, and debris rose high into the air.

A few seconds later Moore's 250lb bomb exploded. Although the flak wagon's armour withstood the blast, the concussion killed the crew and flung the wagon over on its side.

There was no time for jubilation. Although it was still less than two minutes since the Mosquitoes had appeared over the town, all its flak defences, including the second wagon, were now in action, filling the sky with bursting shells and parabolas of tracer. With the element of surprise gone, another low-level attack on any of them would have been little more than suicide. The Mosquitoes' task now was to drop their bombs as swiftly and accurately as possible and then make for home.

The second trio were already doing this. They were carrying 250lb incendiaries. Uncertain what chemicals were manufactured within the plant, Davies had received advice from the boffins that if HE bombs and incendiaries were dropped alternately, one might release gas or chemicals for the other to explode. But although the incendiaries of the second trio began fires in two of the buildings, there was nothing in the flames to suggest they were chemically inspired.

Still more guns had opened up around the industrial complex and on the hillsides. Many were the dreaded 37mms and the third section of Mosquitoes, which Moore led himself, received their full fury. An explosion dead ahead of A-Apple made her falter for a moment like a man receiving a blow in the face. Van Breedenkamp, flying in F-Freddy, lost his upper tail fin from a scything steel fragment but managed to regain control. Another explosion tore the control wheel from St. Claire, badly bruising a hand before he could grab hold again.

With all the aircraft bucking like coracles in an angry sea, it was impossible for their navigators to take precise aim but at their low altitude it was of little importance. When bombs missed buildings, they bounded along compounds or transport bays and crashed through the walls of other buildings surrounding them.

But the fourth attack was not made without loss. As the section swept past the plant a 37mm shell burst right under the nacelle of J-Johnnie. With its cockpit and young crew fused into an obscene tangle of flesh, metal and bone, the Mosquito turned slowly over and crashed into a chimney. As bricks and flaming debris showered down, there was a curse from St. Claire. Without a word to his navigator, he pushed his control column forward and went searching for the flak guns that were killing his friends.

The Mosquitoes of Harvey's trio, the next to attack, were orbiting above like gladiators waiting to enter a bloodstained arena. Noticing St. Claire break formation, the Yorkshireman guessed his intention and rapped out an order. 'Red 4! Get back into line. At the double.'

St. Claire took no notice. The pain in his hand and the violent deaths of Brown and Daglish had triggered off again his nascent hatred of the enemy. Ignoring the protests of his white-faced navigator he went raging back over the burning buildings in search of a gun crew to attack.

By this time Moore had emerged from the worst of the flak and was able to see the reason for Harvey's anger. His own order was equally unequivocal. 'Kestrel Leader to Red 4. You are not to attack flak posts. Break off your action and join Blue Section immediately!'

It is doubtful if St. Claire heard this second order. The blockhouse at the far end of the marshalling yard had been the first flax post to lower its guns on him and had therefore become his target. Having dropped all his bombs, his guns were his only weapon but in the madness of the moment they were enough. Flattening out, leaping over a row of railway sheds, St. Claire opened fire.

The massive recoil of the Hispano cannon jolted the

Mosquito before it sprang forward again. Twenty shells a second, a mixture of ball, incendiary and armour-piercing, speared out and smashed into the blockhouse. But the squat gunpost had been built to withstand bomb blast as well as gunfire and although chunks of brick and stone were torn from its exterior wall, the stabbing gun barrels visible through its visors swung ominously after the Mosquito as it flashed past.

With Harvey and his men waiting for the fourth salvo of bombs to explode before they could attack, Moore was confronted with one of those split-second decisions that come to all field commanders. With Young's Blue Section having completed its task and wisely orbiting out of range, should he recall them to attack the flak posts as St. Claire was doing? There was no doubt the harassment would take some pressure off Harvey's aircraft. Yet attacking flak posts was the kind of gesture only accept-able when the demands of an operation justified it and although no chemicals appeared to have exploded in the plant, its buildings were severely damaged and the fires were spreading. As the recently-planted salvo exploded, inflicting yet more damage, Moore decided it was a move that might lose more lives than it saved. Instead, as Harvey and his men prepared to run the gauntlet, he turned to his navigator. 'Hang on to your seat, Hoppy. I'm going after St. Claire.'

As he kicked the rudder bar and sheered down, he heard Hopkinson's muttered complaint. 'If the bloody fool wants to kill himself, why should we risk our necks?'

Conscious the Cockney had cause for his resentment, Moore tried to judge St. Claire's flight path. Seeing he was banking for another attack on the blockhouse, he dived on an interception course. At the same time he rapped out an order. 'St. Claire! This is your Squadron Commander. Break off and join Blue Section. At the double!'

Huddled behind his reflector sight, St. Claire saw A-Apple suddenly sweep from left to right across his flight path. With coloured chains of tracer following it, the effect was the one Moore hoped for. Muttering some-

128

thing to his relieved navigator, St. Claire swung away from the blockhouse and dived low over the river. A few seconds later he began climbing towards the circling specks of Young's section.

Moore and Hopkinson, both still wearing their high-altitude suits, were bathed in sweat as the flak pursued them. They were making for the northern hillside; their intention to take cover behind it and then make contact with Young. But although Harvey's trio were receiving their full baptism of fire as they neared the plant, the marshalling yard flak posts had become nervous after St. Claire's attack on the blockhouse and were determined that A-Apple should make no similar move. Long coloured chains were casting out to ensnare her and vicious explosions were shaking her like a dog with a bone. Clinging to the control column, Moore had just cleared the hilltop when a tremendous explosion hurled both men forward in their seats and filled the cockpit with choking fumes. Moore, whose forehead had struck some obstacle, felt himself entering the endless black tunnel that had swallowed so many of his comrades. Dropping a wing, A-Apple began its fall to earth.

It was a rush of icy air and an ear-piercing scream that brought the young Squadron Commander back to consciousness. His first move was instinctive: to fight the spin and bring the Mosquito into level flight again. As his eyes cleared he saw a side of the cockpit blister had been blown away and the starboard engine had lost its propeller. As he switched off the Merlin and the hideous scream died, black smoke followed by fire burst out from the shattered cowling. Heart in his mouth he switched on the fire extinguisher. Reluctantly the fire died although smoke and glycol continued to plume out.

Beside him the rush of icy air was beginning to revive Hopkinson. Still half-stunned, he turned shakily to Moore, 'What happened, skipper?'

Moore did not hear him. His head ached sickeningly and his earphones were full of alarmed voices from crews who had seen A-Apple hit. Wincing with the effort, Moore restored order. 'Kestrel Leader to Red Section.

Clear the radio channel. Red Section Leader. Can you hear me?'

Harvey, in dropping his incendiaries and then struggling to escape the flak, had been too busy to take in the shouts on the R/T. Now his voice was sharp with concern. 'Ian! What's happened?'

About to reply, Moore paused. The incendiaries from Harvey's section were beginning to explode. This time enormous spheroids of blue and green fire, like obscene fungi, were swelling outward and engulfing buildings and storage tanks. Moore's voice quietened the shouts of triumph from the Yorkshireman's crews. 'Well done, Frank. It looks as if the boffins were right after all. Now get your boys together and make for home. We could have visitors at any time.'

Harvey was not even listening. At his first suspicion that Moore was hit he had swung round and flown clean through the flak that was sweeping the valley. His masked face could be seen staring across at A-Apple as he closed wingtip to wingtip. 'How bad is it, Ian?'

'We've lost an engine. And we've a hole in the cockpit blister. But she should get us home.'

Ahead, Young's Mosquitoes had now been joined by the remainder of Harvey's section. They were orbiting just below the cloud base and although Moore was flying three thousand feet lower, they were beginning to take on recognisable shape. Mindenberg, covered by smoke through which dull flashes could still be seen, was beginning to slide out of sight among the hills. Harvey's gruff voice came again. 'Are either of you hurt?'

Moore glanced at Hopkinson who somewhat wryly shook his head. 'I don't think so.'

'Then we shouldn't have any problems. You fly between my section and Teddy's.'

'No, Frank, we'd slow you down. Take your boys home. We're coming back the same way, so won't be long after you.'

There was not a man listening who had expected any other answer from their leader. When hunting in enemy territory, the survival of the pack demanded that it was

130

not burdened by wounded comrades. Although it was a rule Moore had been known to disobey when other crews were involved, it was typical of the man to obey it rigidly when he was the victim.

Harvey's reply was unequivocal. 'Don't talk bullshit, Ian. You're coming with us.'

Moore's tone changed. 'You're wasting time, Red Section Leader. Bandits are already overdue. Get your boys out of here. On the double!'

D-Danny remained doggedly wingtip to wingtip. 'You've got a bloody short memory, haven't you, Ian? Who broke the rules to save my skin after the Rhine Maiden shambles? Teddy can take the boys home. I'm sticking around.'

Hopkinson, facing a desperate journey home in a crippled aircraft, never knew how much his plea owed to sympathy or self-preservation. 'He's right, skipper. You owe it to him. Let him tag along.'

Knowing the Yorkshireman's Achilles heel, Moore struck at it hard. 'While you're wasting time arguing here, you're putting your men in danger. I'm giving you a direct order, Red Section Leader. Get back to your men and take them home!'

The curse that came over the R/T sounded distorted. For long seconds D-Danny remained wingtip to wingtip. Then, as painfully as flesh pulling away from flesh, it began to draw away. Hopkinson turned towards the motionless Moore. 'Make it easier for him, skipper, for Christ's sake.'

It was a plea that reminded Moore he was not alone in the aircraft. 'Kestrel Leader to Red 2. Do you read me?'

'Yeah, skipper. Loud and clear.'

'How would you like the job of baby-sitter?'

D-Danny's wings gave a relieved quiver at Millburn's eager assent. 'I'm the best baby-sitter in the business, skipper. Coming right over.'

Ahead, D-Danny suddenly began to climb and to pick up speed. Half a minute later it joined the orbiting Mosquitoes and the squadron disappeared into the clouds.

16

The silence in the Operations Room could be felt as Staines replaced the red telephone receiver. It stood on a long bench that also had radio and W/T equipment manned by a Signals corporal. A series of posters, intended to remind aircrews that a war was on, ran along the wall behind the bench. The one directly in front of Staines read WATCH THE HUN IN THE SUN but from the Texan's expression it seemed unlikely he was contemplating the advice.

Adams, seated at the large table on the platform with Henderson, MacBride and the elderly Brigadier, gave Henderson a questioning glance to which the Scot could only shrug his broad shoulders. Behind them Davies, who had been pacing up and down beneath the large map of Europe, paused and stared pointedly at the American. With his own communication channels silent so far, it seemed certain he would not be able to stifle his curiosity for long. As it happened MacBride spoke for him.

'What's the news, sir? Have your men reached their target yet?'

Stirring himself, Staines swung round and fixed his unfriendly eyes on the soldier. 'They haven't only reached it, MacBride, they've clobbered it. First reports say very heavy damage.'

The American's lack of enthusiasm was clearly puzzling MacBride. 'They've done well. Congratulations.' He turned to Davies. 'When do you expect your report?'

About to put a question to Staines, Davies frowned.

132

'Five or ten minutes. It's difficult to be precise.'

From the floor of the room Staines was eyeing MacBride with increasing hostility. 'You haven't asked me yet what our losses are, MacBride.'

Adams was fascinated at the man's imperturbability as he gazed coolly back. 'Haven't I? What are they, sir?'

'Nineteen B17s and ten fighters. So far!' As Davies gave a wince the Texan went on bitterly: 'Nearly half my goddam force. I'd say they were high losses to clobber a target of doubtful value, wouldn't you, MacBride?'

'Not in the circumstances, sir. If they give us the few days reprieve that we're hoping for, they'll be well spent.'

Staines stared at him, then dropped back into his chair with a grunt of disgust. Glancing at Henderson, Davies went down to the American and the two men conferred in low tones.

Finding the minutes passing with painful slowness Adams tried to smoke his pipe but found he could not. On occasions of this kind his mind's eye usually tended to magnify the danger his friends were facing. Today, however, the American losses suggested that even his vivid imagination had under-estimated the threat.

Six more minutes passed before the blip of Morse was heard. Jumping up, Davies positioned himself at the corporal's shoulder as the man began scribbling on a pad. Henderson and Adams ran down from the platform to join him.

At first Davies was jubilant. 'They've got the plant! Some of the tanks blew up just as the boffins said they would.'

As the blips ceased MacBride rose to his feet. 'Well done, Davies. A damn good morning's work all round.' He turned to the elderly Brigadier who had also risen. 'Now that we've got some ammunition to shoot at De Gaulle, I'm returning to London. I'd like you to come with me.'

As both SOE officers reached the floor of the room, the blips began again. As he read the message aloud Davies' euphoria vanished like a puff of smoke. 'One aircraft shot down and Kestrel Leader lost engine. Will try to make base.'

Someone gave a gasp of protest as the message ended. Davies caught the corporal's arm. 'Send Kestrel Leader this message!' Then he hesitated and finally shook his head. 'No, the less they transmit the better.'

MacBride nudged Simms, who was showing the same concern as the airmen, and said something to him in a low voice. As the older man sighed and followed him to the bunker entrance, Staines gave a growl of resentment. 'You've got your ammunition all right, MacBride. Over two hundred dead kids and perhaps Moore as well. I hope it's going to stick in someone's craw the way it's sticking in mine.'

The man showed not the vestige of emotion. 'I'm sure their sacrifices won't be in vain, sir.' Nodding to the other officers, he acknowledged Staines by coming briefly to attention. 'Thank you for your co-operation, gentlemen. I shall be in touch very shortly.'

Followed by the silent, embarrassed Brigadier, he climbed the steps of the bunker and disappeared. In venting his feelings Staines paid no attention to the Signals corporal still sitting alongside the W/T receiver. 'Sonofabitch!' he announced loudly and hoarsely. 'God-damned sonofabitch!'

The 109 was keeping station a thousand yards back at five o'clock. Gabby's neck was aching from keeping watch on it, and the Welshman's temper was wearing thin. 'What's wrong with the bastard? Why doesn't he attack and get it over?'

Millburn gave him a grin. 'He knows who we are, boyo. He's waiting for half a dozen of his buddies to arrive and square up the odds.'

Scowling, Gabby lifted his eyes to the clouds above. 'You'll be laughing on the other side of your face when they do come, Millburn.'

The American was flying in starboard echelon fifty yards from A-Apple. The two aircraft were three hundred feet below the base of the clouds, near enough

134

for occasional whisps of cotton wool to sweep past their canopies but not near enough to gain protection.

The 109 had latched on to the two Mosquitoes only ten minutes after they had left Mindenberg. Had the crews known it, the pilot was a novice only recently out of flying school. With the Luftwaffe now stretched to the limit by the massive British and American interdiction raids, pilots were being thrown into action within days of their posting to fighter squadrons. In recognition they were unlikely to live long, they were given old, patched-up fighters recalled from OTU units. Karl Lutze was flying such a machine. Although he was willing enough to engage, his present orders had displayed a modicum of sympathy for his circumstances. Should he intercept any enemy aircraft other than a heavy bomber he was not to attack. Instead he would give Control its map references and track it until help arrived.

Fully aware of their danger, the experienced Mosquito crews knew their counter move was to enter the clouds and take evasive action. A-Apple's condition, however, prevented such manoeuvres. Over Mindenberg Moore had been puzzled by the aircraft's sluggishness. Capable of an upward roll with one engine feathered, the Mosquito's one-engine capability was legend and even in its present state A-Apple should have made altitude without difficulty.

The rev counter provided the answer. The exploding shell must have damaged the port engine also. Millburn, who had flown beneath A-Apple, believed the air intake was bent while Gabby thought he could see a fine thread of glycol streaming out. Whatever the trouble the revs were dropping and the engine beginning to overheat. Doubts now existed that A-Apple could reach the coast. Any attempt to coax her higher would almost certainly end in disaster.

Millburn's cheerful voice gave no indication of the perils ahead. 'How're things going, skipper?'

Moore glanced again at the temperature gauge that was slowly climbing into the red. 'It's going to be touch and go. Millburn, this is an order. If more than one kite

135

jump us, you're to take cover and head for home. Hoppy and I will bale out.'

The American winked at Gabby. 'O.K., skipper.'

'I mean it, Millburn. You couldn't save us, so there is no point in trying. Is that understood?'

Millburn sounded hurt. 'Have you ever known me disobey an order, skipper?'

Moore had to smile. 'It has been known. Mind it doesn't happen this time.'

The two Mosquitoes droned on. Behind them young Lutze was chafing with impatience. Where were the aircraft he had called up? Surely they were not going to allow the Tommis to escape? For a moment the young German was tempted to disobey orders and attack. If he shot down one of the formidable Mosquitoes, surely they would not punish him.

Discipline imposed on the young man from his days in the Hitler Youth held him back. His Flight Commander's orders had been unambiguous: if he disobeyed them he might never fly again. Instead he would call up Control again and see where the fighters were.

In fact a *schwarm* of four 190s were already sweeping in from the south west. Having been advised one Mosquito was damaged and was flying below the cloud base, they had not bothered to take cover themselves. A map reference mistake by Control had delayed them for five minutes but now the Mosquitoes were in sight and like a quartet of cavalry riding towards two dismounted soldiers the schwarm were closing in for the kill.

Hoppy sighted the 190s first and yelled a warning to Moore. Hearing him, Millburn immediately heaved back on the control column. As thick mist closed around the cupola, Gabby stared at the American in surprise. 'You doing what Moore ordered?'

Giving him a look, Millburn switched on his fire-and-safe button. Through the swirling mist below glimpses of the enemy aircraft could be seen as they swept round on to A-Apple's tail. They were Focke Wulf A-4s equipped with high velocity Mauser 151 cannon. Extremely fast, they were a match for any Allied plane in the sky at that time. Certain of their prey, three of them swung behind A-Apple while the fourth kept watch for Millburn.

For the American it was a delicate problem of trying to see without being seen. Below, believing Millburn had obeyed his orders, Moore had put A-Apple into a steep dive. The three Focke Wulfs followed in line abreast. The reasoning was simple but deadly. The outer fighters would prevent escape, the inner one would effect the kill. Gritting his teeth, Millburn shoved his throttles forward and went down like a meteor.

It was a desperate attack that caught the Germans completely by surprise. With his eyes on A-Apple that was rapidly filling his luminous gun sight, the *Schwarm* Leader never saw what hit him as Millburn opened fire at point-blank range. As cannon shells smashed into its fuel tanks, the Focke Wulf exploded into a huge fireball. The startled survivors broke left and right. Banking on a sixpence, Millburn went after the latter. His curve of pursuit was too acute for him to line up on the 190's fusilage but the burst of fire he put through its port wing was enough to drive it further away from A-Apple.

For Moore and Hopkinson, as Millburn had known all along, there had never been a chance of baling out. At the best of times the Mosquito was a difficult aircraft to escape from; under attack, with its pilot having to take evasive action, the chances were almost nil. Moore's one hope now was to get down to ground level and try to lose his pursuers by hedge-hoping. He and Millburn had considered it earlier but with A-Apple needing air space as her engine revs fell, they had decided against it. Now it was the only course open but as Moore gazed back he wished he had not taken it. Not only were all three Focke Wulfs now engaging the American but they had called in the lone 109 to further the odds.

Millburn was fighting like a man possessed. Determined to stop the Germans from diving after Moore, he was flying straight at them and scattering them in all directions. Twice he was so near to collision that the petrified Gabby could see the blue oxide flames of enemy exhausts and patched scars from previous dogfights. It

137

was an encounter where survival relied on reflexes honed by combat experience and so the odds were heavily stacked against novices. Bewildered by the speed and ferocity of it all, Lutze lost sight of the dazzling Mosquito for a moment and paid the penalty. Closing up behind him, Millburn opened fire at point-blank range and tore apart the 109's fusilage like a tin can. The young pilot had flown his first and last flight for the Fatherland.

Nevertheless it was a fight that could have only one ending. Every moment that T-Tommy survived she was growing less responsive to her controls as shells tore great wounds in her wings and body. Bathed with sweat Millburn tried to shout at Gabby but found he could do little more than croak. 'Try to bale out, boyo! Make an effort, for Chrissake.'

With earth and sky spinning round like some crazy kaleidoscope, for once Gabby had no reply. Waiting for death, he believed it had come when the massive pounding of cannon suddenly ceased. Nor did Millburn's yell, which almost ruptured the diaphram of his earphones, and the metallic American voices that followed it make any sense to the petrified Welshman. It was only when Millburn's hand slapped his thigh so hard he was jerked against his seat harness that the nightmare broke. 'What happened?' he asked hoarsely.

'Some of the Yank escort came back for us. Harvey gave 'em our co-ordinates.'

Still unable to believe his luck, Gabby gazed at the Mosquito's wings through which naked spars could be seen. 'Do you think we can make Blighty?'

With no other way to vent his feelings, the jubilant Millburn pounded Gabby's thigh again. 'You don't think we're going to crack up now, do you? We'll get back, boyo, if I have to get out and push.'

Gabby's yelp of pain gave evidence of his recovery. 'What the hell do you keep on doing that for, Millburn? You want to cripple me or something?'

Grinning, Millburn put T-Tommy's nose gingerly down and edged alongside A-Apple which had levelled off at 2,000 feet. Above, six Mustangs, which had reformed after driving off the 190s, were spreading out into a protective fan. From their vantage point the two Mosquitoes looked like linen toys that had been mauled by an animal. Although by this time A-Apple's starboard engine was a cooling piece of metal, its port engine was now beginning to smoke. Millburn peered across at it with concern. 'You're going to make it, aren't you, skipper?'

'It's up to Rolls Royce more than us, Tommy. As long as she doesn't seize up, we've a chance.'

'They make a hell of an engine, skipper. And we haven't that far to go. So hang on tight.'

Explosions rocked the Mosquitoes in their unsteady flight. At low altitude, unable to take evasive action, they were a target for every gun along their route. To draw off some of the flak, the American escort sacrificed altitude. But as the smoke from A-Apple began drawing a black line across the sky, the odds against her survival lengthened by the minute.

17

Still wearing his high-altitude suit, Harvey looked like an enraged bear as he ran round the tail of the Mosquito. His snarl made the two mechanics who were attending to the aircraft draw back. 'St. Claire!'

The young pilot's face was pale as he turned. Harvey in a rage was a forbidding sight. 'Yes, sir.'

The Yorkshireman moved towards him. Lacey, his new navigator, followed, ready to grab an arm if the Yorkshireman attempted to strike the pilot. 'You insubordinate bastard! I ought to kill you.'

St. Claire immediately turned defiant. 'I beg your pardon, sir.'

A large vein rose on Harvey's forehead. 'Don't get clever, St. Claire, or I'll smear you all over the airfield.'

The anxious Lacey muttered something in his ear. From the thunderblack look he received it seemed for a moment the Yorkshireman might strike him too. Instead, although shivering with rage, Harvey drew back. 'You're under arrest, St. Claire.' He swung round on Lacey. 'Get him into my office. At the double.'

Nodding, Lacey led the pilot away. With all the Mosquitoes now in, transports were picking up the crews and depositing them outside Adams' Confessional. Their mood was anxious and one topic dominated their conversation: would their popular leader and Millburn get back safely? A few had witnessed the scene between Harvey and St. Claire and as the enraged Yorkshireman started after the pilot, Teddy Young detached himself from the group and caught his arm. 'Take it easy, cobber. You don't know the score yet. Ian might still make it.'

Harvey shook off his hand. 'It won't be thanks to that bastard, will it?'

As a Flight Commander himself, Young held no brief for crews who disobeyed orders. The Australian's concern, knowing the Yorkshireman was never one to count the cost where a friend was concerned, was what harm Harvey might do to himself. 'We all saw it, Frank. You've got a cast-iron case. But for Christ's sake don't thump the guy or you could get the chop with him.'

Harvey pushed him aside and strode across the tarmac apron. As Young watched him, a jeep drew up and Henderson jumped out. 'What's going on, Teddy?'

The Scot showed anger as the Australian explained. 'So it's St. Claire's fault Moore's in this mess?'

Young hesitated. 'He couldn't have known Ian would go down after him.'

'That's hardly the point, is it?' Frowning, Henderson stared after the retreating figure of Harvey. 'You don't think Frank'll go too far, do you?'

'I warned him to watch it. But he's pretty choked up.'

'No bloody wonder,' the Scot grunted. For a moment it seemed he might follow the Yorkshireman. Then he shrugged and turned away. 'I can't interfere. Not yet anyway. Let's get over to the Ops Room and see if there's any more news.'

The door of the Flight Office opened with a crash as Harvey entered. Sam, about to express his delight at his master's return, recognised his mood and slunk under the desk instead. Harvey's scowl was an order for Lacey to leave. As the navigator obeyed and closed the door behind him Harvey marched to his desk, then swung round. 'Well! What's your story?'

The young pilot was standing stiffly to attention. 'I haven't a story, sir. I attacked the blockhouse and Wing Commander Moore flew down after me. When he ordered me to break off the action I obeyed and joined the rest of your flight.'

141

The vein was rising on Harvey's forehead again. 'And he got clobbered! In saving your sodding useless neck.'

Although he was trying hard to hide it, St. Claire was distressed. 'I know now I shouldn't have done it. But at the time I never thought the Squadron Commander would fly down after me.'

'You didn't think! What the hell has that to do with it? Your orders were to orbit away the moment you'd dropped your load. So why didn't you?'

With St. Claire liking and respecting Moore as much as any man on the Station, he had no problem displaying his regret. 'I'm as sorry as anyone for what happened, sir.'

It was an apology that only refuelled Harvey's anger. 'You're sorry! A lot of good that's going to be if Moore gets the chop.' In expressing the possibility Harvey lost his control again. 'If he has, I'll kill you, St. Claire. I bloody will. Unless someone else beats me to it, that is.'

The pilot lowered his head. 'I never meant anything to happen to the Squadron Commander, sir. I really am sorry about that.'

Harvey stared at him, took a turn to the window, then came back. 'What made you do it?'

St. Claire opened his mouth, then closed it again. 'I don't know, sir.'

'You don't know! On two operations you disobey orders but don't know why. You act like a bloody madman but say there isn't a reason? What the hell's going on, St. Claire?? Is it drink, girl friend trouble, or what?'

The pilot's expression turned sullen but before Harvey could say any more the telephone rang. When he replaced the receiver, Harvey's expression had changed. Sinking back in his chair, he lit a cigarette before glancing back at the erect pilot. 'That was the C.O. Moore's made it. He crash-landed on an American emergency airfield fifteen minutes ago.'

St. Claire closed his eyes in relief. Harvey sucked in smoke again. 'Not that that changes anything, St. Claire. You're grounded from now on and I shall send in the papers for your court-martial. In the meantime you'll consider yourself under arrest and confine yourself to your quarters. That's all. Dismiss.'

The young pilot saluted, turned smartly, and left the office. Only when the door closed was Harvey able to give vent to his feelings. With a laugh of relief he bent down and cuffed the dog's head. As Sam came bounding out, he opened a drawer in his desk and pulled out a bottle of whisky.

A draught blew down the full length of Adams' Confessional as the far door opened. Turning, Moore and Adams saw Henderson was entering the hut. Wearing no overcoat, the Scot gave a shiver as he pushed the door closed. 'It's damned charpy today, isn't it? Where the hell has Spring gone?'

When neither man could think of a reply he made his way towards the desks where they were standing. 'I see you've got SPs posted outside. You think we're going to need them?'

'I thought you said Davies and Staines wanted to see us in private,' Adams said.

'They do. But Davies didn't sound particularly excited about it. I get the impression sometimes he's as much in the dark as we are.'

'But the SOE crowd are happy about the Ruhr and Mindenburg raids, aren't they?'

Henderson's grunt suggested he was not in one of his better moods. 'They should be. The photographs show a hell of a lot of damage.' His tone changed as his eyes fell on the contusion on Moore's forehead. 'That's a pig of a bruise, Ian. Are you sure you shouldn't have it X-rayed?'

With the squadron's role in the gas threat still uncertain, Moore had no intention of being grounded for medical reasons. 'No, the headache's gone,' he lied. 'I'm sure it's nothing serious.' He glanced at Adams before continuing. 'I understand Frank hasn't had a chance yet to tell you about St. Claire?'

Henderson scowled. 'What's he done now? Stolen a kite and gone off to bomb Berlin?'

143

Moore smiled. 'Nothing as drastic as that. Last week Sue told Frank what she believed was wrong with him. It was in confidence but after what's happened since she feels we all ought to know.' He turned to Adams again. 'I'd like Frank to tell it in his own words.'

When Adams finished, Henderson was looking horrified. 'They tortured the girl to death? For that? Jesus Christ, what are we up against?' When neither man spoke, the Scot's voice turned bitter. 'I suppose you two would argue we could do that kind of thing as well?'

When both men chose to ignore the remark, Henderson looked ashamed he had made it. 'I take it you both agree with Sue about this?'

Moore shrugged. 'I don't think there can be any doubt about it. He would feel guilty and it would prey on his mind all the months he had to wait before they got him back to England.

'All right, I can see that. But I don't see why it should make him disobey orders.'

'I'm wondering now if he does disobey orders, at least in the way we think. Perhaps he's so full of hatred that when a German fires at him he has to retaliate.'

'Isn't that a bit far-fetched?'

'I don't think so. Not if Sue's right and he had fallen in love with the girl.'

Henderson stared at Adams. 'You never said that.'

'Sue's not certain,' Adams explained. 'But surely it's more than likely. Particularly after the way he's behaving towards Sue now.'

Henderson, who like everyone else on the station had noticed the change in the couple's relationship, frowned again. 'Supposing you're both right. We still can't let him fly again.'

'No,' Moore conceded. 'But I'm wondering if we can't drop some of the worst charges.'

'We have to give some reason for grounding him.'

'Couldn't we have a word with the M.O.? Surely he could find medical grounds − psychological pressure or something of that nature.'

144

'What about Harvey? He's the one who laid the charges.'

'Frank's got a hard shell but a soft centre. I'm pretty certain he'll play ball once he knows the reason.'

The thud of an SP's boots outside as he presented arms checked Henderson's reply. A moment later another draught swept down the room as Davies and Staines appeared, the former carrying a brief case. As he stiffened to attention, Adams thought of a terrier and a Great Dane taking an outing together. Acknowledging their salute, Davies turned immediately to Moore. 'What's the medical report, Ian?'

'Quite good, sir. I'm fit for duty.'

Davies peered beneath the peak of Moore's service cap. 'It's a hell of a bruise. What about Hopkinson?'

'His right arm and shoulder took a bit of a knock. But he'll be all right in a day or two.'

'You were damn lucky,' Davies grunted. 'We all thought you'd bought it. I understand Millburn did a good job?'

'He kept three Focke Wulfs and one 109 away from us until the Americans arrived. I'm putting him in for another bar to his DFC.' Moore turned towards the big Texan. 'We're indebted to your boys too, sir. We'd never have made it without them.'

Staines gave a grimace of satisfaction. 'I hear you had a bit of a thrash with them afterwards. Did they get the Bourbon out?'

'They got everything out, sir. I got a worse hangover from the party than from the knock on my head.'

'There's no better way of getting to know guys. What do you think of Dent?'

'What can I say, sir? He saved our lives and then threw a party for us. We'd pin a V.C. on him if we could.'

As Staines grinned, Davies swung up his briefcase. 'We've brought some photographs to show you. Benson had a Spitfire out early this morning.'

The small party crowded round him as he laid six large photographs on Adams' desk. Taken from oblique angles, with the early morning sunlight casting long

145

shadows, four were of a country estate that had run to seed. Neglected lawns had turned into grassland and ornamental bushes had become thickets. Sheds and tarmac aprons carrying Army transports were additional disfigurements. But the most incongruous feature of all was the modern building that stood in the centre of the estate. Rectangular in shape, three stories high, with a slate roof and heavily-grilled windows, it looked more like a prison or a fortress than a country house. A long, tree-lined driveway linked it to a sentry box and a formidable steel gate. A high wall ran around the boundary of the estate. In one photograph a Nazi Swastika could be seen poised over the main entrance of the huge building.

The other two photographs, taken from above the steep-sided valley, put the estate and building into perspective and showed how they were virtually encircled by the small country town.

Davies anticipated the questions to come. 'Yes, that's the place. For centuries the home of landed gentry and probably the reason why the town sprang up in the first place. Then the family went broke and the Government moved in. They knocked down the old house and built this Institute for Animal Research. Now the Nazis want us to believe it's only a Gestapo Headquarters.' Davies pointed at two long shadows at the side of the building. 'See those? We believe they're the billets for the SS who're patrolling the town and the district.'

Henderson, who was eyeing the steep mountains with trepidation, looked up. 'Do you know yet if our raids stopped the convoys?'

Davies nodded. 'Until now there's been one every Tuesday and Friday. The one due yesterday didn't arrive.'

The Scot looked surprised. 'Then it worked?'

'Apparently it did. At least it's bought MacBride some time. And from all accounts he needs it. He still can't get De Gaulle to budge an inch even though some of our politicians, who seem to realise the danger at last, have also been working on him.'

Adams and Moore exchanged glances. From Davies'

146

tone and Staines' expression it was clear that although their personal feelings towards MacBride might be the same, their attitude towards the gas threat had changed dramatically. 'MacBride showed us some reports from his boffins this morning,' Staines explained. 'They're all certain now that he's right and the Krauts are working to package Sonam into their rockets. It's so goddam serious that if Intelligence and SOE had their way, they'd ask me to send out enough B17s to flatten the place.'

'With the town there, it's just as well they can't have their way,' Henderson muttered.

Davies shifted restlessly. 'We all feel that, Jock. Only remember the alternative could be the failure of the invasion and then a gas attack on London. That would cost a lot more than a thousand or so lives.'

'But you can't be certain the invasion would fail.'

'Of course we can't be certain,' Davies snapped. 'Nothing's certain in war — that's the bloody trouble. But imagine rockets full of nerve gas dropping among troops waiting for embarkation. It would hardly be a brandy-and-butterscotch send off, would it?'

Adams came to Henderson's aid. 'I suppose a precision raid on the Institute has been considered, sir?'

'Of course it's been considered. But if there are stocks of Sonam there, and there are sure to be, it could be out of the frying pan into the five. If I lived in that town and had to choose, I'd rather be killed with high explosives, wouldn't you??'

A brief silence followed before Henderson spoke again. 'So what's our next move, sir?'

Davies' scowl betrayed his frustration with the entire affair. 'I wish to God we knew. According to MacBride there's a whole team of boffins working day and night on the problem. Don't ask me what they're trying to solve — it's all gone hush hush again. But if they come up with an answer and if De Gaulle agrees to use it — so many ifs it makes your head swim — then there's a possibility you or the General's B17s will be used. If it's a B17 job, it should be straightforward. But if we're chosen, MacBride says it will be a quick scramble job. So he wants you to study these photographs and familiarise yourselves with the target so you'll be ready if the green light comes.'

Moore spoke for the first time. 'Is he asking us to destroy the building, sir?'

Davies turned irritable. 'I've just told you — I don't know what he's asking. So for the moment just get to know the building and general lay-out.'

Moore gave no ground. 'I was asking, sir, because MacBride told us French prisoners were kept there.'

Tell-tale red spots were appearing on Davies' cheek-bones. 'I know there are French prisoners, Moore, just as I know I couldn't be more vague with my orders. But that's because I am vague. And it looks as if I'm going to stay vague until those bloody boffins unbutton their mouths.'

Hiding a grin with difficulty, Staines thought it wise to intervene. 'I got the impression from MacBride that the boffins are working on two or three leads. So I guess until they find the right one, there isn't much they can say.'

'If MacBride's right about Werner's timetable, they haven't much time left to find it,' Henderson muttered.

Staines' shrug said it all. Turning to Davies, Adams motioned at his desk. 'Do you want all the crews to study these photographs, sir?'

'Oh, Christ no. That's too dangerous. Just your Flight Commanders and specialist officers for the moment. Don't forget to stress it's all top security. In the meantime I'm having a model made in case we need it later.' Clearly expecting opposition, Davies' tone was aggressive as he glanced at Henderson. 'There's one thing more. MacBride asked me if I thought we could attack this place at night.'

Henderson nearly leapt out of his tunic. 'A precision raid? At night?'

For a moment Davies looked almost apologetic. 'I think he was just exploring all the possibilities.'

'Let's hope so,' the Scot said fervently. 'If he was thinking of a low level attack, those mountains would be a death trap.'

Frustration brought a return of Davies' short-fused temper. 'Do you think I didn't tell him that? But we've got to be fair to him. It is a hell of a threat and he has to know what's feasible and what isn't.'

Although appeased, Henderson left Davies in no doubt of his opinion. 'Well, it isn't possible, sir. Even in moonlight it would be a gamble. In darkness it would be suicide. And by Saturday the moon's gone and it won't be back for eight days.'

18

Sue Spencer paused at the door of the billet. Dusk was falling and the bleak wooden huts were black against the sky. As the girl glanced round to make certain she was unobserved, she heard the notes of a piano. Low and melancholy, the sound seemed to match the mood of the evening and she stood listening for a moment. Then she tapped quietly on the door and entered.

The billet was full of shadows. Engrossed in his music, the pianist did not notice her enter. Then, as she closed the door, he started and turned. 'Don't stop playing,' she said. 'It's beautiful.'

'You shouldn't be here,' he muttered. 'It's against orders.'

She moved towards him. 'I had to see you. What were you playing? Is it something you've written?'

Ignoring her question, he glanced bitterly at the piano. 'It's a wonder they've left it with me. I expect they'll take it away tomorrow.'

The piano owed its presence to Adams. Knowing of St. Claire's growing reputation as a concert pianist when he had been posted to Sutton Craddock, Adams had suggested to Henderson that if he were allowed a small piano in his billet he would be able to keep up a degree of practice. With the Scot's musical taste limited to Harry Roy, Glenn Miller, and other such popular bands of the day, it had said much for his tolerance that he had agreed, although on condition St. Claire did not keep his fellow airmen awake at nights. It was a privilege few men begrudged because until his fall from grace St. Claire had been a popular officer who had never been above playing at Mess parties or dances.

The young pilot lit a cigarette. In the flare of the match his handsome face looked dark and sullen. 'I thought they'd put a guard on the door. What do you want?'

She braced herself. 'I think I might have good news for you. A couple of nights ago I told Frank Adams everything that happened to you in Belgium. And . . . . '

'You told Adams?' His angry interruption made her mouth turn dry. 'Why? You promised to tell nobody.'

'I know that. But I could see you were going to get yourself into serious trouble sooner or later and I wanted Frank to know before it happened.'

His laugh was harsh with sarcasm. 'You weren't wrong, were you? I'm going to be court-martialled for being too aggressive towards the enemy!' Then his tone changed. 'What's the good news? Has Adams put in a word for me?'

'Yes. He's told Henderson and Moore everything. And he thinks they're going to ask Harvey to drop his charges.'

He took a step forward. 'Are you saying they'll let me fly again?'

She flinched. 'They can't do that, Tony. But they can save you from a court-martial.'

His eagerness died as if a switch had been thrown. 'What's the use of that? Tell them I'd rather have it the other way round. Punish me but let me go on flying. That's all I want.'

'Tony, you must know that's impossible. They can never let you fly again after what you've done.'

The darkness prevented her seeing the effect of her words and his cry of distress was as unexpected as it was moving. 'I must fly again, Sue. I must. Can't you all see that?'

She knew she had to make him face the truth. 'Tony, have you never asked yourself why you have this obsession to go on fighting? And why you have developed such a hatred of the Germans?'

He turned away sharply. 'If you'd had six months over there, you wouldn't need to ask that question.'

'I know what an ordeal it must have been. But there's another reason, isn't there? You've changed because of what they did to Francoise.'

His voice turned hostile. 'You've got Francoise on the brain.'

'No, Tony. It's you who can't forget her because the two of you were in love.' As he cursed and went over to the window, she followed him. 'I'm not blaming you for it. It can happen when a man and a woman share danger together. Your problem is you won't admit it.'

'You sound as if you want me to,' he muttered.

'If it's true, I do. We can't get anywhere unless we're honest with one another.'

He fell silent a moment, then shifted restlessly. 'I don't know how we felt. We never talked about it.'

'Perhaps you didn't but you can't help knowing she was in love with you.'

His pain made her wince. 'Because she died for me? Is that what you mean? It should never have happened. If those damn friends of hers had told me sooner I could have given myself up and saved both her and her family.'

'That wouldn't have saved her. It would only have confirmed the Gestapo's suspicions. And in turn they'd have tortured you to find out who her colleagues were.'

'At least I could have saved her from torture.' As memory made the young pilot suck in his breath, his hatred exploded. 'Damn those murdering bastards! I hope they burn in hell!'

As she put a hand on his arm, he regained his self-control and turned to gaze out of the darkening window. 'She loved her country,' he muttered. 'She loved it passionately. I'm sure that's why she helped me and others to escape. So we could go on fighting to liberate it.'

She shook her head. 'I think you're wrong. As a member of an escape line she would know that very few airmen are allowed to fly over Germany again. I believe she took those risks because she saw you and other airmen as friends in distress. It was her war effort to help you escape but it wasn't done for selfish reasons. She wasn't using you to gain revenge on the Germans.'

'What do you know about her?' he muttered.

'I know I owe her your life,' she said quietly. 'And I know that if I had been her I wouldn't have wanted the man I loved to escape full of hatred and thoughts of revenge.'

The glance she received was full of contempt. 'How do you know how she felt? It's a different world over there.'

'Yes, I know that. But I won't believe that Francoise was any less of a woman than myself, and I wouldn't want my sacrifice to end up like this.'

His expression changed as he stared at her. When he spoke again, his voice lacked conviction. 'You don't know what you're talking about. So drop it, please.'

She took a deep breath. 'Tell me something, Tony. Do you still love me?'

He turned away. 'Of course I do.'

'Are you sure?'

He started to answer, then suddenly clapped his hands against his face. 'For God's sake, stop it! Stop asking all these questions!'

Alarmed, she caught his arm. 'I'm sorry, darling. But I'm so worried about you. And I don't know if I mean anything to you any more.'

She could feel his arm trembling beneath her hand. 'I know that and I'm sorry,' he muttered. 'But all I can think of at the moment is that I want to go on flying. Perhaps it'll be different later; I don't know. But I can't stop thinking day and night what she did for me and what I owe her.'

'But Tony, she's dead. You must face it. You can't spend the rest of your life trying to make it up to her.'

She felt him stiffen, then he tore his arm away. The look she received turned her as cold as ice. 'Leave me alone. Please.'

At the door she turned back. He was gazing through the window at the approaching night as if he had already forgotten her existence. The cry of a jay, settling down in the hedge alongside the road, was a harsh and desolate sound. Closing the door, she turned and ran towards her billet.

* * *

153

There was not a pilot or navigator in the Messerschmitt 410s who was not on edge that night as he orbited his airfield at Gouda. The previous night an RAF intruder, hovering unseen above the flarepath lights, had pounced like a hawk on Jogen Pohl as he came in to land and left him and his crew in a funeral pyre on the left of the north-south runway. Tonight pilots refrained from switching on their navigation lights until the last moment, a ploy that added the extra peril of collision. Nervous crews could be heard shouting warnings to one another as Messerschmitt after Messerschmitt came sliding cautiously down to land.

Neumann's was the last aircraft in. His port engine had begun over-heating just after his Staffel's attack on Lincoln and knowing the Allied night fighters would be in hot pursuit, he had ordered his unit to make for home without him.

In fact his engine had provided more power than he had expected and the last aircraft had been down no more than five minutes when Control picked up his radio signal. As he flashed his identification lights, the flarepath blazed on again, a thin river of light in a plain of darkness. Banking towards it, he settled the Messerschmitt down. With the threat of attack ever present, the lights were extinguished almost before his tyres and brakes finished squealing. With the darkness a solid force around him, he had to rely on the headlights of a truck to guide him to his dispersal point.

Blipping his engines for the last time, Neumann applied his brakes then followed his weary crew out on the hard standing. As he handed his face mask to a mechanic and took deep breaths of the night air, a corporal came up and saluted. 'The Generalmajor is waiting for you in his car, Herr Major.'

Turning, Neumann saw a car with extinguished headlights waiting at the far side of the dispersal point. As he approached it, the rear door opened and Peltz leaned out. 'Join me in the back, Neumann.'

The young major obeyed. Peltz slid the glass partition closed before turning to him. 'How did it go tonight?'

Neumann's voice betrayed his weariness. 'We reached Bath without too much trouble. But they must be moving guns in all the time because the flak was very heavy. And their fighters attacked us on the way back. I saw four go down. And Pelman crashed just after crossing the coast.' He paused a moment to accept the cigarette Peltz offered him. 'Do you know our total losses tonight, Herr Generalmajor?'

The flare of Peltz' lighter, dazzling to the pilot after hours of darkness, hid the older man's expression. 'Not all the reports are in. But so far the number is twelve.'

Neumann drew in smoke. 'That means we've lost well over 10% again. How long can we keep this up, sir?'

Peltz ignored the direct question. 'As far as you're concerned you are being taken off general operations again from tonight. Until this airfield raid is over I can't afford you to lose any more trained men.' A trace of amusement entered the Generalmajor's voice. 'Our political masters have been showing impatience ever since the *Tommi* Mosquitoes ruined the Fuhrer's birthday celebrations in Copenhagen. And their latest raid on our Dutch filing system has been the last straw. They are demanding we keep our promise. How many of your original crews are left?'

Neumann's cigarette glowed in the darkness. 'Less than two-thirds after tonight.'

'Then you had better have a final rehearsal on that dummy airfield. With everyone in the Gestapo from Welter downwards with their eyes on us, we can't afford to make any mistakes.'

'We'll do a good job, sir. When do we go?'

Peltz motioned at the dying sickle of moon that had momentarily slid out from behind a bank of clouds. 'I'm holding out until we have a full night of darkness. So have your men briefed and ready to attack on Saturday.'

19

The evening wind came sliding through the pantiled roof
of the attic and made the paraffin lamp hanging from the
rafters flicker. Below it a portable radio stood on a rough
table. A middle-aged man with a flat cap of iron-grey
hair and a weatherbeaten face sat before it. With a cigarette in one nicotine-stained hand, he was holding up a
pair of earphones with the other. Jean Poix made a practice of listening to the BBC's foreign news even though he
expected no messages for himself that evening.

Voices on the landing outside and a tap on the rickety
door made him turn. A moment later the door creaked
open and a girl wearing a coat and a head scarf appeared.
Poix gave a start. 'Lorenz! How did you get here?'

The girl sank wearily down on a pile of grain sacks. 'I
got a lift on a German troop carrier.'

The Frenchman stared at her. 'You got a lift from
Germans?'

'Why not? I'm a German myself.'

'You take too many risks, Lorenz. You should have sent
one of the men. One day you are going to be caught.'

The girl turned impatient. 'There wasn't time. In any
case I've got identification papers. When do you next
transmit to London?'

The man glanced at an old alarm clock on the table.
'In forty minutes. Have you got some more news?'

'Yes. Listen to me carefully.'

When the girl finished speaking, Poix' smoke-
roughened voice was hoarser than usual. 'Do you believe
him?'

'Why should he lie to me? He knows I'm a German.'

'If he's right, what do you think London will do? Bomb right away?'

'No. They'll have to get permission from De Gaulle first.'

The Frenchman gave a humourless grin. 'I wouldn't like his job. Ferot and his comrades don't exactly love him as things stand now and they believe it's the Communists the Boche prefer to experiment on. If De Gaulle and London don't play it right, there could be trouble when the invasion begins.' Before the girl could reply, he leaned across the table and picked up an envelope. 'Bonel asked me to give this to you. It came in with an agent he collected yesterday.'

Looking puzzled, she tore open the envelope. As she scanned its contents she gave a sharp exclamation. Poix leaned forward. 'What is it? Bad news?'

Shaking her head and waving him to be quiet, she continued reading. As the Frenchman watched her, a grin began spreading across his weatherbeaten face. 'Good news then?'

Although there were tears in the girl's eyes when she finished the letter, all the weariness had left her face. 'Oh, yes. Very good news.'

'London must be getting a heart at last. I've never known them send private mail before.' Then Poix' tone changed. 'Don't hang on to it, for Christ's sake.'

Giving the letter a last glance, the girl folded it and slipped it into her coat pocket. 'Don't worry. I'll destroy it before I go back.'

Nodding, Poix fumbled in his pocket for a pouch and rice paper. Rolling a cigarette expertly, he offered it to her. When she refused, he slid it into his mouth and struck a match on the side of his chair. In front of him was a tin lid full of stubs and dead matches. The girl smiled again. 'Is this why you do this job? To keep yourself in tobacco?'

Poix's grin showed his teeth to be as stained as his fingers. 'If I do, it's a better reason than most. Men can change their politics and heroes can turn into cowards but addicts like me can never do without their smokes.'

Outside a dog had started barking. Motioning to the girl to keep quiet, Poix picked up the lamp and set it on the landing outside. Then, closing the door, he threw open the blacked-out window. As a cold breeze stirred in the attic again, the girl caught the earthly, comforting smells of a farmyard. The night was dark but the Frenchman was not relying on his eyes. As he listened he heard the eerie, distant screech of a vixen. The dog barked again, then went silent as a woman called to it from a doorway below. Satisfied, Poix closed the window and brought back the lamp. 'Tell me what you want me to say. Only make it as short as you can because Bonel says he saw German D/F detector vans roaming around yesterday.'

Davies gave a grunt of shock. 'So soon?'

Staines was less restrained. 'And that's what I lost all those ships for? To save three days?'

The elderly Brigadier sighed. 'I know it seems little. But in the race we're in, they might be vital.'

With the heavy loss of his crews still troubling him, Staines turned away. 'They could matter if they held Werner up,' he muttered. 'But supposing he had a reserve of chemicals to keep him going until more supplies got through?'

The way the Brigadier passed over the question was an admission the possibility existed. 'I'm afraid this isn't the only news Anna Reinhardt has sent us. She has seen the German laboratory assistant again and it seems he was jubilant. He told her Werner believes he has made a breakthrough and needs only to carry out a few more experiments to be certain. He hopes to have them completed by the weekend.'

Both airmen gave a start. Staines sounded bitter. 'Then he had reserves in hand. Does De Gaulle know about this?'

'MacBride and his Committee have asked to see him this morning. I understand the Secretary for War will also be present.' Simms made a gesture of apology. 'That is why I called you so early this morning. I felt you would want to hear the news right away.'

The three men were in the library of High Elms. Dawn

had broken only fifteen minutes ago and birds were in full chorus in the elms outside. Both Staines and Davies showed evidence of their hasty summons: they were unshaven and the Texan's tunic was unbuttoned. With the Werner affair now of crucial importance, both men had visited High Elms the previous day to inspect the model of the Institute that a local craftsman had hurriedly made for them from the photographs. As the Brigadier had intimated there could be news from MacBride and the boffins at any time, they had decided to stay the night at the SOE centre. Instead news had come from Anna via London less than thirty minutes ago.

'So what happens now?' Staines asked.

The Brigadier poured both men a second cup of coffee. 'I wish I knew. De Gaulle holds the key, of course, but his choice isn't simply the life of a town on the one hand and military expediency on the other. There are complicated political factors involved which the Germans will be only too quick to exploit if he makes the wrong decision.'

Staines had been watching him closely. 'You don't think he'll give permission, do you?'

The soldier sighed. 'Frankly, sir, I'm not optimistic. But we can only wait and see.'

There was a sound like sandpaper being rubbed as Staines scratched his chin. 'Yeah, it's a tough one all right. I can't say I'd like to be in his shoes.'

'What do we do if he says no?' Davies asked.

'Then we shall have to hope our boffins come to our rescue in time.'

'But if Anna's right, they've only got until the weekend. And what can they come up with in that time that'll satisfy De Gaulle?'

The Brigadier turned away. 'So far MacBride has kept this to himself. I can hazard a few guesses but as I'm not a chemist I doubt if they have any value.'

'Then you've no idea why he sounded us out about a night raid?'

'Not one I'd care to discuss at this stage.'

Davies could not help asking the last, inevitable

question. 'Supposing the boffins don't find an answer? What then?'

Simms moved towards the French windows through which the shapes of budding elms could be seen. 'We would then have to hope that our bombing of the V.I. sites is effective enough to make a full scale gas attack impossible.'

'But the V.Is aren't the only rockets Jerry's got,' Davies pointed out. 'What about the larger ones we've detected? The ones that don't need fixed sites?'

Silhouetted against the French windows, the Brigadier suddenly looked a frail and weary figure. 'I think we shall have to meet those problems if and when they come, Davies.'

Staines gave Davies a warning glance. The brief silence that fell gave the elderly soldier time to compose himself and his voice was firmer when he turned. 'With luck we should have news of De Gaulle's decision by lunch time. Is it possible for you gentlemen to stay until then? If he gives permission, we shall need to plan our attack without delay.'

Although with his usual courtesy the soldier had asked his question of both men, Davies knew that he, personally, had no choice. Staines gave a resigned grimace. 'Yeah. O.K. I'd better hang around just in case. That all right with you, Davies?'

Davies nodded. Looking relieved the Brigadier indicated a door at the far end of the library. 'Thank you, gentlemen. We shall do our best not to make the waiting seem too long. Might I suggest we retire now and meet again over breakfast?'

As Simms drew back to allow Staines to pass through the door, he touched Davies' arm. Waiting until the big Texan had disappeared, Davies turned to him. 'What is it, sir?'

The Brigadier smiled. 'There was a postscript at the end of Anna's message. It read: "Additional communication noted and reciprocated. Lorenz". '

Davies looked puzzled. 'What does it mean?'

160

'It means she has received Harvey's letter.'

Davies' face cleared. 'Christ yes, I'd forgotten. He'll be like a dog with two tails when we tell him.'

Staines glanced at his watch. 'He's making a meal of it, isn't he?'

Davies checked the time himself and saw it was 14.25. 'At least he can't have said no right away.'

'Not unless everyone's so shattered they've forgotten to tell us,' the American grunted.

The Brigadier shook his head at the suggestion. 'No, gentlemen, you can rely on MacBride to be in touch the moment a decision is reached.'

The three men, wearing greatcoats, were walking along a path flanked by daffodils. Although the day had turned out fine and sunny, a chilly wind was rustling the branches of the elms and agitating the daffodils. As the Brigadier led them on to a wide lawn, his musing voice made them glance at him. 'They will all be impatient with him because he is De Gaulle and has a reputation for being difficult. But how many of them would like to make the decision themselves?'

Thinking it was a gentle reprimand, Staines frowned but his face cleared as the soldier's quiet voice ran on: 'It seems to me that almost daily decisions are becoming less of a choice between right and wrong and more of a choice between evils. We blame those who make decisions but shouldn't we also blame ourselves for allowing the world to become a place where right and wrong are no longer valid concepts?' Seeing Staines glance uncomfortably at Davies, the Brigadier gave a self-deprecating smile. 'Forgive me, gentlemen. In times of waiting I have a habit of turning philosophical. I assure you I quickly become a pragmatist again when the waiting is over.'

As if to prove his words there was a shout from the terrace. Seeing a young officer running down the steps to the lawn, the Brigadier started forward. 'I believe we have our answer, gentlemen. Please excuse me.'

The two airmen watched the men exchange a few quick words, then move hurriedly towards the house.

161

With a grimace, Staines turned to Davies. 'Here it is! For better or worse. Shall we wait for him in the library?'

It was ten minutes before Simms emerged from the Communications Room. Seeing the airmen sitting at the table he said a word to the young officer at his side, who withdrew and closed the door.

Both men rose from their seats as he approached them. 'Well?' Staines demanded. 'Was it MacBride?'

The Brigadier nodded. 'Yes. De Gaulle has come to a decision. We must go ahead and attack as soon as possible.'

It was the last thing the airmen expected. Staines looked astonished. 'We've got the green light? What changed his mind?'

'It appears MacBride had word from the boffins half-way through the conference. Until then the general had categorically refused to consider an attack.'

'Then the boffins must have made a breakthrough. Do you know what it is?'

'No, there was no time to go into details. MacBride was leaving London immediately.' The Brigadier turned to Davies. 'He would like your squadron put on immediate alert. And he wants Henderson, Adams and Moore to attend his preliminary briefing here.'

Before Davies could respond, Staines broke in. 'What about my boys?'

'I can't say if MacBride would like your help or not, General. But it seems that on one point De Gaulle was adamant. The raid on the Institute must be a precision one by Mosquitoes.'

Like Davies, Staines seemed unable to decide whether the decision pleased or dismayed him. 'Always the bridesmaid and never the bride,' he muttered. 'What time are you expecting Ghengis Khan?'

The Brigadier hid a smile. 'As he is leaving London immediately, I would say by the early evening.'

Staines turned to Davies. 'Then you'd better get in touch with your boys right away. Now McBride's got the green light he probably won't give 'em the chance to pee before he sends them out.'

Davies was already making for the Communications Room. 'Will you stay on, sir?'

Staines' grimace was both wry and comical. 'You think I could sleep tonight if I didn't hear what those boffins have cooked up? Of course I'm goddam well staying.'

20

As was his way, MacBride wasted no time on prelimi-
naries. Saluting Staines and acknowledging the salutes of
the other airmen, he threw his greatcoat over a chair and
walked to the head of the table. 'Sorry if I've kept you
waiting, gentlemen, but I got here as quickly as possible.'
His eyes met Staines'. 'I'm glad you could stay, General,
although I hope what I have to say won't make you feel
your time is wasted.'

Adams, who along with Henderson and Moore, had
arrived at High Elms an hour ago, wondered how much
sarcasm was wrapped up in the remark. Staines' expression suggested he too had his suspicions. 'The message I
got was that the boffins had made a breakthrough. Don't
tell me you've got it wrong and we're back to square one
again?'

There was both elation and malice in MacBride's
smile. 'No, General. If you'll be patient a few minutes
longer you'll see we're far from square one.' His gaze
moved to Henderson. 'Have you put your squadron on
alert, Group Captain?'

The Scot nodded. 'Yes, sir. All outside communications are cut.'

'Good. Now let me tell you what has happened to
change De Gaulle's mind.'

In the brief silence that followed the distant ringing of
a telephone could be heard. Watching MacBride, knowing how much he was savouring his role, Adams was
nevertheless forced to admit that with his height, his big
jaw, beetling eyebrows and forceful voice, the man could
hold an audience. MacBride glanced again at Staines

before he began.

'As De Gaulle has given us permission to bomb other French establishments, we've known all along it has been the gas threat that has held his hand here. Accordingly our boffins have been working day and night on a way of neutralising it. This morning we heard they believe they have found an answer.'

Excited murmurs broke out. Staines leaned forward. 'What kind of answer?'

'I haven't the full details yet although, as we carry stocks of the gas ourselves, they are certain to be classified. But although I gather the toxic effects of the gas are not affected by heat, the boffins have isolated a reagent chemical which, when mixed with it, makes a highly-inflammable mixture. If that mixture is then exploded, the gas is either detroyed or rendered harmless.'

Forgetting his dislike of the man in his excitement, Staines drove a huge fist into the palm of his hand. 'Bingo! How do we drop the stuff?'

'That problem hasn't been solved yet. Our first move was to get De Gaulle's permission. The boffins are now working on a method of delivery.'

Davies, whose earlier apprehensions of the mission had been swept away by this news, was now showing disappointment. 'Then we can't go yet?'

'No. But I wouldn't think the delivery problem will hold up the boffins for long. With luck we might even hear from them tonight.'

With the mission cleared and the threat to French civilians minimised, Davies was his old, thrusting self again. 'What are they looking for? The right bomb casings?'

He received an impatient shrug. 'I don't know. I'm not an armourer.'

Davies glanced at Staines. 'Perhaps we could use our SCIs.'

The Texan scratched his chin. 'Yeah, that's a thought. Only I guess it depends on the viscosity of the chemicals.'

The technical problems of the mission were momentarily set aside as Moore raised a hand. 'Did De Gaulle make any mention of the French Resistance workers imprisoned in the Institute, sir?'

He received a hard stare. 'He's concerned for their welfare, of course, as we all are. But there's a limit to the precautions we can take if this threat is to be removed.'

'There could be dozens of them, could there not?'

'I doubt it. The Germans probably bring them along as they need them. But in any case it's likely most of them are Communists.'

It was a remark that made his audience exchange glances. Staines raised a bushy eyebrow. 'And that makes a difference?'

'It could make a great deal of difference after the war, General. The Communists and the Resistance are fighting a war within a war to decide who shall take over France after the liberation. As an American I'm sure you'll agree that we're hardly justified in risking a crippling gas attack on our invasion troops for the sake of men who are working for the overthrow of our political system.'

Moore's cultured voice saved Staines the need of a reply. 'As the commander of the raid, sir, I would want consideration for the welfare of these men to be included in our tactical plans.'

To Adams' relief, Henderson came out in support of his squadron commander. 'I agree with that, sir. We must do all we can to save them.'

MacBride's hostile stare moved from one to the other. 'Give what consideration you like but remember this, both of you. At this point in time your squadron is under my orders and this means your prime objective is the total destruction of this Institute and the scientists working inside it. You will do nothing that will in any way prejudice this objective. Is that clearly understood?'

Davies intervened with some haste. 'There's no question of the operation being prejudiced. You have my word on that. What we need to know is how soon we have to be ready.'

MacBride turned to him. 'You have to be ready as quickly as possible so that when the chemicals reach you,

166

in whatever form, you will be able to take off at a moment's notice. This is essential because we ourselves don't know when the attack can be made.'

Like the others, Davies was looking puzzled. 'You mean we can't attack at the time that suits us best?'

The soldier's brusque reply made Davies flush with resentment. 'If you thought about it for a moment, you wouldn't ask that question. To release the gas and the diffusing elements your men have first to blow open the laboratories. This means that if a wind is blowing, the gas will drift over the town before you can explode it. If this happens De Gaulle will hold you and your men responsible. You are to attack only when the wind over the target is 5 knots or less.'

'But that could be at night,' Henderson protested.

MacBride gave a grim nod. 'It could well be at night. That's when the wind tends to drop in that part of France.'

The Scot's protest was uncompromising. 'That's out of the question. We lose the moon tomorrow night. How can we make a precision raid in total darkness?'

The big soldier turned towards him with a scowl. 'Now you listen to me, Henderson. When your unit was handed over to me I was told you were specialists who prided yourselves on doing jobs other squadrons thought impossible. In fact it was your reputation that helped me change De Gaulle's mind. So now, instead of bellyaching how impossible it is, I suggest you start thinking how it can be done. Because if you fail, we'll all be for the big drop together.'

On their arrival back at Sutton Craddock that night Moore and his colleagues found the squadron was once again preparing for instant action. In the armoury men were packing the huge 20mm gun magazines with shells. In the photographic section gun cameras were being checked and loaded with film. In the parachute section Waafs were checking packs and in some cases re-folding the great silken canopies. In the Intelligence Office Sue Spencer was preparing escape equipment for the crews.

In a dozen brightly-lit rooms specialist officers were being kept at full stretch answering queries and issuing requisitions. Out on the field or inside the draughty hangars, Maintenance NCOs were shouting orders or giving quiet advice according to their temperaments. 15cwt and 25cwt trucks were rushing all over the field, dropping off ammunition drums and spares, then speeding back for more.

The objects of all this intense activity were the sleek, dew-covered Mosquitoes, anchored out on the field at their dispersal points. With their spring-loaded panels and engine cowlings removed, mechanics were swarming all over them, servicing their Merlins, checking their airframes, loading their guns. Petrol bowsers trundled hither and thither replenishing their fuel tanks. The night was full of shouts, lights and the cough and roar of engines. As a precaution that no airman could sneak out and explain to his girl friend why he had broken his date, SPs were patrolling the airfield perimeter.

The only men left with the time to grumble were the aircrews. With the Adjutant as ignorant as everybody else why the alert had been called, he had taken the precaution of closing the Mess bar. As a result many of the disgruntled crews were either playing cards, darts, or discussing the reasons for the sudden flap. Others, more sensitive to its implications, had returned to their billets to write letters. A few of the pilots, mostly veterans, were out on the airfield supervising the preparation of their aircraft.

Discovering Harvey was one of these, Moore drove out to D-Danny's dispersal point in the Station jeep. He found two mechanics working on the Mosquito's port engine in the light of a pressure lamp and Harvey talking to his Maintenance NCO on the hard standing below. Hearing the jeep pull up, Harvey turned. 'Hello, Ian. What's all the flap about?'

Jumping out, Moore nodded at the shadowy airfield perimeter. 'Feel like a walk?'

With a word to his NCO, Harvey fell into step beside him. Beneath their feet the grass was wet from the heavy dew. As the glare of the lights dropped behind them and a gunpost appeared out of the darkness, Moore turned to the Yorkshireman. 'I've news for you, Frank. Anna's received your letter.'

There was a gruffness in the Yorkshireman's voice that had not been there before. 'Who told you?'

'Simms. This afternoon.'

'Did she send a message back?'

'She acknowledged receipt of it in a radio transmission, so obviously couldn't say any more. But the Brigadier expects her to reply the next time an agent's due to fly into London from her sector.'

Harvey lit a cigarette, then, remembering, offered the pack to Moore. 'Is she all right?'

'She must be. She's doing valuable work for the SOE.'

Harvey sucked in smoke, then jerked a thumb at the activity on the airfield. 'She's connected with this flap, isn't she? What's going on, Ian?'

The sandbagged gunpost was rising in front of them by this time and Moore could hear voices issuing from it. Turning down the perimeter road, he waited until the post fell back among the shadows. 'Yes, she's involved.'

'How? Can you tell me?'

'Yes. You and Teddy. No one else until the briefing. Even then I don't think Davies will tell the boys everything.'

When Moore finished Harvey's voice was harsh with shock and recrimination. 'They're letting Anna get mixed up in a filthy thing like this? Christ, don't they realise what'll happen if the Gestapo catch her?'

'I don't think they gave her this job, Frank. As far as I can make out, she found out about it herself.'

The bitter Yorkshireman was in no mood to apportion the blame. 'They let her take the shit because she's a German. In their eyes she's expendable.'

'Come off it, Frank. They think the world of her at SOE. In any case she's a highly valuable agent. So why should they treat her as expendable?'

Harvey gave him a look of dislike. 'You've a bloody short memory, Moore. They had her right in the middle of the Rhine Maiden target area, didn't they?'

'Yes, but this is different. There must be plenty of French agents in the area who can tip us off about the wind.'

In his fears, Harvey could not be comforted. 'If there's a risk, she always takes it herself. It's because she's a German — she feels responsible for what they're doing. So you can bet she'll be there on the night.'

Although the same thought had occurred to Moore, for the Yorkshireman's peace of mind he denied it. 'I doubt it this time. In fact I heard the Brigadier say that when this operation is over he might bring her back here for a rest.'

The tall, raw-boned figure gave a start. 'Do you mean that or are you bullshitting me?'

'No; it's true. They feel she's done enough for the time being. They also want to check she's fully recovered from an attack of jaundice she had.'

Harvey sucked in smoke again, then nodded at the moving lights on the airfield. 'Then let's get the bloody job done. Her luck can't last for ever.'

For a full minute neither man spoke as they continued walking along the perimeter road. The dark mass of Bishops Wood could be seen opposite them when Harvey turned his head. 'You know this operation's crazy, don't you? How the hell can we do a precision raid in the middle of the night?'

With Harvey's fears for Anna momentarily eased, Moore knew the Yorkshireman was now thinking about his men. 'It might not be at night. But if it is, it's not impossible. Davies has come up with a few ideas that might just tip the scales.'

With his memories of the Rhine Maiden affair awakened, Harvey was in no mood to be tolerant to the small Air Commodore. 'That glory-hunting bastard. Trust him not to miss the chance of getting himself another ring on his sleeve.'

Moore shook his head. 'No, you can't blame him this time. He was as shocked as the rest of us when MacBride said it might be a night operation.'

'But, Christ, think of the risk. Supposing we make a

170

balls of it and that gas spreads across the town.'

Haunted by the same fear, Moore turned away. 'De Gaulle and the War Cabinet know the danger and they've accepted it.'

Harvey's reply dripped with scorn. 'You think those bastards will accept the blame? If things go wrong they'll pile it on us with steam shovels.'

The sudden sharpness of Moore's voice made Harvey stare at him. 'You think I don't know that? But what alternative do we have? Refuse a direct order and be court-martialled?'

The thunder of a Merlin across the airfield made Harvey pause. When the sound died away his tone had changed. 'Supposing the wind doesn't drop? What then?'

Regaining his control, Moore turned to walk back. 'I can't even guess. Perhaps, town or no town, they'll still send us out. If they don't, Werner will have gone and so will our last chance of stopping him.'

21

In the Operations Room the light from the huge map of Europe made the rows of intent faces look pale and apprehensive. As Davies nodded at Adams and the Intelligence Officer switched off the map, the momentary darkness was filled by the buzz of puzzled voices. The noise died away as the main lights came on and Davies walked from the map towards the edge of the platform.

'All right, men, you've heard what your target is and shown where to find it. Now we come to the method of destroying it. We shall be using HE, of course, but with it we shall be dropping special chemicals. These will be sprayed over the target by SCIs which all your aircraft will carry or dropped in special containers code-named TX bombs.' Here Davies glanced at Moore who was sitting at the table along with Henderson, Adams, and other specialist officers. 'Your Squadron Commander will be giving you operational details in a moment. Before he does I want to make two things very clear. Because we cannot know until the last moment when the weather conditions are right, you will stay in instant readiness after this briefing. I know it's a bind but we've no option. Secondly — and this is vitally important — I want that building totally destroyed and gutted into the bargain. All right?'

As men nodded, some dubiously, Davies motioned Moore to take his place. Although the Squadron Commander's heavily-bruised forehead brought a reminder of past perils shared, there was a noticeable relaxation of tension among the crews as he stepped forward. The man was their battle leader, and the indefinable camaraderie

172

that fighting men share gave them an odd confidence in the mission that had been lacking before. Moore's pleasant, humorous voice added to the effect.

'Well, chaps, you know your job by this time: now it's just the simple matter of how we carry it out.' Moore smiled at the groans and cat-calls that followed. 'I don't know what you're worried about. As I see it, it's better than a rest cure. No girl friends and no booze — you'll be fit for the Olympics when it's over.'

Dismayed murmurs followed, then a cry of agony. 'You mean you're keeping the bar closed, skipper?'

Moore glanced round at the grinning Henderson. 'We might let you have a small ration to keep the D/Ts at bay. But that's something we'll decide later. At the moment I want to talk about our battle procedure. We are going to use all our aircraft plus our P/R Mossie and one of our reserve crews — eighteen aircraft in all. Squadron Leader Harvey and myself will have a special role that will be explained later. The rest of you will be divided into sections of four: red, blue, green and orange. The leaders and crews of these sections will be decided later.'

A few nervous coughs sounded as Moore continued. 'If the green light comes during the daytime we shall go out at low level with a Mustang escort, much as we did during the Copenhagen operation. Like ourselves, the Americans will be standing by. On the other hand, if the alert comes at night, we shall go out alone at high level. Over the target we shall stack in orbit before we attack. The order from low to high level will be Red Section, Blue Section, Green Section and, right at the top, Orange Section.'

While Moore had been talking, Adams and Marsden, the Signals Officer, had brought up a large blackboard. Sketched on it with considerable skill was a plan of the French Institute and the mountains around it. Taking a pointer from Adams, Moore turned to the drawing.

'Here's your target, plumb in the middle of a French town. Later on you can come up here and examine a model we've had made. As our method of attack is going to be the same whether we go out in daylight or at night,

I'm going to brief you on a night attack because obviously that'll be the more difficult.'

An ironic laugh sounded. 'You ain't kidding, skipper.'

The quip could have come only from one man. Moore took advantage of it.

'I know most of you think we've gone crazy planning a precision raid at night. And if our firework boffins hadn't recently come up with some new flares, it would have been impossible. One, a parachute flare, burns far longer and much brighter than the ones we've been using, so it can be dropped from a greater height. A second has been developed for precisely this kind of operation. It ignites on impact with the ground and gives high illumination for a radius of nearly two hundred yards. We believe half a dozen of these plus the new parachute flares will give us all the light we need.' As hands immediately shot into the air, Moore shook his head. 'If you're going to tell me the Germans will put the flares out, wait to hear why they won't. If you've any other queries, wait until question time.'

As the hands were lowered, Moore turned again to the blackboard. 'Squadron Leader Harvey and I will lead the attack. Along with our SCIs we shall be carrying rockets. While Red Section drops parachute flares, we shall plant ground flares around the perimeter. As soon as they're burning, Red Section will come down and attack with their cannon the Institute's gun posts.' Moore's pointer moved to four places within the boundary wall of the estate. 'From information pieced together from French refuse collectors and food suppliers, Intelligence believes the sites are here. Some might have been overlooked, however, so be careful. If we're quick off the mark, we might catch the crews with their trousers down. But in any case they must be knocked out, not only for our sakes but for another reason.'

Moore's pointer moved to the building itself. 'As you've already heard, we believe there could be quite a number of French prisoners inside. If Amiens is anything to go by, the Gestapo will keep them on the top floor as a deterrent against air attack. So, after we've dropped our flares, Squadron Leader Harvey and I will attempt to blow holes in the east and west wings while Red Section is keeping the gun crews occupied. This should give the prisoners a fighting chance to escape before the real attack begins.'

A voice rose above the sudden buzz of conversation. 'But the building's three stories high, skipper.'

'I know that, Van Breedenkamp. But if other raids of this nature are an indication, some men will escape. I'm afraid it's the most we can do for them although to give them a reasonable chance we shall wait one full minute before Blue Section engages. Its four aircraft will come in at low level in line astern and drop 500lb time-delays. These delays will be staggered so that all the bombs should explode together *if* you follow one another nose to tail. If you don't, the rear kites will go up with the Institute, so make sure your timing is precise.

'With any luck this first attack will demolish the top stories. So when Red Section follow up with SAPs, they should reach the laboratories and gas tanks. As this will release the gas, the next stages are absolutely critical. The moment Red Section's bombs have exploded, Green Section will fly over the Institute in line abreast at exactly two thousand feet and spray it with their SCIs. It doesn't matter if the chemicals spread out a bit over the town — apparently they're harmless on their own. But it is vital you fly at two thousand feet. The boffins have carried out tests and established that in zero or near zero wind conditions, four 250lb SCIs at that height will blanket the Institute and the grounds around it for a radius of one hundred yards.'

Matthews put up a hand. 'What about the flares, skipper?'

'By this time Orange Section will be at the bottom of the stack and it'll keep the flares going. As soon as I'm satisfied the area is thoroughly sprayed we shall withdraw in the hope the fires already started in the Institute will explode the treated gas. It seems there is some doubt about this — the gas might need a higher temperature than ordinary fires can give. If it does, I shall send in

175

Orange Section to drop the KOFQR bombs — better known as coughcure bombs — that we shall all be carrying. For anyone who hasn't used them before, they're highly-efficient incendiaries. These will be dropped from 2,500 feet. No lower because if everyone has done his job properly and the boffins are right, there should be a big whoosh and up should go the Institute, the Gestapo Headquarters, the gas, and all.'

'What if they don't?' a Welsh voice asked sotto voce.

'I was just coming to that, Gabby. If we've no luck then I shall either send in Orange Section to do another spraying job or get them to drop the special TX bombs that this section will be carrying. But this is something I shall have to play by ear.'

Teddy Young raised a hand. 'What are these TX bombs, skipper?'

'Frankly, I haven't a clue,' Moore confessed. As he glanced back at the table, Lindsay, the Armament Officer, rose somewhat apologetically to his feet.

'I can't help you much either, Teddy, except that I'm told they mustn't be dropped above 800 feet or they'd be ineffective.'

'What are they supposed to do?' the ginger-headed Australian asked.

Lindsay's hesitation betrayed the lack of information given him by MacBride. 'I'm assuming they have the same function as the chemical sprays but in a more concentrated form. As we're told to drop them only if everything else fails, I'm taking it the boffins have only had time to do a makeshift job with them. Needless to say, if you do have to drop them, they'll be tail-fused to give you plenty of time to get away.'

Moore gave Young a smile. 'I'm going to carry one myself, Teddy. So if gremlins jump out and send the Gestapo chasing their tails, you'll know what to expect.'

As laughs broke out, another hand was raised. 'What about night fighters, sir? You said we'd have no escort if we go at night.'

'That's right. Instead we're going to have a flight of Sterlings with Mandrel radar jammers flying across our route. With luck they'll send Jerry's monitors haywire and his fighters off to Russia. Yes, Preston, what's your problem?'

'If we don't know when we're going, skipper, how are we to work out our navigation plots?'

Moore's wry smile was an acknowledgment of the problem facing the navigators. In the cloudy conditions they were almost certain to experience at this time of the year, plots were worked out on wind speed and direction which in turn decided petrol consumption, and with Met. reports changing almost from hour to hour, navigators would have to be constantly updating their charts. 'I agree, Preston, it's not going to be too easy. But we've got ideas on this and when we call in the Navigation Officer, I think you'll find we've got a solution.' Moore indicated a wiry figure on the front bench. 'Anyway, there's always Hoppy to get us there.'

He allowed the cheers and catcalls to die away before continuing. 'All right, if you've no more questions, come up and examine the model. It's a work of art, so don't knock any bits off.'

The model to which he referred stood on the platform. By this time of the war it had been discovered that wedding cake decorators were particularly skilful at creating three-dimensional models and the seven-foot, plaster of Paris specimen of the Institute and its surroundings was a gem of its kind.

It was another hour before all the men had examined the model and the specialist officers had completed their technical briefing. When every man was seated again, Henderson walked to the edge of the platform. His tone, sombre when it was usually hearty, was an indication of the big Scot's distaste of the operation.

'Your code-sign will be Cobra and the Station's will be Ratcatcher. You can all have a good sleep until the morning when you'll be called at 06.30 to airtest your aircraft. After that you'll be on stand-by until further orders. That's all for the moment. Off you go.'

As the crews rose and came to attention, Davies hurried forward and whispered something to the Scot.

His face tightening, Henderson turned back to his curious audience. 'There is just one last thing. When you come down and attack the Institute, you'll keep your face masks in position and your oxygen turned on. You all know why, so make certain you don't forget.'

22

When the crews were called the following morning, Saturday, rain was pouring down from a grey blanket of sky. Cursing, they drank their mugs of tea, picked up their parachutes, and trudged out to the waiting transports. Few words were exchanged as they passed round cigarettes. The earliness of the hour, the weather, and the operation they faced which would almost certainly entail the loss of brave Frenchmen, combined to depress even the most resilient of them.

Two by two, they were dropped off at their dispersal points. Here fitter engineers were already running up the Mosquitoes, and with the propellers lashing back the rain, mechanics were struggling to protect their faces. At T-Tommy's dispersal point, Millburn pushed into the hut for shelter. A fire had been lit only a few minutes earlier and was giving off sulphurous fumes. The NCO in charge pushed a damp DI form at Millburn. 'We've checked that cable connection, sir, and she's O.K. now.'

As Millburn handed the form back, Gabby sank down on an unmade bed. 'Did you say those chemicals have come in?'

Millburn nodded. 'During the night, according to Harvey. He says the SCIs are already filled.'

Gabby jerked a thumb at the half-open door. 'I don't know what all the panic's about. The job can't be done today.'

Millburn gave a sardonic grin. 'If they can send us out at night to do it, boyo, they can send us any time.'

Gabby showed dismay. 'It's mountainous country over there; the clouds'll be right down on the deck. Anyway, how the hell could we find it in this weather?'

'You've got a point there,' Millburn agreed. 'Most of the time you've trouble finding France.'

The Welshman, in one of his Celtic moods, scowled at the grinning American. 'Funny, funny! You've got a bloody nerve, Millburn. You get lost walking over to the Mess.'

Millburn winked at the grinning NCO. 'At least I don't get lost walking back. Why don't you learn to take your drink, you little Welsh fairy? All you had last night was a couple of bottles and look at you.'

Apart from a gibe at his sexual prowess, no remark could have offended Gabby's machismo more. 'You think that colourless piss gave me this headache? It's your bloody snoring, Millburn. Christ knows how your women put up with you. You sound like a pregnant sow.'

Similar astringent views about the operation were being bandied about by the other crews as they prepared for their air tests. One by one, with wheels hurling back spray and water running in rivulets from their wings, the Mosquitoes gathered speed and disappeared into the low clouds. Half an hour later, with the DI forms signed, the crews were allowed to troop in for breakfast. They were then ordered to their billets to make certain their personal effects were correctly labelled 'to be destroyed' or 'to be sent to nearest relative' in the event they did not return. As most men kept their effects in separately-labelled drawers, this was an occasion to lie on the bed, smoke a cigarette, and wait until the next order came over the tannoy.

This was to report to their respective flight offices where Sue Spencer handed each man his escape kit. Apart from the usual small files, escape maps and money, this time each man was given a tiny compass in the guise of a button to be sewn on his tunic. Although the Intelligence Section were always producing new gadgets, this one seemed to have special significance that morning and to hide their feelings crews made remarks that caused the red-faced girl to make her exit as quickly as possible.

Although the navigators were prepared for a frustrating day of updating plots, orders came at 10.30 that weather conditions prohibited flying until the afternoon when a fresh assessment would be made. Freed for a few hours to do as they wished, crews were thrown back on their own resources.

The extroverts suffered the least. West and Jones of A Flight, both Londoners, argued with anyone who would listen that Arsenal was the finest soccer team in the country. Teddy Young organised a sweepstake on one of the new season's flat races. Larkin, a fanatical card player, borrowed a bottle of whisky from the Mess Officer and used it as bait to inveigle Millburn, Gabby, Hopkinson and Baldwin into his billet for a cut-throat game of poker. Once again, in their battle behaviour, the crews of 633 Squadron were running true to form.

Out at their dispersal points the Mosquitoes were now fully operational. Bombs and SCIs had been hoisted into their bays, rockets slid on to launching rails, magazines snapped on to their deadly 20mm cannon, films loaded into camera guns. The only act left, as final as the cocking of a rifle bolt, was for the safety pins of the stores to be removed and the bomb doors closed.

Lunch came and went. Although the Met. officer announced the glass was rising as the depression drifted eastwards, the rain still fell and the sky remained blanketed in cloud. As the afternoon dragged by, men's nerves began to fray. Jokes that had brought a laugh before were now received with a glance or with silence. Small but significant arguments began to break out between the card and dart players. Harvey, hardly known for his sartorial elegance, snapped at Sam for repeatedly brushing his wet body against the Yorkshireman's slacks.

When Henderson entered Moore's office in the late afternoon he was showing signs of wear and tear himself. 'Davies has just been on the blower. He says MacBride's getting hourly reports from the valley but the wind's gusting at around twenty knots.'

Moore gave a slight start. 'Who's sending them? Do you know?'

Knowing what was in the young Squadron Commander's mind, Henderson shook his head. 'MacBride wouldn't say. But it's probably one of his French agents. Twenty knots! Christ, we could wait days for that kind of wind to drop.'

Moore nodded. 'I suppose we could. I don't know much about the weather conditions in that part of France but even here we don't get a wind speed of less than five knots that often.'

The Scot scowled. 'It's a hell of a thing for the men. They know that however careful they are they're still going to kill some Frenchmen and, if things go wrong, a couple of thousand civilians as well. A day or two of this and they'll be bomb happy.' A thought struck Henderson as Moore made no comment. 'I'm going to talk to Davies again and see if we can't stretch that wind limit a knot or two.'

As the Scot disappeared Moore sank back with some relief and began gingerly massaging his temples. Although the headaches he had suffered from his injury had eased to some degree, they were still painful and the sleep he had missed the previous night seemed to have aggravated them again.

His fear was that the pain might affect his judgement when it was most needed. Moore had no illusions about the operation should it fall at night. To his knowledge such an attack had never been attempted before and although the new flares sounded adequate, Moore was only too aware of the gap that could exist between promise and fulfilment. Night flying at low level was always a supremely hazardous business. And flares were no answer to the lethal black mountains that rose on either side of the town.

Moreover the nature of the assignment was raising doubts he could never remember having before. The stakes were not between failure and success: between the lives of Allied or German soldiers. If a mistake should occur — and in war mistakes were endemic — it would be women and children who would die in a way too horrible to contemplate. He wondered if he should have raised more objections to the mission. Wasn't MacBride indulging in a wild gamble that at best might only delay the threat and at the worst end in disaster? In either case – although at that moment it seemed unimportant – Moore had little doubt on whom the blame would fall.

Yet what was the alternative? If the nerve gas threat were not removed the Germans would certainly feel justified in using it against the Allied invasion force. In turn the Allies would show no more scruples in deploying it themselves. Eventually one side or the other would use it against a city and then the terrifying escalation would begin. Wasn't it yet another of those hideous mathematical formulae that wars throw up – that some must die that many shall live?

Moore knew this was the reason he had not protested before. Yet with his imagination made feverish with pain, the operation seemed to hold so many possibilities of disaster that he knew he was afraid of it.

In an attempt to change his mood he thought of Anna Reinhardt. It was not difficult. Images of her had come to him in unguarded moments ever since she had been flown back into Occupied Europe. His first meeting with her in The Black Swan when, dressed in black with her only jewellery an emerald brooch, she had looked as regal as a queen . . . . The honesty in her grey eyes when she had defended Harvey's social attitudes . . . . Her courage in going back to face the monstrous threat of the Gestapo. Like Harvey, Moore lived with the knowledge that in her passionate desire that Germany should be rehabilitated in the eyes of the civilised world, she would take any risks. The thought she might be the agent in St. Julien who was sending on the hourly messages added to his apprehension.

The tap on his ante-room door came as a relief. 'Yes, what is it, Tess?'

'Flying officer St. Claire is asking if he can see you, sir?'

Moore hesitated, then nodded. 'All right. Send him in.'

He lit a cigarette as the handsome young pilot came to attention. 'Stand at ease, Tony. What do you want?'

'I want first to thank you for dropping the charges, sir.'

'Don't thank me. Thank Squadron-Leader Harvey.'

'I already have. He told me you were responsible.'

'No. I only told him what happened over there. He did the rest.' Moore was eyeing the pilot with some sympathy. 'A man you ought to thank is Frank Adams. If he hadn't taken the trouble to question Sue, you'd have been for the high drop. Why didn't you tell us yourself?'

St. Claire avoided his eyes. 'It isn't something one likes to talk about, sir.'

'No, I suppose not. But now we do know, it has made a difference, hasn't it?'

The young pilot's impassioned reply took Moore by surprise. 'No, sir. It's made no difference at all. You're still not allowing me to fly.'

'Tony, you've twice disobeyed orders while on active service. It's beyond my power to reinstate you now.'

Desperation showed on the man's handsome face. 'I won't do it again, sir. Please let me fly. If only on this operation.'

Moore leaned forward. 'Why, Tony? Because it's against the Gestapo?'

For an instant St. Claire's eyes lowered to his own. They lifted immediately but not before Moore had seen what was in them. 'I just want to fly again, sir. That's all.'

'No, Tony, that's not all. You want your revenge on them, don't you?'

Bitterness put an end to the pilot's control. 'Do you blame me? They tortured her to death. Can't you understand what that does to a man?'

'Yes, I think I can understand. And none of us blame you for how you feel. But that's why we can't let you fly in this theatre again. We're not fighting a personal war, Tony. You'll get your chance to fly again but it'll be against the Japanese. Your posting will come through in a few days.'

'For God's sake, sir, my war's here, not in the Far East. Let me come with you. Please.'

Moore rose to his feet. 'I'm sorry, Tony. Now you'd better go.'

Opening his mouth to make a last protest, St. Claire realised the futility and left the office. Sighing, Moore picked up his phone. 'Hello, sir. Have you been in touch with High Elms yet?'

Henderson gave a grunt of disgust. 'You can bet MacBride had thought of it. He had a word with the boffins earlier and they told him a higher wind speed could only be tolerated if the spray was dropped from a lower altitude – the theory, I suppose, is that the chemicals would take less time to reach the gas. But, as the boffins point out, that's out of the question. Even with the crews inside their cockpits the gas might get to them. And if it didn't, they might be incinerated. All we can do is sweat it out, although if the weather's like this in South-East France I can't see us getting away tonight.'

'Then do you still want me to keep the boys on standby?'

'Oh, Christ, yes. If the green light were to come and we weren't ready, MacBride would throw the book at us.'

Replacing the receiver, Moore left his office and walked out on the footpath outside. Although a bleak wind was gusting across the airfield, the rain had ceased. Seeing the light was fading he glanced at his watch and saw it was only 18.45. The heavy clouds that still lay across the sky were ensuring darkness came early. Suppressing a shiver, Moore turned and made his way towards the Mess.

23

That same night the Operations Room at Gouda was
hazy with tobacco smoke. Resting on a table in the centre
of the floor was a papier mâché model of Sutton
Craddock airfield. Young German airmen, some wearing black leather jackets and others their Luftwaffe
uniform, were crowded around it. Some were talking
more volubly than usual, others were betraying their
nervousness by their silence. A few, who had faced
danger so often that it had drained them of both fear and
excitement, were standing in a group talking about anything but war. Neumann was among them. Feeling
someone nudge his elbow, he turned and saw the tall
figure of Peltz standing in the doorway. Alongside him
was the stocky figure of Obergruppenführer Welter.
Both men's greatcoats were stained with rain. The
depression that had drenched Britain earlier in the
day had now drifted south-east to the Netherlands. As
Peltz fastidiously brushed the rain off his lapels and
knocked his cap against his arm, Neumann called his
men to attention. Acknowledging them, Peltz led the
Obergruppenführer over to Neumann and drew him
aside.

'The operation is scheduled for tonight, Neumann.'

Neumann gave a start. 'But the weather, Herr
Genëralmajor! There's eight-tenth cloud out there.'

Welter's harsh voice broke in. 'You are ready, aren't
you? Your men and your aircraft?'

'Yes, Herr Obengruppenführer. We have been ready
for days.'

'Then what's your problem? The British fly in this

weather. Are you saying our German pilots are not so skilful?'

'We are talking about a low-level attack, Herr Obergruppenführer. One third of my crews are replacements straight from flying school. They have no experience of such weather.'

The Gestapo officer jerked his close-cropped head at the group of whispering men. 'You were granted a delay until the moon was down but not a day longer. Your presence in here tonight is proof you knew that.'

'No, Herr Obergruppenführer. My men are in here because since we were taken off general flying duties, I have used the time to make certain they know every stick and stone of the target. But I did not expect they would have to fly tonight.'

'Well, they must. Time is critical. Moreover the weather is improving. By midnight or at the latest the early morning you will have a clear run.'

Peltz nodded as Neumann glanced at him. 'Our submarine reports confirm the cloud base is lifting off the east coast of England. Conditions won't be perfect but they should be good enough. We'll delay your departure as late as possible. If you leave just after midnight you'll have plenty of time to get back before dawn.'

'I still think it's too risky with new recruits, sir. Couldn't we leave it until tomorrow night?'

Peltz's dry comment brought him a rancorous glance from the Gestapo officer. 'Must I remind you again, Neumann, that, like the Army, the Luftwaffe is no longer run by its own officers but by policemen and politicians. In their wisdom they decree we do the impossible and so we must do the impossible. You will fly tonight as ordered.'

Davies phoned Henderson on the Scot's red telephone just after 21.00 hours. 'Jock, I want you to rig up accommodation for Staines, MacBride and myself. We're coming right over.'

Henderson stiffened. 'Does that mean the operation's on tonight, sir?'

'No, it doesn't,' Davies grunted. 'Although the weather seems reasonable enough over there, the damn wind's blowing as hard as ever. No, it's just that there's nothing more we can do here but wait and we're better doing that where the action's going to be. The old Brigadier's going to pass on the reports to us.'

Unsure of his attitude towards the operation, Henderson could not hold back his question. 'Do you think we're going to make it before Werner moves out, sir?'

'How the hell do I know, Jock? We're in the hands of the bloody weather gods and we all know how fickle they can be.'

The Scot sighed. 'Very well, sir. We'll get the beds organised right away.'

The evening wind was tugging at the eaves of the old stone cottage. Poix, sprawled out in a tattered armchair alongside his radio transmitter, rolled a cigarette and slipped it into his mouth. As he struck a match he glanced at Anna staring out of the window. 'Stop worrying, Lorenz.'

Her voice was sharp as she turned towards him. 'I can't understand why neither Etienne nor Delacourt has left a message for us.'

The wiry, weatherbeaten Poix shrugged. 'They probably felt it too risky. Boche patrols often visit these hill farms.'

Anna turned restlessly back to the window. 'Someone should have contacted us. They knew we were moving in today.'

Five more minutes passed, then Poix sat up sharply in his chair. The girl addressed him in a whisper. 'What is it?'

Motioning her to keep quiet, the Frenchman drew a pistol from his trouserband and stood alongside the door. The girl could now hear footsteps on the flagstones outside. A moment later the door burst open and Pierre Delacourt appeared. Anna gave a gasp of relief. 'Where have you been? Where's Etienne?'

The young Frenchman was panting hard from his

climb up the mountainside. 'I thought he was up here until I ran into him in the village. The Gestapo brought him down this afternoon.' When both his listeners stiffened, Delacourt shook his head. 'No, it's nothing to do with us. They wanted mutton from him and made him go to their headquarters. Thank God you didn't arrive sooner.'

Poix was watching him closely. 'So what's all the panic about?'

'A large convoy arrived at the Institute while he was there.'

'You mean they're still bringing in chemicals?' Anna interrupted. Her look of hope died as the young Frenchman went on: 'No. Etienne says the covers weren't tied down. All the transports were empty.'

Anna gave a gasp. 'That means they're moving out!' Running to a chair, she snatched up her coat. Poix stared at her. 'Where are you going?'

She was panting with urgency. 'London must order the attack tonight. They must!'

'How can they when the wind's blowing so hard. They'll poison the whole town.'

The girl gestured at the cottage. 'We've been sending our reports from here, over eight hundred feet up. The Institute's on the floor of the valley.' She swung round to Delacourt, her words as much a plea as a question. 'Isn't it possible it is more sheltered down there? Have you ever noticed a difference?'

Delacourt gave a start. 'It's possible, I suppose. I haven't noticed any difference today but it might be quieter at the other side of the valley. I suppose it could depend on which way the wind's blowing. But we can't go near the Institute, Lorenz. There are SS patrols everywhere and the curfew's on.'

Anna ran to the door. 'Tell London about the convoy and then stay at the window,' she told Poix. 'If I flash my torch three times, instruct them to go ahead.'

As she pulled the door open, Delacourt caught her arm. 'No. I'll go myself. You stay here with Poix.'

Her voice turned scornful. 'You – a Frenchman out

after curfew? You've just said it yourself. You'd never get through the patrols.'

Knowing she was right, he hesitated. Then his grip tightened again. 'It's my town, Lorenz. I'm the one to take risks for it.'

With an impassioned cry, she tore her arm away. 'And it's my people who are experimenting with that filthy stuff down there. So don't try to stop me, either of you.'

24

Maisie gave a sigh of relief when the last of the locals said good night and she was able to close the door of the bar and draw a bolt across it. 'Gawd, it's seemed a long night. I thought they were never goin''

Kearns, whose lounge bar had emptied five minutes earlier, smiled as he put a match to his pipe. 'It wouldn't be because none of the lads came over, would it?'

Maisie tossed her dark head. 'What's that got to do with it?'

'Knowing you, lass, I'd say just about everything.'

Giving him a look, Maisie turned away. 'What's goin' on over there?' she muttered. 'It's the second night they've been kept in camp.'

Kearns had the typical Yorkshireman's sense of humour. 'Whatever it is, I wish they'd get on with it. I'm losing business while they're making up their minds.'

'Is that all you can think about? Your pocket?'

Kearns' eyes twinkled. 'No; I'm just as much worried about you, lass. If they keep the lads from you much longer, you could pine away.'

Over on the airfield the strain of waiting had begun to tell on the crews. Tired of darts or cards, their main complaint had been the closure of the bar. Feeling that tension was a greater threat than alcohol, Henderson had increased the evening ration to three bottles of beer. With most aircrews heavy drinkers three bottles had barely touched the sides and the grumbles that filled the flight offices and the Mess had been loud and long. As early as 10.00 hours men had begun drifting to their billets. Their orders, although few obeyed them, were to

191

remain fully dressed and to keep their parachutes and Mae Wests by their bedsides. By midnight twenty-four hours of waiting had had its effect and most crews lay in an exhausted, if uneasy, sleep.

As always there were exceptions. Allison, who shared a billet with his pilot, Matthews, was listening with envy to the young man's steady breathing. Matthews was a man blessed with a sense of immortality. Mayhem and death could be raining from the skies but he would walk through the downpour without a qualm. Allison was of a different order. Cursed with a nervous disposition, he had only one close relative, a fragile menopausal mother who relied on him for both financial and emotional support. Possessing a sense of responsibility as well as a deep affection for the pathetic woman, Allison found Matthew's temperament a mixed blessing. It helped his confidence when it was most needed but it also led Matthews to take chances that made a more imaginative man cringe. Tonight, listening to his pilot's untroubled sleep, Allison was wondering why life should be so bountiful to some and so miserly to others.

Harvey was another who could not sleep. In spite of what Moore had said, he did not believe Anna would allow others to take over the final and dangerous stage of her mission. She would be somewhere near the Institute — the Yorkshireman was certain of it — and her life might rest not only on his skill and the skill of his comrades but also on factors beyond anyone's control. With the knowledge of what nerve gas could do, Harvey was hoping the weather conditions would make the mission impossible. Although thousands of lives might be lost as a consequence, Harvey was honest enough to admit he could only sorrow for those he knew and loved.

There was no sleep at all for the executive officers. At first MacBride and Davies had decided to copy Staines and snatch some sleep on the camp beds erected in Henderson's office. But just after 23.00 hours Simms had rung through with the latest news from St. Julien. Staines, Henderson, and Adams had all been called immediately to the Operations Room and each man was

192

now showing his brand of concern. Staines, tieless and with his tunic unbuttoned, dropped somewhat heavily into a chair. 'Empty transports? Then they could be moving out tonight.'

The blackness of MacBride's scowl conceded the possibility. 'Yes. But it's late on Saturday night and old habits die hard. I'm still banking on them loading up tomorrow. After all, there must be tons of stores and equipment in there.'

Adams wondered how much the man was talking to keep his spirits up. Staines shrugged. 'Tonight, tomorrow. What's the difference if this wind keeps up?'

MacBride's jaw jutted out a full couple of inches. 'If we don't get off tonight, I'm taking it to Churchill himself. I've got no choice.'

'You mean a saturation job?' When MacBride nodded, Staines gave a whistle. 'You think he'll risk turning the French against us?'

'I think he'll have to when he knows the alternative.'

The silence that followed was full of frantic questions. Adams broke it more out of duty than conviction. 'Perhaps they won't have time to get the rockets ready. Packaging them with the gas can't be an easy job.'

He received the full brunt of MacBride's frustration. 'You think they won't have been working on that? Damn it, man, now they've made this breakthrough, neither hell nor high water will stop them.' He turned back to Staines. 'We'll wait until 04.00 hours. If the green light doesn't come by then I'll get through to his private secretary.'

'If you're thinking of a B17 raid, you'll have to tell me soon,' Staines pointed out. 'Otherwise they'll all be out on their interdiction raids again. What about a Mosquito job with an escort? I've got Dent standing by for that.'

MacBride turned moodily away. 'We've got a few hours. Let me think about it.'

With either type of raid dooming the town to destruction unless the weather conditions changed, Adams was opening his mouth to protest when he caught Henderson's glance and closed it again. Staines, with a night's growth adding to his grim appearance, gave a nod at the telephone linked to High Elms. 'You know something? It could be a long night.'

The only sounds Anna could hear were her footsteps and the occasional bluster of wind. The small town had been placed under curfew after Ferot had ambushed the convoy, and with the Gestapo and SS presence everywhere, only fools or desperate men ventured out after dark.

She kept to the narrow cobbled lanes that ran between pantiled cottages towards the town centre, pausing at each road intersection to check for patrols before running across and continuing her descent. Occasionally she heard voices or music behind the shuttered windows but apart from a couple of stray cats she saw no sign of life until she reached the broad floor of the valley. Avoiding the market place she reached a wooden bridge crossing a fast-flowing river. A timber mill stood on its far side. As she paused she heard German voices and in the starlight saw the shadowy figures of two sentries on the bridge. Knowing all the bridges would be similarly guarded she took a deep breath and stepped out. A few seconds later there was a guttural shout in German. 'Halt! Who is that?'

'It's all right,' she called. 'I'm a friend.'

'Step forward and identify yourself.'

She obeyed. As she stepped on to the bridge a torch shone in her face, blinding her. 'Who are you?'

'I am a translator in Albertville. I've come to see a friend who works in the Institute.'

'How did you get here?'

'I got a lift,' she lied.

'Show me your papers.'

The SS sentry shone his torch on them as she obeyed. When he glanced up again his tone had changed. 'Your friend is a lucky man, fraulein. I hope he treats you well?'

She smiled. 'I hope so too.'

'If he doesn't, come back and see me. I'm always good to pretty girls.'

She eyed him speculatively. 'I'll remember that,

Sturmann. May I have my papers back now?'

Grinning, the sentry obeyed and stood aside. 'Auf Wiedersehen, fraulein.'

'Auf Wiedersehen.' As the girl walked away she heard the man whisper something to his colleague. A moment later both of them broke into raucous laughter.

She made her way through more narrow streets until the cottages and shops gave way to the macadamised road that ran the full length of the valley. A stretch of grassland lay beyond it, then a lichen-stained wall that ran parallel to the road. A bright light shining in the grounds behind showed it was topped by strands of barbed wire. Keeping an eye open for traffic she followed the road until it brought her to the Institute entrance.

Here the road bisected, one branch following the wall round the front of the estate. Opposite was a low hedge interspersed with trees, and taking care the sentry at the gate did not see her, she took cover behind it.

It was her first sight of the Institute at close quarters. Until now, after making contact with the laboratory assistant, she had made a point of seeing him in the near-by and larger town of Albertville so as to avoid giving him any grounds for suspicion. The one time he had asked her to meet him in St. Julien she had kept well away from the estate. Now she was barely thirty yards from the entrance with its closed steel gate, sentry box, and flagstaff. The flag it carried was whipping in the wind and although it was hidden by the darkness the girl knew it would be the hated Gestapo pennant that was never lowered.

Behind the gates floodlights stood in strategic positions among the grounds, making it virtually impossible for an intruder to enter unseen. They gave glimpses of untrimmed lawns, parked vehicles, and newly-erected Army huts. They also enabled her to gaze down the straight, tree-lined driveway to the Institute, although with all its windows shuttered it was only a black silhouette against the sky.

In the silence that gripped the town, the wind brought

occasional gusts of laughter from the distant SS billets. Trying to judge its direction, she decided it was blowing diagonally across the valley and wondered if the town only gained protection from it when the flanking mountains lay right across its path. If so, her vigil was likely to be in vain.

Light shone from one of the distant huts and she heard orders being shouted. Half a minute later a squad of soldiers came marching down the driveway, to halt behind the gates. As their NCO barked another order, they stood at ease.

The sound of engines made the girl crouch down. Two troop carriers were approaching from the western end of the town. As the foremost vehicle flashed its headlights, the sentries opened the gate. The transports rolled inside, then halted again. Steel-helmeted SS soldiers began jumping out, talking and laughing. As they exchanged cigarettes, their replacements climbed into the vehicles, which turned and made back for the town.

As the men drifted towards their billets and the sound of the transports died away, the silence that returned seemed to lack some meaningful sound. It took the girl a moment to identify it — the Gestapo pennant was no longer whiplashing in the wind but was now hanging limp on the flagpole. Hardly daring to believe her senses, she swung round towards the nearby trees and saw their branches were also motionless.

Her impulse was to signal her news to Poix immediately but she made herself wait another five minutes. When the air remained still she slipped back along the road until she was out of sight of the gates and had a clear view of the southern mountain. Pointing up her torch, she flashed it three times. When no reply came, she repeated the message. This time three tiny sparks answered her. Satisfied, full of hope again, she took cover behind an old barn and waited.

25

The promontory reached out from the dark mass of land like the leg of a huge animal. Around it the sea was the colour of gun metal. Ulrich jabbed a finger forward. 'Flamborough Head, Herr Major.'

Neumann nodded. 'What time is our ETA?'

'Seven more minutes, sir.'

Neumann glanced upwards. The submarines' weather forecasts had been correct. The wet front had drifted clear of the British Isles and here and there patches of starlight could be seen through the dark clouds. For the German crews the improved conditions were a mixed blessing. It would aid their navigation to the target but it would also help the enemy defences. It was true they had flown two dog legs to disguise their intentions and it was unlikely the enemy would guess their target was a mere airfield. At the same time the British radar defences were ruthlessly efficient and fighters would already be vectored towards them. If once they came in range of the fighters' A.I. detectors, the mission could end in disaster.

The slow minutes dragged past as dry-mouthed navigators shared their attention between the coastline and the deadly skies around them. As the short promontory that was Filey Brigg appeared, the aircraft swung 70 degrees to port. As always crews held their breath until the manoeuvre was safely completed: changes of direction at night were a frequent cause of collisions.

To the south the blast furnaces of Scunthorpe momentarily turned the clouds blood-red. Below tiny lights twinkled in the black folds of hills and a thin white plume of smoke betrayed the passing of a train. Just over a minute later, Ulrich gave an exclamation of relief. 'I think that's it, Herr Major. Over at one o'clock.'

Neumann broke radio silence. 'Jaguar leader calling. Target identified. No. 2 follow me down. The rest of you prepare to attack.'

The scream of airfoils grew as his 410 began to dive. At 5,000 feet it levelled out and Ulrich dropped his first parachute flare. As it burst into blinding light, Sutton Craddock leapt from the darkness into stark relief with its hangars, billets, and landing strips. On the road that ran along the northern perimeter a single, slate-roofed building looked tiny and vulnerable. It brought a yell of relief from Ulrich. 'There's our marker, sir. The Black Swan.'

Neumann immediately put his 410 into another dive. Behind him a second aircraft was banking towards the southern perimeter. In the icy light, black canisters could be seen falling. Within seconds, pools of green fire were burning in all four corners of the field.

It was the signal to attack. With bomb doors open and bomb-aimers crouched over their sights, the raiders swept in. Below them, like a man with his head on the block, Sutton Craddock lay spot-lighted and helpless.

Maisie sat upright with a start, unaware at first what had awakened her. Then she heard the rising scream and fall of a siren. Jumping out of bed she threw on a dressing gown and ran into the front bedroom of the inn.

The scene from the window was one of intense activity. Hangar doors were rolling back, truck engines starting up, men yelling orders. Out on the dispersal points storm lanterns had already been lit and mechanics were clustered around the Mosquitoes, tearing off engine covers and opening hatches. As armourers yanked out the safety pins of the rockets and bombs, fitters started up the engines. In no time the air was shuddering and windows rattling under the blast of thirty-six Merlins. As crews leapt down from their transports and exchanged places with the fitters, the first Mosquito began waddling like a huge awakened bird into the darkness.

It was followed by another and yet another. As the eighteen aircraft reached the far end of the field, the flarepath lights clicked on, blinding the rapt Maisie. Within seconds the first Mosquito came back into sight, its engines snarling as it picked up speed. Heavy with its load it fell back twice on the wet runway before it finally broke free and roared triumphantly over the perimeter fence.

The rest followed in quick succession, their sleek wet shapes a blur in the dazzling lights. When the last one rose into the night the lights snuffed out, leaving darkness that looked almost solid to the girl. As the ear-splitting roar of the engines began to fade, she heard Kearns' voice beside her. 'I wonder where they're going, lass.'

She felt dazed by the noise and the excitement. 'I know where I'm goin'. I need a cup of tea.'

He followed her into the old-fashioned stone kitchen and watched her put a kettle on the hob of the still glowing fire. Seeing the shudder she gave as she turned away, he fumbled in the pocket of the trousers he had pulled on over his pyjamas. 'You feel like a cigarette, lass?'

She took one from him and dropped into a chair. Her expression was moody as she dragged in smoke. 'If only we knew where they were goin'. We're allowed to mix with 'em, get friendly with 'em, even go out with them. But when they go on operations, we're not even allowed to know whether we ought to worry or not.'

He knew she was thinking about Gillibrand, the Canadian pilot she had once loved. 'They can't let civilians know, lass. If they did, the Jerries would know ten minutes later.'

'For Christ's sake, we're not likely to tell anybody, are we?'

'That's not the point. They can't make exceptions.'

She drew in smoke resentfully. 'No. I suppose not.'

The kettle boiled five minutes later. As she was filling the teapot the drone of engines could be heard again. As the sound drew nearer she gave Kearns a puzzled look. 'That isn't them comin' back again, is it?'

'They might have been recalled,' he said.

She listened a few seconds longer, then put the kettle back on the hob, 'Hang on. I'm going upstairs to take a look.'

Puzzled, he waited. The night sky seemed full of aircraft again. A sudden scream of airfoils sounded almost overhead. It was followed by a flat explosion, then a scream from upstairs. 'Joe! What's happening? Oh, my God! Joe!'

The first German attacks were made on the airfield gun posts. The Junkers 188 escorts were given this task and after hours of practice on the dummy airfield their pilots knew exactly where to find them. Diving from the darkness into the dazzling glare of the flares, they swept along the perimeter and dropped their bombs with pin-point accuracy.

The ground gunners were taken completely by surprise. The last attack they had suffered had been in the spring of 1943. Since then, with the Allied Air Forces winning control of the skies over Britain, their task had seemingly turned into a pointless chore. Moreover there was always a tendency to relax when the last aircraft had taken off safely and the flarepath lights were switched off. The sound of approaching engines a few minutes later had been attributed to Lancasters or Stirlings assembling for their nightly raids into Europe, and many men had been smoking cigarettes and drinking tea when the first flare had exploded. Dazzled by the blinding light, paralysed by the enormous snarl of engines, they caught only blurred glimpses of the 188s as they roared past, and before they could recover the time bombs began exploding. Sandbags and bodies were hurled into the air; the long Hispano cannons were bent and twisted like soft wire. Two posts did manage to survive the attack but the tough 188s soon ended their resistance as they swept back with hammering cannon.

At this moment Davies was back in the Operations Room, along with Staines, MacBride, Henderson and Adams. Marsden, with one of his Signals corporals, was also present. While no communication was expected or desired from the Mosquitoes until they reached St. Julien, the Operations Room, with its complex radio and telephone links, was the place where any emergency or change of plan could be handled. Armed with flasks of black coffee, the small party were prepared for a long vigil.

It meant, however, they were the last people on the airfield to learn of the German attack. Because the room was the operational heart of the Station, two-thirds of it was built underground like a bunker. With its low entrance and such walls that were visible heavily protected by sandbags and its stout roof covered with turf, it was almost soundproof and the roar of the approaching German aircraft had sounded no louder than an engine under test. It was only when the first marker exploded, a low, flat report, that the men had exchanged puzzled glances. As Henderson rose to his feet to investigate, the telephone linked to the Control Tower began ringing. Answering it, the Signals Corporal swung round on Henderson, his face pale. 'It's the Duty Officer, sir! He says the Station's under attack!'

The scramble to the entrance was dominated by Henderson. Frantic for the safety of his Station, he forgot rank, protocol, and everything else and both Staines and Davies were shoved unceremoniously aside in his dash for the steps. He reached the top just as the first 410 launched its attack.

In the dazzling light the airfield looked like a stage-set. Fires were burning on its perimeters and from every quarter the tiny figures of men and Waafs could be seen running for the deep shelters. As Henderson stared in disbelief, a stick of bombs came raining down. They missed the hangars and the Administration Block but burst in a series of explosions alongside the north-south runway. Tiny figures were swatted away, to lay crushed and motionless, and dispersal huts were tossed up like matchwood. The ground kicked and heaved and the blast came like blows to the face.

'Oh, my God,' Henderson said hoarsely. As he

suddenly began running towards the Administration Block, Davies let out a startled yell. 'Jock! Come back! That's an order.' When Henderson ignored him, Staines showed why he had been such a power on the gridiron twenty years earlier. Hurling his two hundred and forty pounds after Henderson, he brought him down with a crunch that drove the breath from the Scot's body. 'You can't do a goddamned thing,' he shouted. 'So get back under cover.'

Debris rained down as another stick of bombs exploded. Crouched alongside Davies, Adams was about to run out himself when the Air Commodore grabbed his arm. 'Where do you think you're going?'

'I left Sue Spencer in my office,' Adams shouted.

'That was over an hour ago,' Davies snapped. 'She could be anywhere now. Get back under cover.'

Six yards away Henderson had recovered his breath and it took the combined efforts of Staines, MacBride and Davies to drag him back down the steps. As he was flung into a chair, Staines gave a sympathetic grunt. 'I know how you feel, Jock, but you've got a professional outfit here. They all know their job. So why get yourself killed reminding 'em of it?'

The Texan was right. Although it was barely more than a minute since the first marker had fallen, the Station personnel had rallied and were carrying out their emergency procedure. Armourers were snatching automatic weapons from the store and throwing them to reserve gunners and SPs. Drivers were leaping into trucks and petrol bowsers and trying to disperse them. Inside No 1 hangar, where two Mosquitoes were being serviced, mechanics were frantically hitching up tractors in the hope of dragging them to safety. In Adams' Confessional Sue Spencer had snatched up a clutch of the latest Intelligence reports and begun running towards the Operations Room with them. Seeing her coming through the smoke, Adams gave a cry of relief and ran out to help her.

The attack was now developing in earnest as clutches of bombs came toppling down from the night sky. To Maisie it was like looking at an illuminated lake, seething and erupting under some massive thermal disturbance. Since the attack had begun Kearns had been urging her to take shelter but she had ignored him. Now, grabbing her arm and twisting it behind her back, he pushed the sobbing girl down the staircase and towards the Anderson shelter at the bottom of the garden. As they reached it a petrol tanker was hit. In seconds devouring flames leapt as high as the hangars and the sky became a red-stained canopy reflecting the havoc below.

26

From the Mosquitoes, which had not yet crossed the broad, steel-grey Humber river, the shuddering flashes could be seen clearly as they ran along the underside of the clouds. With raids on Britain a rarity by this time of the war, Hoppy was looking puzzled. 'It can't be York, skipper — it's not far enough west. And there's nothing but moors further north. So what can it be?'

With the same thought as the Cockney, Moore broke radio silence. The Signals corporal in the bunker, still manning his switchboard although the ground was heaving below his feet, turned his pale face towards Henderson. 'It's Cobra Leader, sir.'

The Scot grabbed the radio telephone from him. 'What is it, Cobra Leader?'

'We can see explosions. Are you under attack.'

With his station in peril, Henderson could feel only relief at that moment. 'Yes, Ian, we are. Heavy attack.'

At the foot of the steps Marsden was answering an urgent enquiry from Davies. Scampering like a terrier down the bunker, Davies snatched the phone from the indignant Henderson. 'What is it, Cobra Leader?'

'Shall we turn back and help? We can jettison our stores in the sea or in the Humber.'

By this time, at a request from MacBride, Marsden had switched on the loudspeaker. The Mosquito crews were also listening to the conversation. Davies' hesitation was human. If the Mosquitoes jettisoned their bombs and rockets they would be transformed into highly efficient fighters and even without A.I. equipment would be able to contain the raiders until regular night fighters arrived.

Moreover men have affection for the things they create and Davies was seeing his Station blasted before his eyes. Then he noticed MacBride's expression and his face hardened. 'No, Cobra Leader. You've a job to do. Get on with it. That's an order.'

Alongside MacBride, Staines gave a low whistle of admiration. Shouts of protest could be heard from the Mosquito crews. A good five seconds passed before Moore, after silencing his men, acknowledged Davies' order in a flat, curt voice. 'Very well, sir. Good luck.'

Avoiding Henderson's accusing eyes, Davies handed the phone back to the corporal and walked back to the bunker steps. To Staines his walk seemed slightly unsteady although the American was prepared to concede the heavy explosions could be the cause. The Texan turned to the stunned Henderson. 'He'd no choice, Jock. You'd have done the same in his shoes.'

The Scot's voice was bitter. 'I only hope it's worth it, sir.'

Through the bunker entrance vivid flashes could be seen splitting open the darkness. Finding Sue near the top of the steps, Davies turned angrily on Adams who was crouched by her side. 'What the hell's she doing here? Get her downstairs.'

Half-deafened by the explosions, Adams was forced to shout at him. 'She's worried about her fiancé, sir.'

'She can't help him here,' Davies yelled back. 'Get her downstairs!'

Had the girl known it, St. Claire was in No I hangar where 'Chiefy' Powell, the squadron's veteran flight engineer, was struggling to save the two Mosquitoes. The young pilot's impulse was suicidal — had either of the aircraft been fit to fly it would not have moved forty yards down the field before being blown to pieces by the rapacious 188s. But with the enemy now threatening his fiancée and his friends, reason had no part in St. Claire's behaviour. Ignoring Powell's protests, he was demanding the tractors were disconnected and that every effort was made to get one aircraft serviceable. It was an order so absurd that Powell was considering having the frantic

205

pilot dragged off to a shelter when a tremendous explosion blew in one side of the hangar. As the concrete floor buckled, a great mass of steel girders and corrugated iron sheets crashed down and buried the Mosquito beside which St. Claire was standing. Choking in the black, acrid fumes, the half-stunned Powell took a moment to realise what had happened. Yelling at his two equally dazed mechanics to do what they could, he ran off to get help.

The hit on the hangar marked the high tide of Neumann's success. For the last minute urgent warning had been coming from his fighter escort that their Naxos radar sets were picking up enemy A.I. transmissions. The knowledge these pulses could only be detected when fighters were closing in had unnerved the 410 crews and there is little doubt that their haste to release their bombs and to climb into relative safety was the reason Sutton Craddock was saved from total destruction that night.

Nor was their nervousness unjustified. Once the first bombs had fallen, the British night fighters no longer needed their radar equipment. Heading straight for the fires, they adopted the 'Wild Boer' tactics of their German counterparts and dived on the raiders when they were silhouetted against the reddened clouds or the burning airfield. As two torches went twisting downwards, Neumann knew it was time to withdraw and his aircraft made for cloud cover. Falling back on their radar 'eyes' again, the British fighters followed them right across the North Sea to their base. Before the last weary crew landed, twenty per cent of Neumann's force had been destroyed.

But the scoresheets of death and destruction could not be measured yet. As the all-clear siren wailed out at Sutton Craddock and dazed men and women emerged from the dense smoke and fires, a massive explosion blew half-a-dozen billets into matchwood. As Lindsay had feared, the Germans had dropped bombs with a variety of time delays and some of these had yet to explode. All Waaf personnel were immediately sent back into the shelters and officers and men alike were given the highly unpleasant task of seeking out craters where unexploded bombs might be lying. At the same time, while an SOS call was made to the nearest Army Bomb Disposal Unit, those armourers unfortunate enough to have had a course on enemy bombs were formed into two-man crews under an NCO. Lindsay's orders to them were painfully explicit. Any bombs unlikely to cause casualties or serious damage to valuable equipment were to be cordoned off and left for the Army. If any were found in the other category, an immediate attempt must be made to defuse them.

Such a bomb was found almost at once, a 1,500 kilo monster buried almost up to its fins near the photographic section. Lindsay examined it, decided it could be defused, and ordered two armourers to join him. Never dreaming in their worst nightmares they would ever be given such a task, the white-faced men were brought up in a truck whose driver drove off as fast as he could engage his gears once the two men had jumped out.

During this time, Henderson was here, there, and everywhere, supervising the fire-fighting crews, the clearing of wreckage, and trying to make certain all the Station personnel were accounted for. The distressing fact soon emerged that the sick bay had received a direct hit and the MO and all his orderlies had been killed. With only one ambulance left undamaged, Henderson ordered his serviceable transports to ferry the dead and wounded to the hospital in Highgate.

While all this frantic activity was raging, Powell's news had reached the Operations Room. Deciding MacBride and Marsden could monitor the mission at its present stage, Staines, Davies, Adams and Sue Spencer had rushed to No I hangar where a huge hole gaped in the roof and in the wall below, which had been blown inwards by the blast. A massive crater at the foot of the wall was still pouring out smoke. The tons of wreckage, now surrounded by storm lanterns brought up by Powell's men, were piled like a grotesque tent over the crushed Mosquito.

At first glance it seemed impossible anything could

have survived the downfall and Davies was about to order the distressed girl away when a faint cry was heard. Exchanging glances, men snatched up lanterns and began examining the pile. A shout from Staines brought them hurrying towards him. They found the American lying on his stomach and peering through a gap no more than a foot high at the base of the wreckage. Coughing from the dust and smoke, he edged his head inside, then held a hand behind his back. 'Anyone got a torch?'

One of the mechanics pushed one into his hand. Wriggling gingerly, Staines drew his arm into the opening. A moment later he gave a grunt of satisfaction. 'There's a horizontal shaft here where the wing seems to have held up the stuff. It's as narrow as hell but I think I can see him. Yeah, I can. And he looks to be alive.'

Glancing at the girl, who seemed afraid to breath in case it was a false alarm, Davies dropped on his knees alongside the American. 'Can we pull him out?' he asked as Adams joined him.

'Not a chance. The wing and a girder seem to be holding things up but it's a hell of a low shaft.' As Staines shifted his position to gain a better view, there was an ominous rending and the entire structure settled a few inches. As a sheet of corrugated iron came clattering down, missing him by only a few inches, Staines drew back and grimaced up at the startled faces. 'I did say seem!'

As he climbed to his feet, the girl snatched the torch from him and peered through the opening. She gave a gasp of dismay. 'There's blood everywhere. He must have a ruptured artery.'

Staines nodded when Davies glanced at him for confirmation. Leaning down, Davies tapped the girl's shoulder. 'One of us will try to reach him, Sue. Out you come.'

Her pale, dust-smeared face turned towards him. 'None of you can get through. It'll be a tight squeeze even for me.'

'I'm hardly a giant, am I?' Davies snapped. 'Come out

and I'll see what I can do. In any case the breakdown trucks from Highgate should be here in a few minutes.'

Her voice was already muffled as she pulled herself forward with her elbows. 'If he has a ruptured artery, he won't last that long. And I've had medical training.'

As another screech of metal came from the unstable pile, Davies grabbed her ankles. 'Come out of it, Sue. The whole thing's going to collapse at any moment.'

The girl tried to free herself. Afraid her struggles might bring about the very accident Davies was trying to avoid, Staines caught his arm. 'I'd leave it, Davies,' he muttered. 'It's her fiancé in there. And there's a chance she might save him.'

Davies hesitated, then drew back. As the girl's feet disappeared, the men watched the pile with bated breath. Whispering as if he feared his voice might bring it down, Davies turned to Powell. 'Get over to the main entrance, Chiefy, and bring a crane over here as soon as the trucks arrive.'

The NCO nodded and ran off. Ignoring the danger, Staines flattened himself again and peered along the narrow shaft. 'How's it going, honey?'

Half-frantic for the girl's safety, Adams heard her unsteady voice. 'It's all right, sir. I think I can reach him.'

The minutes that followed were the longest of Adams' life. Voices were yelling orders all over the airfield, sirens were sounding, trucks dashing hither and thither, but Adams might have been in a soundproof chamber as he listened to the groaning of metal under stress. Staines' gravelly voice, announcing the girl had reached the injured man, broke his vigil. 'How is he?'

Adams had to press close to the American to hear her reply. 'He's badly hurt. But I think I can stop the bleeding.'

Glancing round at Davies, who was watching anxiously for the breakdown trucks, Staines gave the thumbs-up sign. He turned back to the shaft. 'Is he still conscious?'

'No, sir.'

'Good. Then he isn't in any pain. Just stay still, honey, and you'll both be O.K.'

As Adams took the Texan's place, Staines drew Davies aside. 'When's that goddamned help coming?' he muttered. 'That pile can't stay up much longer.'

With one crisis following another the strain was beginning to tell on Davies and he was about to snap how the hell could he know when a massive explosion almost blew both men off their feet. Over by the photographic section Lindsay and his two armourers, in trying to slide the exploder from the 1,500 kilo bomb, had forgotten that as a deterrent to disposal squads, some German bombs were fitted with the treacherous Zus 40 fuse. For a split second every fire on the airfield paled beneath the brilliant flash. As the thunderous blast echoed across the hangar, a high-pitched scream of metal made Adams jump back. A second later the entire pile began to collapse on itself, filling the air with choking dust.

Shouting for help, men tore at the jagged pieces of metal with their bare hands. Shock had numbed Adams: blood was running from a gash in his hand but he felt no pain. More mechanics ran up and joined in the rescue attempt. Davies was burying himself in the debris like a terrier and Staines was doing the work of three men but in their hearts all the helpers believed their efforts were in vain.

Meanwhile the first breakdown truck had arrived at the Station gates. Commandeering it immediately, Powell jumped aboard and guided it through the bomb craters and into the hangar. Sizing up the situation at once, the veteran NCO took charge. Climbing on the pile of wreckage he selected a girder and directed the truck towards him. He then slipped the hook of the crane beneath the girder, shouted at Davies and his party to draw back, and indicated the driver to begin winching.

The girder lifted, checked, then lifted again. As sheets of corrugated iron fell away, sections of the crushed Mosquito became visible. Heartened, the officers and men added their help until a sudden shout from Powell checked all operations. Seeing the NCO's jubilant expression, Adams clambered over the twisted metal sheets and saw the girl lying across the prostrate body of St. Claire. Although a trickle of blood was running down her dust-stained face and her tunic was filthy with rust and oil, her look of relief told him she was not badly hurt. As Adams reached her the reason became apparent. Although the final collapse of the pile had snapped the Mosquito's wing, the girder that had fallen over the port engine had given protection to the couple huddled beneath it.

The girl's posture puzzled Adams until he realised she had her thumbs jammed on a pressure point on the unconscious pilot's right shoulder. Although by this time her muscles must have been screaming with pain, her refusal to relinquish her grip told Adams she had held it even when the wreckage had collapsed on her.

Relief at her survival made the next few minutes somewhat unreal for Adams and his next clear memory came when he was bending over her in one of the County ambulances that had been rushed to the airfield. On the bed opposite her St. Claire, still unconscious, was receiving blood plasma from a nurse. Although her hair and face were caked with dirt, her eyes were shining as she gazed up at him. With her throat choked with dust, he had to bend down to catch her words. 'I'm lucky, aren't I, Frank?'

Knowing what she meant he was too moved to speak. Instead he squeezed her hand.

Weariness closed her eyes for a moment. Then her joy surged back. 'I never dreamed I'd get the chance. Oh, Frank, I'm so very lucky.'

Outside Adams could hear Davies shouting for him to return to the Operations Room. Bending down he kissed her, then climbed out into the fire-swept night. Unable to see clearly, he blamed the smoke for misting his spectacles.

27

A high pressure area had moved in over France and from the great height the Mosquitoes were flying the ground below looked like an endless black sea. Far to the north a small island appeared to be suffering volcanic activity. Glowing with larva, it was hurling thousands of fiery sparks into the sky. Banks of clouds were pulsating with red fire as if they were radioactive.

Moore knew it was a German city being pounded by one of Bomber Command's massive raids. Bundles of red and gold marker flares were tumbling down and the cauldron seethed as if stirred by a giant ladle. Thin blue searchlights were striking back and a yellow flare burned its baleful eye as a night fighter detected a raider. A few seconds later a torch no larger than a match twisted and fell into the cauldron it had helped to make.

Moore's eyes turned back to the dark horizon. Hoppy, who possessed the serviceman's ability to relate the misfortunes of others into personal terms, gave a grunt of satisfaction. 'We're in luck, skipper. That raid ought to keep Jerry's night fighters busy.'

The dryness of Moore's reply had less to do with the Cockney's insensitivity than with war itself. 'They've always a few to spare, Hoppy. So keep your eyes open.'

Ninety minutes had passed since the Mosquito crews had witnessed the attack on their airfield and still none of them knew the outcome. Hoppy's discontented opinion was shared by all. 'You'd have thought Davies or someone would have let us know how things went, skipper.'

Moore shrugged. 'Davies is playing it safe. He knows there has to be some reason for the attack. If he contacts us, someone might put two and two together.'

The Cockney was not so easily comforted. 'It could also mean something else, skipper. That the Ops Room was wiped out with the rest.'

The burning city dropped back into the night as the Mosquitoes droned on. Below, a tiny strip of light appeared, shone for a few seconds, then vanished again. Moore knew it was night fighters taking off but because of the Mosquitoes height, speed and the Mandrel cover they were receiving, he felt interception unlikely. Their return in daylight could be a different story.

By 03.50 hours they were well into the high-pressure area that was covering south-western France. At 04.10 Hoppy tapped Moore's arm. 'ETA in ten minutes, skipper.'

Moore nodded. Ahead the pre-dawn was visible, a red wound splitting the dark skin of night. Silhouetted against it were the distant peaks of the Alps. Hoppy's voice came again. 'Thank God we aren't arriving in darkness, skipper.'

Moore smiled. 'Amen to that, Hoppy.'

Six more minutes and the angry orb of the sun began to appear. Below, the folds of hills and shallow mountains were beginning to rise from the black sea. At one o'clock a tiny cluster of lights were suddenly extinguished. Hoppy, who had had his eyes fixed on the lights for some time, guided Moore in their direction.

A-Apple reached the valley only four minutes after its ETA. Circling at 5,000 feet in the lowest orbit of the stack, Moore waited for his last crew to arrive. When all were present the stack ranged from himself to Teddy Young flying at 12,000 feet.

Below the floodlights that guarded the Gestapo Head-quarters had been extinguished by orders from ground control although not before the lynx-eyed Hoppy had spotted them. Now, as the enemy aircraft assembled above, German SS patrols raced through the small town to ensure no lights were flashed up at them. At the same time flak crews were playing safe and were warming up their predictors. Tension was high both in the town and in the huge, darkened Institute.

With the German defences now alerted, Moore broke radio silence. 'Cobra Leader to Green I. Release your flare and attack. Red Section get ready.'

With a nod at Hoppy, who had one of the new flares poised over the chute, Moore dropped a wing and went down. At the far end of the valley Harvey was taking similar action. The flares the two aircraft dropped exploded at 3.000 feet within six seconds of one another. Hoppy gave a whistle of appreciation. 'Those flares are really something, skipper. Take a look at that.'

The icy brilliance of magnesium candles had burned away the last of the night and every detail of the valley was exposed: the tiny cottages that clung to its lower slopes, the bright flashes of the swift-flowing river, the timber yards along its banks, and the huge rectangular building that was set in relief by its black shadows. With a last careful look at his photographs, Hoppy pointed down. 'That's it, skipper. No question.'

Moore addressed his R/T again. 'Target positively identified, Green I. Drop your ground flares.'

On reciprocal courses, the two Mosquitoes dived on the Institute. As an aid against collision, both pilots switched on their navigation lights. With the parachute flares illuminating their target, neither pilot had any difficulty in planting his ground flares inside the boundary walls. As they shot past one another the building seemed to rear upwards in the dazzling light.

Experienced in the manoeuvre, both pilots were counting. At fifteen seconds they turned on a wingtip and came diving back. This time their approach was not unopposed: flak gunners opened fire the moment they switched on their navigation lights. Moore's orders were terse as chains of tracer swept towards him from the grounds of the Institute. 'Cobra Leader to Red Section Leader. Pinpoint the guns, sort out your targets, and attack.'

Ahead the illuminated building was growing larger by the second. Trying to ignore a line of coloured shells that seemed to be clawing at his eyes, Moore steadied A-Apple so that it was heading directly for the upper story. As two

214

luminous lances darted out from his wings, he banked steeply to port, switched off his lights, and climbed away.

He was unable to see the result of his attack but a yell from Hoppy confirmed that his rockets had struck just below the eaves. At the far side Harvey had fallen a few seconds behind in his attack. With A-Apple out of his way, the Yorkshireman left off his navigation lights but their absence made little difference. Light was beginning to seep down the valley and with Moore no longer a threat the flak gunners were giving D-Danny their full attention. Moreover two light machine guns had started firing from the roof of the Institute. To survive, Harvey had to take evasive action and although he pressed home his attack with his usual tenacity, only one of his rockets struck home. Drenched in sweat, the Yorkshireman vented his feelings in typical fashion as he climbed away. 'I thought they said there were only four gunposts down there, Ian. The place is full of the sods.'

It was a grim fact that Red Section, led by Millburn, were already finding. As they went for the guns like dogs worrying rats, the rest of the Mosquitoes moved one stack down in their orbits and waited. To aid Millburn and his men they began dropping parachute flares at regular intervals.

Red Section's orders were to attack not only the guns but also the SS barracks. While some of the soldiers had found the time to reach the air-raid shelters, others could be seen running for the Institute and being cut down by the Mosquitoes' guns.

Moore and Harvey had one last role to play before joining the main attack on the Institute. Flying at low level, both released rockets that blasted holes in the high boundary walls. Ignoring the ground fire, both pilots circled low to see if their desperate measures were having any success.

The red sun was now poised at the end of the valley but explosions, drifting smoke, and the dazzling chains of tracer made visibility difficult. Then Hoppy gave a sudden yell. 'There's some of the prisoners, skipper!

Climbing down on to that outhouse! And there's more running across the grounds!'

Moore caught a glimpse of half a dozen ragged figures heading across a lawn towards a crumbled gap in the wall but a few seconds later smoke hid them and the Institute from view. But faith in the Cockney's remarkable eyesight was such that cheers could be heard from the crews orbiting above.

Putting out a call to his Red Section to be careful not to strafe any civilians, Moore took note of the time. In the elongated way time behaves in moments of danger, it was still less than ninety seconds since the last rocket had struck the Institute and Moore's instincts were to give the prisoners all the time possible to make their escape. But reason dictated otherwise. Fighters would already be racing in and unless all the phases of the operation were completed before they arrived, the outcome might be disaster.

He was calling down his Blue Section when one of Millburn's Mosquitoes was hit. With the entire front section of its fusilage blown away and its port engine trailing flames, it swept past the Institute and crashed into the grounds beyond. Wincing at the ball of fire and then the thick column of smoke that rose from it, Moore gave a violent start, then shouted an order. 'Red Section Leader! Break off your attack!' He then swung round on the surprised Hopkinson. 'Get me base! Right away!'

Panting from his exertions, Henderson paused at the foot of the Operation Room steps. 'Any news yet, sir?'

Davies, who was examining the flight track of the Mosquitoes on the huge map of Europe, spun round. Still outraged by the attack on the airfield, he answered impatiently. 'Give them time, Jock. They probably aren't there yet.'

Henderson, his uniform torn and filthy, showed resentment. Since the bombers had been driven away, the Scot had been working heroically to save what was left of his station and this was his first opportunity of visiting the bunker. 'I was only asking, sir.'

At that precise moment the red telephone connected with High Elms began ringing. All eyes turned as MacBride snatched up the receiver. 'Hello, Simms. MacBride here. Yes, yes — what?'

In the silence that fell Henderson moved anxiously forward. Meeting his enquiring glance, Davies shook his head. Adams, who had a presentiment, felt his heart beating hard and fast.

MacBride slowly lowered the receiver. With his hard face full of bitterness and disappointment he sat staring at the wall for a moment. Then he turned to Davies. 'It looks as if we might have to abort the mission.'

Staines beat the startled Davies to the question by a short head. 'Why, for Chrissake?'

'Our agent has sent another report to London. The wind's picking up again.'

Although Staines gave a grunt of dismay, Adams saw relief on Henderson's unshaven face. Davies moved forward. 'How strong is it?'

MacBride lit a cigarette and exhaled smoke. 'It's not a gale or anything like that. But Lorenz is certain it's well over five knots.' Exhaling smoke again, he gave Davies a challenging stare. 'You know something? If it's not blowing that hard I'm tempted to risk it.'

Although Davies gave a start, he ignored Henderson's exclamation of protest. Adams was trying to read the small Air Commodore's face. He knew that on the one hand Davies would like nothing better than to withdraw his crews from the operation: the odds on success were impossible to define and failure, particularly if it resulted in the destruction of St. Julian, was certain to rebound heavily against him and his squadron. On the other hand there was no denying Davies was ambitious and success would mean another feather in his cap. To give him time to respond, Staines intervened. 'What about De Gaulle?'

MacBride's scowl betrayed his Achilles heel. The big Frenchman was the last man to show clemency if his orders were ignored. For Davies it was the factor that weighted the scales. 'If he'd accept the responsibility, we might be able to risk it. But as he won't, we've no option but to abort or he could foul up the invasion himself.'

MacBride shook his head. 'You haven't thought this through, Davies. Didn't it come out at the briefing that if the chemicals were dropped at a lower altitude it could counter a higher wind speed?'

This time Henderson could not contain himself. 'You're not asking my boys to incinerate themselves, are you?'

He received a hard stare. 'There's no certainty of that.'

'There's no certainty of anything,' the Scot said bitterly. 'They might fly into the gas itself!' He turned imploringly to Davies. 'We can't ask them to take a risk like that, sir. It's inhuman.'

To Adam's relief, Davies had already made up his mind. 'No one's going to, Jock. We'll have to abort.'

His decision brought out the worst in MacBride. 'You seem to have forgotten who's in charge of your squadron, Davies. If I say they attack, they attack.'

It was a remark that fired all the latent animosity Staines felt for the man. His growl might have come from an outraged bulldog. 'You don't out-rank me, MacBride, and I don't come under your goddamned Administration either. If you give that order I'll see everyone from Eisenhower down to buck private bears about it. That means if things go wrong and the gas poisons the town, they'll crucify you.'

As the two men's eyes locked, Adams was certain the temperature in the bunker rose ten degrees. With a curse, MacBride crushed out his cigarette and rose to his feet. 'All right, Davies. Abort the mission. Only remember to blame yourselves if that gas gets among our troops on D-Day.'

If Davies was thinking of a reply it was silenced by sudden blips of Morse in the Signal Corporal's earphones. There was a stir in the bunker as the man turned towards Davies. 'It's Cobra Leader, sir.'

Through the smoke haze that filled the bunker, Adams watched Davies run to the NCO's side. The moment the man finished scribbling down the message, the small Air

Commodore tore it off the pad and scanned it. His expression was hidden from Adams as he turned and handed the sheet of paper to MacBride. 'Moore's spotted the wind change too. He estimates it between 10 and 12 knots.'

Staines whistled. 'That's higher than we thought, isn't it?'

Without a word MacBride tossed the message on the bench. Reading the gesture for what it was, Davies turned back to the corporal. 'Send this reply. "Ratcatcher to Cobra Leader. Abort mission and return to base immediately." '

28

There was an air of anti-climax in the bunker as the
corporal ceased transmitting although Henderson and
Adams were showing undisguised relief. As the Scot
moved towards the entrance, MacBride's harsh voice
checked him. 'As it's a washout, I might as well get back
to High Elms. What's the transport situation?'

Henderson turned. 'Your car's burned out, sir. And all
my undamaged vehicles are on fire or ambulance duty.'

'What does that mean? I can't get back?'

Adams was certain he detected malice in the Scot's
reply. 'I'm afraid it does for the moment, sir. Unless you
can organise transport from High Elms.'

As the smouldering MacBride eyed him, the blip of
Morse was heard again. The corporal turned to Davies.
'It's Cobra Leader again, sir.'

Davies looked puzzled. 'What does he want now?
Acknowledge.'

The Morse key danced beneath the NCO's practised
fingers. Ten seconds after he ceased transmitting the
blips sounded again. Listening to them Adams saw the
operator start and suddenly the acrid taste of high explosives turned dry in his mouth. As the message ended, the
NCO turned to Davies. 'Cobra Leader is asking your permission to carry on, sir.'

The effect was like an electric shock in the bunker.
Snatching the sheet of paper from the NCO, Davies
scanned it, then swung round on Henderson. 'Listen to
this! "Men have volunteered to fly lower. Believe we
have a chance. Request permission." ' Pride was glowing
from the small Air Commodore like a light. 'You hear

220

that, Jock? They've volunteered! Every man jack of 'em.'

All the colour had gone from Henderson's cheeks. To Adams it was like re-living an old nightmare. To the day almost exactly a year ago when another band of young men had volunteered to fly into almost certain death in the Black Fjord and established a squadron tradition of sacrifice. He wanted to protest but discipline held him motionless.

Henderson was less inhibited. 'They're doing it because it's expected of them, sir. But we can't allow it. Not with nerve gas present — it's too hideous a risk.'

MacBride, who appeared to have grown a full three inches since the news, broke in exultantly. 'You can't refuse, Davies. Not when the stakes are so high.'

As Davies hesitated, the breath grew tight in Adams' lungs. Staines opened his mouth, then closed it again. A moment later Davies' sigh could be heard the full length of the bunker. 'I don't see how I can. Not when so much might depend on it.' He turned back to the waiting corporal. 'Send this message. Permission to attack granted. Good luck. Ratcatcher.'

A red-cored explosion outside A-Apple's cockpit, followed by a vicious crack of steel, made both Moore and Hopkinson flinch. It brought a wry comment from the Cockney. 'With all these guns they must have something to hide, skipper.'

Moore nodded. If any doubts had remained about the threat contained in the Institute, they were dispelled now. Coloured shells and stabs of tracer were shooting out from both sides of the valley: a concentration of guns that could not possibly be put out of action by the number of Mosquitoes available.

Forced to fly above the flanking mountains to avoid the danger of collision, the orbiting sections, among which was Millburn's withdrawn Red Section, were now in sunlight. As bright shafts caught their sharklike bodies and spinning propellers, the 37mm and 88mm crews revelled in the targets presented to them. In T-Tommy Gabby gave a startled grunt as an exploding 88mm shell almost turned the aircraft over. 'We're crazy to volunteer. We're like ducks in a shooting gallery up here.'

'You didn't volunteer,' Millburn told him. 'I twisted your arm.'

Gabby forgot his indignation as another shell sent T-Tommy reeling. 'Why have I to be mixed up with a crowd of eager beavers? If we get a whiff of that gas we could be zombies by breakfast time.'

Above his face mask Millburn's eyes twinkled wickedly. 'You should worry, boyo. Who'll notice the difference?'

Below, in the few seconds since he had received Davies' permission to attack, Moore had been hard at work re-structuring his battle tactics. If the original plan were adhered to and the gas were not to spread across the town, his Green Section would have to fly almost on the heels of his Red and Blue Sections, which would put them at risk from the exploding time delays. Moreover, with the higher wind speed facing them, some gas might still drift away before their chemicals settled. In an effort to avoid either contingency Moore had decided to send in a second spraying section downwind of the Institute to catch any gas that might escape. It was a move against all the advice of the boffins but having asked permission to launch the attack, Moore felt he owed it to the townsfolk to take all measures possible for their safety. Because of the high risks involved he had decided to lead the downwind section himself while Harvey led the Green Section directly at the Institute. Hopefully this concentration of eight aircraft would be enough and the fires from the Institute itself would ignite the activated gas. If they did not, Moore still had the SCIs of his Red and Blue Sections and the unused TX bombs.

It was typical of Moore that once he had made his assessments he acted on them without further hesitation. As his terse but cogent orders rapped out, Van Breeden-kamp, the leader of Blue Section, called his crews to formate behind him and the four Mosquitoes went plunging down. Flattening above the floor of the valley, they raced in line astern for the Institute.

The fires on the upper stories had now been extinguished, although the SS barracks in the grounds were still ablaze. The ground flares had also burned out but with the huge building now silhouetted against the red sun, the need for artificial light had gone.

Only one of the SS gunposts in the grounds was still firing: Millburn and his men had done sterling work before they were recalled. Apart from the two LMG posts on the roof, the main threat to Van Breedenkamp's aircraft now came from the hidden guns lined along the hillsides. Recognising his section as the immediate threat, all guns but the high-angle 88s were lowered to form a gauntlet down which the Mosquitoes had to fly. As their bomb doors opened, the shadowy hillsides became alight with the rapid flashes of automatic fire. Black explosions wreathed the slim aircraft and lethal chains of shells swirled in from all directions.

Ahead Van Breedenkamp could see a score of tiny grey-uniformed figures running out of the Institute. His forehead beaded in sweat as he fought to control the bucking Mosquito, the young South African let out a yell to his tense navigator. 'Ready . . . . Ready . . . . Now!'

As the Mosquito soared over the huge building, the 500lb bombs held in its belly dropped and smashed through the roof. Blue 2, flying only fifty yards behind, had the same success. Blue 3 and 4, flying to a pre-set plan, released their bombs a couple of seconds later so that they smashed into the far wing of the building.

As Van Breedenkamp dived back to the floor of the valley to gain all possible cover from the flak, he was counting. At ten there was a triumphant yell from his navigator. Twisting his head the South African saw the Institute being rent apart by a series of massive explosions. The debris had barely settled before Millburn's Red Section swept in and dropped their stores on the shattered building. This second salvo of bombs were of the semi-armour-piercing type. With the top stories already demolished, they were meant to penetrate into the Institute's laboratories and with their high shrapnel content rupture any tanks that might be proof against ordinary high explosive. To breathless Frenchmen, peering out through shuttered windows, the destruction of the hated Gestapo headquarters seemed complete.

But there was no hint of jubilation among the Mosquitoes' crews who knew their most dangerous moment was yet to come. If the SAP bombs had done their work, the stocks of nerve gas would already be mixing with the flames and dense smoke that were rising hundreds of feet into the air.

The last bomb had barely exploded before Moore and Harvey were leading their Orange and Green Sections towards their target. To shorten the dropping time, they were flying at 1,200 feet. The four aircraft from each section were flying line abreast which meant, as they were flying on a parallel course, that eight aircraft were strung side by side across the town. Moore and Harvey were flying eight hundred yards ahead of their sections. Realising at the last moment that he had no way of knowing how far the chemicals would float before they made contact with the drifting smoke, Moore had decided to use himself and Harvey as target sighters. From the drift of their chemicals Young and Machin would be able to adjust their sections' flight paths accordingly.

As the twin lines of Mosquitoes raced through the scabrous hills towards the red orb of the sun there was not a man who was not glad of the face mask that hid his expression. To spray the target meant they would have to fly straight and level and since the shattering attack on the Institute the gunfire from the hillsides had risen to a new level of fury. But razor-sharp steel and phosphorous-filled bullets that could burn inside a man's body were not the only horrors the crews were being asked to face. The prospects of incineration or death by slow paralysis made fear claw at men's bowels as Moore's terse order came over the R/T. 'Cobra Leader to all crews. Tighten your face masks and turn on your oxygen.'

Men smelt the staleness of metal and rubber tubes as they obeyed. Low-angled guns were now raking them on all sides. Sweeping chains of shells blinded them and vicious explosions made them flinch and duck. Like a giant hand slapping a toy, a 37mm shell struck the tail unit of V-Victor. Cartwheeling down, the Mosquito hit the floor of the valley and exploded.

The elongated shadows of cottages and barns were beginning to appear below. Ahead Moore and Harvey were suffering even greater pressure than their shell-shocked crews. Both were afraid that in her determination to do her part in defeating the gas threat, Anna Reinhardt might still be present in the danger area surrounding the Institute. The two men also had the technical problem of being able only to guess how much forward drift their airspeed would give to the falling chemicals.

Across on his port side Moore caught a glimpse of Harvey's D-Danny. To allow for the wind, the Yorkshireman was flying a hundred yards to the left of his preset course. Moore himself was heading for a point approximately halfway between the blazing Institute and the southern boundary wall.

Pantiled cottages and narrow streets flashed below. With neither crew knowing what to expect, both Mosquitoes seemed to be flying at twice their rated speed. As the tree-lined drive to the stricken Institute appeared beyond his port wingtip, Moore took a quick glance at Hopkinson. The Cockney was crouched in his seat with one hand pressed against his face mask and the other gripping the SCI release. Moore's voice was very calm. 'Steady, Hoppy . . . . steady . . . . Now!'

Almost at the same moment Harvey fired his own SCI. To the crews following half-a-mile back the effect was startling. Like enormous contrails, two wide belts of cream-coloured particles streamed out from the Mosquitoes. Tinted pink in the early morning sunlight, they began drifting and sinking towards the billowing smoke. Expecting a massive conflagration, men waited with held breath.

But as Moore and Harvey climbed away under full throttle their navigators reported no change in the scene below. Moore, who noticed his chemicals were sinking into the smoke sooner than he had wished, gave a sharp order to his Orange Section Leader. Teddy Young had noticed the shortfall, however, and his Mosquitoes were already spewing their chemicals nearer the southern boundary of the grounds.

To the north Harvey had experienced better luck and his reagents had straddled the Institute. When no explosion resulted, his Green Section swept in and saturated the blazing building. With the need to fly straight and true during their attack, both sections suffered heavy flak damage. Machin had half an aileron blown off but somehow managed to regain control. Tracer hammered through the unarmoured seat of young Richards, killing him instantly. C-Charlie had an entire wing blown off and went spinning down into the dense smoke. The rest of the two sections managed to survive but when they dived thankfully away, there was not an aircraft that had not suffered damage.

Moore, who was flying at mountain top height to gain a better view of the operation, was watching the white steam that rose as the chemicals sank among the leaping flames. The bitter voice that came over the R/T confirmed that Harvey was sharing his fears. 'It's a dead loss, Ian! The heat's burning the stuff up before it can sink down to the tanks.'

With his Orange Section having suffered no such problem, Moore's first thought was to try to incinerate the smoke that was already drifting toward the southern boundary wall. If it would burn, it would not only hold back the danger to the town for another minute or two but also prove that the gas was escaping. Then he realised his mistake. The tanks were the very heart of the matter. If they had been ruptured, it was more than likely they would continue to pour out gas and dispersants for some time. With the flames preventing the reagents from reaching them, they would remain untreated and therefore immune to fire. An inferno in the grounds, therefore, might only make it more difficult to activate them later. With fighters racing in, Moore realised now that he had no time left for a repeat performance with the unused SCIs of his Red and Blue Sections. If the tanks were ruptured, they had to be destroyed or the town would die along with Werner and his secrets.

'Cobra Leader to Green Section Leader. Climb and give cover. Orange Section, stand-by. I'm going down to drop my TX bombs. Keep clear for ten seconds. If I've no luck, follow me down and drop your bombs in a salvo.'

Moore then turned to Hoppy. With A-Apple well above the mountain tops the Cockney had slipped off his face mask for a moment to breath fresh air. Now his freckles had turned black against his pale, thin face. 'All right with you, Hoppy?' Moore asked quietly.

Hoppy swallowed once. 'O.K., skipper.'

Moore gave him a nod of appreciation. 'Then put your mask back on. It would be a bit tricky down there.'

The two men's eyes held for a moment, then A-Apple dropped a wing and dived down. Levelling off at 800 feet, Moore made straight for the Institute. At his nod, Hoppy opened the bomb doors, fused the two TX bombs and waited. Bullets drummed against the Mosquito's fusilage but the Cockney, a veteran of over eighty missions, barely noticed the raging guns. Paralysis was his personal horror and the great cloud of smoke ahead, shot with vivid flames, seemed at that moment to be the portals of hell itself.

To gain all the cover possible, Moore held A-Apple down until the last moment. Then he hauled back on the control column, at the same time shouting at Hoppy to release the bombs. Outside, the horrified Cockney saw smoke envelop the cupola as he pressed the bomb release. As A-Apple leapt upwards, Hoppy closed his eyes and waited for incineration or worse.

Acutely conscious of the gas threat, the crews above were almost as tense as Hopkinson and shouts of relief were heard when the Mosquito emerged unscathed and began climbing towards them. Eyes turned back to the blazing building but although two flashes were seen in the smoke there was no noticeable increase in the fires already burning.

With his bruised head pounding from his exertions,

Moore was nearer to desperation than he could remember. He had taken on the responsibility of continuing the operation and although it seemed likely that Werner and the gas threat had met their end in the gutted Institute, failure to save the French towns-folk from the cost of that success seemed imminent. The implications, both in terms of human suffering and De Gaulle's outrage, were almost too calamitous to face.

Below Young and the two survivors of his Orange Section were circling round at the end of the valley to make their own attack. Although it was a last card he had to play, Moore had little hope of success after the failure of his own TX bombs. When their attack was over, he would send his Red and Blue Sections down in an effort to ignite the smoke that was now almost at the southern boundary wall. Although it would be a Pyrrhonic victory if they should succeed, at least it would mean there would be less gas left to poison the town.

The progress of Young's Mosquitoes, flying in line astern, could be followed by the flak raging around them. The starboard engine of the Number 2 was trailing glycol but Roberts, the pilot, stayed close behind his leader. Looking as if they were tied together by rope, the three Mosquitoes hurled themselves into the smoke. As the blazing Institute appeared beneath them, each pilot released his two bombs.

To the crews circling above, the three Mosquitoes disappeared completely from sight. Five seconds later, just as Young's aircraft appeared again, the horrified men saw a series of shuddering flashes light up the great canopy of smoke. A moment later, with a roar that could be heard over the noise of engines, a raging fireball swelled upwards and outwards with bewildering speed and ferocity. The heat was such that, three thousand feet above, the orbiting Mosquitoes were sent reeling about like paper toys. When pilots regained control, almost the entire estate was a sea of flames. There was no sign of Young or his number 3 but Roberts was still airborne although with its charred and naked spars, his Mosquito was a hideous sight. Seeing it was circling back over the

228

estate as if the pilot were blinded, Moore put out an urgent call. For a reply, the Mosquito wearily dropped a wing and plunged down into the inferno.

A few shouts and curses sounded, then the radio channel went oddly silent. The sudden loss of six comrades, in particular Teddy Young, was difficult to grasp. A member of the original squadron, the only man to bring his aircraft back from the Swartfjord, the tough, popular Australian had seemed indestructable and men could not believe he would no longer be there to take their bets on the horses or to exchange banter with his crews. It was a loss that also reminded men of their own mortality and when a voice called "Bandits, skipper" stunned pilots found it difficult to respond.

Providentially an American voice, replying on the same frequency, announced the alarm was one of mistaken identity. 'We're your escort, Cobra Leader. It looks as if you boys have done a hell of a job down there. Why don't you call it a day now and come home?'

Dent's familiar voice, full of concern, told Moore that Staines had kept his word to help in every way possible. He knew he should be feeling relief but the loss of Young had killed all emotion in him and his flat orders gave evidence of it. While Mustangs wheeled protectively over them, weary crews attended to their wounded and began the long flight home.

29

The last pilot, Larkin, unshaven like the rest of the crews, trudged down from the platform and made his way towards the bunker steps. As he disappeared, Adams picked up one of the de-briefing forms and read it again. Setting it aside, he slipped the rest into a file.

Behind him Davies was talking to Staines and MacBride. On a bench below Henderson was asking Moore questions in a low, distressed voice. The Operations Room had been chosen for the crews' de-briefing because, although Adams' Confessional had escaped serious damage, all the windows had been blown in and the hut stank of high explosive fumes.

The squadron had landed in England less than three hours ago. Diverted to Leconfield, a bomber base nearby, they had been given coffee and sandwiches and then ferried by road transport to the battered Sutton Craddock. Here they had been immediately called for interrogation. The order had come from MacBride but as it was normal practice for crews to be questioned about an operation while their memories were still fresh, neither Davies nor Henderson had found any reasonable grounds for complaint. As a consequence Adams had spent the last hour trying to prise answers from the dog-tired men.

Even then their ordeal had not ended. Before Larkin could be questioned about his navigator's death, the High Elms telephone had rung. Two minutes later, in spite of Adams' protests, MacBride had mounted the platform to give the crews his latest Intelligence reports. They indicated the raid had been an unqualified success and there was every reason to believe the gas threat had been eliminated. With some men almost too weary to keep their eyes open, it is doubtful if many cared one way or the other but the self-satisfied MacBride seemed oblivious of their condition. Staines, who, in spite of his heavy commitments, had stayed on to congratulate Moore, had quickly sized up the situation. Pushing massively forward, he had cracked a joke at the resentful MacBride, then turned to the comatose crews. 'Before you guys drop right off to sleep I want to say what a hell of a job I think you've done. In fact when you've grabbed some shut-eye I would like you and my boys to get together for a celebration party. It shouldn't be any problem because your C.O. tells me he's standing you down for a few days.'

Nothing could have brought about a quicker restoration. A quip from Millburn brought the first laugh of the day. 'Are you going to be there yourself, sir?'

'I'm going to do my best, that's for sure.'

'Try hard, sir. Then your boys will push the Bourbon out.'

Staines' leathery grin had broadened. 'I'll see you get your Bourbon, Yank.'

With MacBride upstaged, Davies had been able to bring an end to the proceedings. As the tired men filed out, Adams had at last been able to learn the grisly facts of Richards' death. Now, with Larkin gone, Adams picked up the spare debriefing form and turned to Davies. 'May I have a word with you, sir?'

Davies moved up to him. 'What is it?'

Adams handed him the form. Looking puzzled, Davies scanned it, then gave a start. 'Are these his own words?'

As Adams nodded, Davies called Moore to the platform. As the Squadron Commander approached, he held out the form. 'What does this mean — that you made a grave error in sending in your Orange Section at 800 feet?'

With shadows beneath his eyes the colour of the bruise on his forehead, Moore was looking more tired than

231

Adams had ever seen him. 'It means what it says, sir. I made an error that killed six men.'

'How? You were told to release those bombs from that height. And you'd just dropped a couple yourself without coming to any harm or doing any damage. As I see it, you'd have been justified in sending Young in even lower.'

'No, sir. The effect would have been the same from a safe height.' Seeing MacBride was moving in closer to listen, Moore turned towards him with a bitterness that drew the attention of every man in the room. 'The reason we were ordered to drop them at that height was because it was known their cases were so frail they could break up on impact.'

Davies gave a violent start. 'Are you saying that was the reason Young and his men were killed?'

'What other reason could there be? If the cases had withstood the impact, the reagents wouldn't have been released until the time-fuses exploded. As it was, they went straight to the tanks and gave Teddy no chance to escape.'

With Davies feeling the loss of Young as much as anybody, he showed little finesse as he swung round on MacBride. 'He's right, by God. Are you sure the boffins said 800 feet? Didn't they warn you about the danger at that height?'

The burly soldier's hostility and bluster convinced Adams he was lying. 'What sort of question is that? Of course they didn't warn me. All I did was pass on their instructions.'

Adams knew he would never forget the look Moore gave the man. Davies, whose suspicious eyes were missing nothing, picked up the debriefing form again. 'You're being far too sensitive about this. Everyone of us should have guessed what was behind it, particularly Lindsay. You're feeling this way because of Teddy. Go and get a good sleep and you'll see things more clearly tomorrow.'

Although Moore spoke quietly, Adams could hear every bitter word. 'No, sir. As Squadron Commander I should have seen through the deception. I would like that report to go through as it stands. May I go now?'

Frustration got the better of Davies. 'That bump on your head must have addled your brains. All right, if you want to put a blot on a brilliant career, that's your business. Yes; off you go.'

With a glance at Staines, Moore saluted and left the platform. No one spoke until he disappeared up the bunker steps. Then Davies swung round on Adams. 'I'm not losing my best squadron commander because some deceitful bastard tricked him into sending six good men to their deaths. I want you to tear that report up, Adams.'

In spite of his relief, Adams showed surprise. 'The book does say we have to send in uncensured reports, sir.'

In his state of mind Davies had forgotten there was anyone else in the room. 'I don't give a duck's arse what the book says. Forge his signature if you have to but send in another report.'

Adams glanced at Henderson, who was also showing relief. 'All right, sir. I'll fix it somehow.'

By this time Davies had remembered Staines' presence but he showed no contrition as he faced the American. 'I've got no choice, sir. You've seen yourself the kind of man he is.'

On the floor of the bunker the High Elms telephone had began ringing again. Staines gave a broad grin as his eyes followed MacBride down to it. 'I never thought I'd see the day, Davies. A Limey tossing the book out of the window? Now I know we're going to win the war.' His tone changed as MacBride reached the telephone. 'Do you know something, Davies? I'm going to help you find that double-crossing sonofabitch myself.'

MacBride gave him a glance as he lifted the receiver. As he spoke in low tones, Adams saw him start. Thirty seconds later he replaced the receiver, sat back in his chair, and gazed reflectively at the men on the platform. His look of grim satisfaction gave Adams one of his premonitions. As he rose and mounted the platform again, Staines turned towards him aggressively. 'Well! Is it anything we should know?'

Adams could see the big soldier was enjoying the moment. 'It was a report from Lorenz. Rather a sensational one, I'm afraid.'

Everyone was gazing at him now. Henderson sounded apprehensive. 'Not about the civilians? They're still all right, aren't they?'

MacBride's voice was dry. 'They're hardly that, Henderson. It seems over three hundred of them have died in the last few hours.'

The hush that fell was like a bomb exploding. Davies sounded afraid of his own question. 'Three hundred? Not from the gas?'

MacBride shook his head. 'No. It seems that the Das Reich SS have rushed more men into the town. Deciding that some of the townsfolk are responsible for the raid, they're taking reprisals. In fact they appear to be doing another Lidice. Batches of fifty, men, women, and children, have been shot throughout the morning. According to Lorenz, the executions are still going on.'

A chair gave a groan of protest as Staines dropped into it. 'Jesus Christ,' he muttered. Henderson had gone pale. Davies was looking horrified. 'Is she sure of this?'

MacBride shrugged. 'You know Lorenz. She's hardly one to exaggerate, is she?'

'Then all that effort and cost to destroy the escaping gas was wasted! We still haven't saved their lives?'

MacBride sounded like an instructor lecturing a dense pupil as he picked up his cap. 'It was anything but wasted, Davies. If we had been the cause of their deaths, as sure as De Gaulle is De Gaulle we'd have had no help from the French Resistance when we invade. But now, as it's the Nazis who are doing the killing, the French will fight like tigers.'

As he reached the steps he turned, his deep-set eyes moving from one shocked man to the other. 'I don't want to sound callous, gentlemen, but the truth is the enemy are being unusually generous. They're presenting us with fifteen or more divisions of fighting men right behind their lines.'

Although a chilly breeze was sweeping through the shattered windows of the Intelligence Office, Adams did not feel it as he sat huddled behind his desk. In his mind's eye he was seeing women and children being dragged screaming from their homes to be brutally murdered and the knowledge it was happening as he sat there overwhelmed him. Moore was right. There was a beast in all men that was only waiting the right moment to escape. At that moment the sensitive Adams would have welcomed a catastrophe that wiped mankind off the face of the earth and left its gentler creatures to inherit it.

Running footsteps outside made him glance up. A moment later Sue Spencer appeared in the doorway. Catching sight of him she paused, her voice breathless. 'I'm sorry I wasn't here for the interrogation, Frank. I didn't think the crews would be back so soon.'

He tried to tell her it did not matter but no words came. Looking concerned she started towards him. 'What is it? What else has happened?'

He could not tell her. 'How is Tony?'

Her expression changed. 'He's going to be all right. Although he'll never fly again.'

'Does that matter?'

'Matter?' she said quietly. 'It's the best thing that has happened to me for years.'

He gazed into her face and knew the truth. 'It's all right again, isn't it? Between the two of you?'

The joy in her could no longer be contained. With a sob she threw her arms around him. 'Yes. Isn't it wonderful?'

Adams swallowed hard. 'Yes. Yes, it is.'

She gazed into his face, then suddenly drew back. 'Listen to me! Talking about happiness after we've lost Teddy and the others. Love makes us selfish, Frank. It's such a little thing in a world full of suffering.'

'Little thing,' Adams repeated. He wanted to laugh

but knew hysteria would claim him if he did. Instead he took a deep, steadying breath and reached into his tunic pocket for his pipe and pouch. 'Sue, it's the only thing in the world that matters. Sit down and tell me all that's happened.'

The end

633 SQUADRON OPERATION CRUCIBLE
by FREDERICK E. SMITH

AUTUMN 1943:

A vindictive press campaign in the States had placed the blame for heavy U.S. losses over Europe on lack of support from the RAF. To restore American confidence — and guarantee the supply of B.17s to Europe — joint special operations were planned by RAF and 8th Air Force top brass, calling in 633 Squadron, whose Rhine Maiden mission had won them a shining reputation. Operation Crucible was to be a Dieppe-style landing launched by the Americans, and 633 Squadron were assigned their most hazardous role yet — giving ground support to the troops against totally unforeseen odds . . .

0 552 10741 7   80p.

633 SQUADRON OPERATION VALKYRIE
by FREDERICK E. SMITH

The memory of Operation Vesuvius — the successful but suicidal attack on the Black Fjord — still haunted 633 Squadron. For there were those who could remember how, on a cold July morning in 1943, only a single crippled Mosquito had finally made it home . . . But now, barely a year later, it seemed as if the nightmare of that fateful mission would have to be lived through again. The Germans were once more processing the secret 'element' known as IMI — and were about to move their stocks from Norway into the safe heartland of Germany. If successful, the manoeuvre could turn the tide of war . . . For 633 Squadron it meant another 'impossible' mission; but it also meant a flight into the dark, unforgotten past . . .

0 552 11075 2   £1.50

THE FIGHT OF THE FEW
by RICHARD HOUGH

The summer of 1940. The Battle of Britain. For Flying Officer Keith Stewart and his American friend Mike Browning it meant pitting their comparatively slow, poorly-armed Hurricanes against the vicious might of Goering's Messerschmitt 109s in the skies above Southern England.

Hopelessly outnumbered, desperately exhausted, the pilots of the RAF continued to out-think and out-fight the Luftwaffe. But day after day, fewer of them returned, and the certainty of death grew with every flight, every sudden dog-fight. But so, too, did the will to survive . . .

0 552 11307 7   £1.25

ANGELS ONE-FIVE
by RICHARD HOUGH

When a young Englishman, Keith Stewart, and his American friend Mike Browning joined the RAF, they thought of it as embarking on a glamorous adventure, and exciting crusade. Learning to fly, to master their fast, efficient Hurricanes was a thrilling experience — but nothing in their training equipped them for what was to follow . . . the tense, desperate moments of aerial combat, the butchery, the fear of failing nerves, the endless killing. What began as a crusade ended as a personal battle for survival . . . a battle in which their flying skills, the speed of their fighters, their courage and their luck would all be tested to the limit . . . and then beyond it . . .

0 552 11094 9   85p.

HURRICANE SQUADRON
by ROBERT JACKSON

MAY 1940

To Sergeant George Yeoman, cruising high above France in his Hurricane fighter, on his way to join his first operational squadron, the war seemed a million miles away. But at that very moment, the squadrons of the Luftwaffe were gathering to strike the first devastating blow in Hitler's Blitzkreig on the Western front . . .

HURRICANE SQUADRON —

The story of a fighter squadron at war; of a handful of pilots struggling desperately against hopeless odds; of a young man's rise from the innocence of peace to the experience of war.

0 552 11195 3   85p.

SQUADRON SCRAMBLE
by ROBERT JACKSON

France, and the nightmare of Dunkirk, turned Sergeant George Yeoman into a veteran fighter pilot — an ace with several kills to his credit. But for him and the rest of the battle weary pilots of 505 Squadron there would be no rest. In the fateful summer of 1940 the Luftwaffe hurled its might across the Channel and all that stood between England and defeat was the Battle of Britain . . .

0 552 11231 3   80p.

A SELECTED LIST OF FINE NOVELS
THAT APPEAR IN CORGI

While every effort is made to keep prices low, it is sometimes necessary to increase prices at short notice. Corgi Books reserve the right to show new retail prices on covers which may differ from those previously advertised in the text or elsewhere.

The prices shown below were correct at the time of going to press. (Aug. '81)

ORDER FORM

All these books are available at your book shop or newsagent, or can be ordered direct from the publisher. Just tick the titles you want and fill in the form below.

CORGI BOOKS, Cash Sales Department, P.O. Box 11, Falmouth, Cornwall.

Please send cheque or postal order, no currency.

Please allow cost of book(s) plus the following for postage and packing:

U.K. Customers—Allow 40p for the first book, 18p for the second book and 13p for each additional book ordered, to a maximum charge of £1.49.

B.F.P.O. and Eire—Allow 40p for the first book, 18p for the second book plus 13p per copy for the next 3 books, thereafter 7p per book.

Overseas Customers—Allow 60p for the first book and 18p per copy for each additional book.

NAME (block letters) ....

ADDRESS ....

(Aug. '81) ....